Verushka

Jan Stinchcomb

JOURNALSTONE
YOUR LINK TO ARTIST TALENT

ISBN: 978-1-68510-090-2 (sc)
ISBN: 978-1-68510-091-9 (ebook)
Library of Congress Catalog Number: 2023937557

First printing edition July 7, 2023
Published by JournalStone Publishing in the United States of America.
Cover Artwork and Design: Don Noble
Edited by Sean Leonard
Proofreading and Cover/Interior Layout by Scarlett R. Algee

JournalStone Publishing
3205 Sassafras Trail
Carbondale, Illinois 62901

JournalStone books may be ordered through booksellers or by contacting:
JournalStone | www.journalstone.com

For Kurt

Verushka

Verushka: 2004

The trick is to get between mother and child.

Verushka understands this, but only after many years of hard work. It is not enough to snatch a girl away; she has to confuse her heart. The girl needs to say yes. The girl must come willingly.

This time she will build a little house. Children can't resist houses. And then she will have a girl all to herself. A girl to raise.

The years will fly by.

The child will be a teenager in no time. A maiden. Beautiful and promising and ready to return to the oldest forest.

Ready for the darkest marriage.

Caroline and Devon: 2004

The chalet was only a temporary escape.

Jack found the place through a friend at work. The owners were away in some cold country like Sweden or Iceland. It was a steal, way cheaper than the apartment they had fled, and it was nice to be in a house for a change. They all deserved a break, something new, even if it seemed reckless to move to a neighborhood in a high-risk fire zone after what they had been through. Jack assured Caroline there were no trees anywhere near the house. The lot had been recently cleared of brush and appeared safe. No rosemary in sight.

It was a long drive to the city from Topanga, but it was worth it. No neighbors. The simple blue A-frame sat on a hill with the woods behind it and, if you walked up the hill far enough, there was a sliver of the ocean to the west. The house was wide open, almost like a barn, all wood with exposed beams. There were two bedrooms downstairs with a bathroom between them, and the entire second story was one big open room, accessed by a wooden staircase with little trees carved into the balusters. Caroline loved it.

Devon ran all over the little house squealing until Caroline, surprised by her daughter's reaction, had to warn her about running up and down stairs. "I want you to be very careful. Respectful. Don't scratch anything, don't dent anything. This is someone else's home. It doesn't belong to us. I want you to protect it."

"Like a guard dog?" Devon asked, baring her teeth.

"Or a guard cat."

Devon went around meowing on all fours while her parents stood and stared, too tired to unpack. Their Volkswagen carried what remained of their possessions after the Venice duplex had burned down. The smell of smoke, like a campfire indoors, had woken them, and then adrenaline took over.

Caroline was wearing her favorite dress. She had fallen asleep on the couch, her contacts still in, after coming home from a party in Culver City. She had time to grab her purse and her little Nokia phone. Jack took his keys, phone, and the PowerBook off the kitchen table. Devon had her favorite animal, Bear, in her arms.

When all the residents were standing on the lawn in front of the duplex, the fire engines not yet audible, Caroline thought of running back inside for the wedding picture. She imagined it disappearing, curling at the edges before turning into a black ball, an evil spell intended to destroy her marriage and family. Devon cried about her village of stuffed animals and her little dollhouse. Jack poured reassurances over them in the hot night: they had renters' insurance, Grandma Carol would send more toys, they had their lives. Everyone got out safe, even the Burkes' cat, Simon, who surveyed the flames with his golden eyes.

"Maybe she won't remember," Jack whispered to Caroline.

"Of course she will. I don't know why people always say that about children."

After the fire they stayed in Beverlywood with Diane, Caroline's old roommate from grad school. While Diane and Jack were at work and Devon napped, all Caroline could do was lie on the couch and stare. She wanted to sob in the privacy of Diane's little house, but the tears refused to come. "It's probably shock," her mother told her. "You should stay with me for a while. I can watch Devon while you try to get on your feet again." Resentment, so bitter and quick it surprised her, rose up inside Caroline. She knew it was an overreaction and so she chose her words with care. It was better not to get in a fight with her mom.

"That would never work. Jack's job is here. You know he's trying to make partner. And I'm waiting to hear back from preschools for Devon. She's turning four. It's time."

"Well, where are you going to live?"

"I don't know, Mom. I don't know."

She tried not to think about her material losses because when she did, her heart plunged deep inside her ribcage. She had nothing left, not even her jeans. Her books were gone, as were the pricey Revere Ware pans her mother had bought her when she started college. Her little troupe of docile, dedicated cacti must have turned to ash. And the wedding picture still haunted her. They had stored the negatives in the closet, unfortunately, instead of the safe deposit box.

She decided to make a list of everything she wanted to replace, but she soon found herself drowning in an endless stream of remembered objects. What had happened to the keepsakes and weird wedding gifts, all those things she and Jack used to laugh at? "I want to downsize," she announced to Jack one night while they were at the dinner table. "I mean really. Like not acquire anything unnecessary."

"Sounds good to me," Jack said. "We'll never have the space for it anyway. Not in LA."

A few days later, when Caroline was alone with Devon in the little Beverlywood house, she found herself bent over the toilet, where she gagged but produced little more than long strings of saliva. She felt funny. It was a familiar feeling which had been building for days. *Oh no.* She sat up, still nauseated, and tried to list the essentials. You had to have a car seat or they wouldn't let you leave the hospital. A bassinet. A stroller. Diapers. Onesies. A teething ring.

That was when she cried, ugly cried, in great choking gasps she didn't even try to hide from Devon. Her daughter came running up to her carrying a small wooden car she had found on Diane's desk.

"What's wrong, Mommy?"

"Stomach ache." Caroline noticed Devon was wearing a pair of pull-ups even though she was potty-trained and only needed them at night. She must have put them on herself. She was very self-sufficient for a little kid. As Caroline stood up to wash her face, she could hear Devon playing with Bear in his new car.

* * *

After they had been in the chalet for a week, Caroline found a plush rabbit nestled under the blankets in Devon's bed. She turned it over in her hands. It had silky fur of a purply beige no real rabbit would have. It was an expensive toy, a treat, bought for no reason one day on the 3rd Street Promenade.

And Caroline was sure it was one of the precious toys that had burned in the fire.

"Where did this come from?" she asked, walking out to the main room, where Devon was playing with the new tea set her grandmother had sent her. "It looks exactly like your old rabbit."

"It's Henry," Devon said.

"Devon," Caroline began. Then she paused. Maybe it was all right. Why couldn't this replacement rabbit be Henry? Or Henry II? Perhaps this was the right way to deal with their trauma and the long process of remembering, on a daily basis, all that was lost. Caroline was constantly reaching for objects that no longer existed in her new kitchen. Things as simple as a preferred cheese grater could ruin her mood by their very absence. So many memories were attached to each item, replaceable or not. The narrative of their lives could be told through these objects. She gave the new Henry a little squeeze.

"I found him outside," Devon said.

Caroline knelt down next to her daughter. "Devon, I told you not to go too far. I know you're a little adventurer. In the fall you'll be in school with other kids, and then you won't be so bored. For now, though, you have to stay in the yard."

"I didn't leave the yard, Mommy. Henry was on the picket fence. He was waiting for me."

Caroline smiled. "Okay," she said, and let it go.

There was a small patch of grass, dotted with wildflowers, out the back door. A simple white fence that was waist-high separated the property from the woods. They called it a picket fence, just as they called the A-frame house a chalet. Devon copied everything they said and did. "What's she going to do when she goes skiing and sees a real chalet?" Jack would joke.

Shortly after moving in, they had taken a family walk in the woods. There was a trail that led partway up the hill behind the chalet and then disappeared into a scattering of oak and black walnut. Coast live oak, to be exact—Jack had looked it up. He worried about the possibility of mudslides, as well as fire, but this was the beauty of a month-to-month lease. Maybe they would find something else before too long. Caroline worried about wild animals.

"You mean mountain lions?" Jack asked.

"It's possible, isn't it? They've been spotted in the city. I'm sure they're out here too."

"I think you should be more worried about coyotes." The trees around them hummed with insects and birds. Jack stood and breathed in, balancing Devon on his back. "We can make a rule. No walking in the woods alone. And Devon, you never go beyond the picket fence. No coming up here without Mommy or Daddy." And then they hiked back down to their life in the chalet.

When Jack came home from work, Caroline showed him the rabbit she had found.

"You know what?" He slipped off his work jacket. "It took me over an hour to get here from Century City. There must have been an accident. Unbelievable."

"Jack. Devon says she found it on the picket fence."

"I'm sure she's only playing."

"You're not listening to me."

"Can this wait until after I've had something to eat?"

"Jack, it's exactly like her old one. The one that burned in the fire."

"It must have come in that box of stuff your mother sent."

"I would have noticed when I opened it."

"What are you saying?" He stopped and looked at her, then set the rabbit on their new kitchen table. "Maybe one of the neighbors left it for her."

"People don't do that kind of thing around here. And I haven't met any of the neighbors."

Jack went to the refrigerator and took out a beer. "We're all really tired. A lot has happened to us. You're overthinking this. I, for one, am glad to see Henry here."

"I'm surprised you remember his name."

"Who could ever forget Henry?" Jack said. He went back to the table and put the rabbit on his shoulder. Devon came downstairs and saw her father, and then the two of them started to play. They were so loud and happy they couldn't hear Caroline asking if it was Jack who had bought a replacement Henry and perched him on the fence.

That must have been what happened. Of course. Jack was pulling her leg.

* * *

There was a certain liberation in having lost everything, but it was outweighed by grief. Jack was organized enough to have stored the essentials in a safe deposit box at the bank (including, wisely, Devon's baby book), but all the personal correspondence and old college papers were gone forever. The photographs. That one wedding picture. Caroline's mother had copies of the best photos from Devon's babyhood, but there were so many others they would never see again.

In particular, there was a little album Caroline had made of her life with Jack, her wedding present to him, and after Devon was born she kept on adding to it. Lost: a few strips from photo booths she had dragged him into at the pier; an old Polaroid taken at a retro Halloween funhouse, where she was dressed as a flapper and Jack was wearing a bearskin coat; Devon's pictures with Santa; the yearly trips to the pumpkin patch.

"It's like our whole life burned up, Jack."

"That did not happen. What an exaggeration. God, Caroline. It's amazing nobody died."

She knew he was right, but there was no denying her grief. Of course their lives were the most important thing, but the loss of those pictures was too painful. It was disorienting not to have her visual reference points, and she worried she would forget too many details of their shared past. Her mother offered her all the pictures she had, dating back to

Caroline's childhood. "Look through everything. Take whatever you need."

"I don't want to spend energy on this right now, Mom."

Her mother-in-law, Elaine, who was travelling, called from Dublin one night. After Devon talked to her, Jack retreated to the bedroom to speak to his mother in private. Caroline started washing dishes and told Devon to brush her teeth.

Jack came back out sooner than Caroline had expected. She couldn't read the expression on his face. "What's she up to? Visiting friends? Is she still going to Athens?"

"I'm not sure. I don't think she ever got tickets for the Olympics. She won't admit it but it's hard on her to travel alone."

"I think it's hard on everyone now. Those lines at the airport." Caroline left the pans in the sink for Jack. "Did she say anything? About the fire?"

"She was shocked, but grateful. What were you expecting?"

"I don't know. For her to say something positive, like she always does. Some hippie shit."

"Jesus Christ, Caroline."

"No. I didn't mean anything bad. I like your mom."

"Well, she did offer me money."

Caroline laughed and let the matter drop. She resolved to move forward and even said a little prayer to that effect after climbing into bed. Her unconscious didn't comply though, and her dreams were filled with charred clothing, doll heads, and pets from childhood. In one dream she was walking through the remains of their old duplex, still smoking from the fire. She came across a modest strand of pearls, Jack's wedding present to her. She picked them up, but they were hot to the touch and blackened. When she rubbed them against her dress, they became white for one second before turning into a fine powder which joined the ashes at her feet.

* * *

Devon has witches and fairies and ghosts in her world. They come to her at different times. At night she sees them in the dark corners, and in the daylight she sees them in the trees. Parks are good. Grass is great.

She loves the chalet. A whole new world greeted her when they drove up to the property that first time.

Her feet feel better on the ground. She loves dirt and rocks. There is nothing like a handful of soil. It has a particular smell (and taste—don't tell her mother). When she is older, she will learn this is called terroir. She starts collecting plants in a little bag. She counts weeds as plants and is only deterred by the ones with pricklies. Anything with a flower is notable.

She likes to raise her face to the sky, to the sun. Her daddy tells her about the planets. So far she has seen Jupiter and Venus. The stars are something to eat and to wrap around oneself. Their shape keeps appearing in her world. She had a dream where she was wearing a black dress covered in stars, and in the morning she cried because it was gone. Her mother promised her she would buy her a star dress if she ever saw one.

There is something untruthful about her mother.

One time there is a rainbow so huge that Devon can see the full arc. Her parents make a big deal of it, but it seems natural to her. She knows instinctively there is no pot of gold at its end and yet is disappointed, both at the material loss and at the lie the grown-ups have told her.

In the distance, to the west, is the ocean. It has always been there. The first time she ever sees it, before she can speak, its power makes it hard for her to breathe. She is not afraid of drowning, but she knows her mother thinks she will drown in the saltwater. Devon loves everything about the beach. Everything. She wants to take all of it back to her bedroom. The sand. The tiny shells. The foam. The seaweed. The gulls. The repeating waves. The blue houses where the lifeguards live.

The blue of the chalet is almost the same shade, but not quite.

The ocean is the biggest thing she has ever seen, will ever see. While they live in Venice it is part of her everyday world. The first time her father shows her a world map, he spreads it out across the floor. This is in the old apartment, the duplex, what Devon calls the first house. And when she sees that endless expanse of blue, the ocean represented on paper, Devon feels fear, especially when her father's index finger moves to show her the tiny spot on the map where they live. The world is big and she is so small. There is so much water. Can she survive it? She tells her daddy she is afraid and at first he laughs, but then he praises her for what he takes to be caution.

She knows the truth. Daddy is often afraid.

The chalet is mostly wood inside, not dominated by white walls like the first house. Her new room is pure joy. She has one big window, special in its own way. It opens up in the middle and then pushes outward, into the world. There is no screen and that is why she cannot sleep with her window open at night. Her mother warns her not to drop anything outside the open window, especially not the nice new toys from Grandma Carol.

Something horrible has happened but it did not kill them. It is the worst thing that has ever happened, and it settles into her bones forever. Devon knows it is terrible because her parents, instead of telling her strange little stories about the event, say almost nothing at all. Her mother, especially, has been changed by that night. The flames dance around in Devon's head, especially when she closes her eyes to go to sleep.

For years the smell of smoke, any smoke, will flood her solar plexus with doom.

She has Bear. Bear is so much more than a toy. He is a baby, a sibling, a king. When she holds him against her chest on the Horrible Night, she hears his voice for the first time. He is older than she expected. He doesn't use the same words her parents do, but she knows what he means. And he knows more than either of her parents. For days she hangs onto him. For days she doesn't speak. Years later she will remember lying on her side, staring into the distance, making up stories about Bear.

Then, one morning, everyone is eating breakfast together at the new kitchen table and there is sunshine. Devon looks up and experiences time, understands how it moves, slow and fast at once. She will learn to call this life.

The yard at the new house makes up for the sea being so distant. Her parents tell her she can still see the Pacific at the very top of the hill behind the property, but she won't be able to hear the waves crashing. The yard ends at a fence with peeling white paint. The picket fence, as her parents call it, is slightly higher than her head. Beyond the picket fence, up the hill, is an ocean of trees, green instead of blue but, like the ocean, the color of the woods changes according to the light.

Devon doesn't fear the woods.

One day everything changes forever. This is the second great change of her short life, the first being the fire. She goes out to play in the yard and sees Henry sitting upright on the picket fence. Henry, of all her lost animals. Her beloved rabbit. She hasn't seen him since the Horrible Night.

Devon walks over to the fence and reaches up to take the soft rabbit in her arms.

* * *

Caroline kept her secret. While they were still staying with Diane in Beverlywood, she threw up only once. Nobody noticed her looking pale or acting weird.

Everyone assumed she was traumatized by the fire.

Everyone was right. How awful to lose all your possessions when you were a struggling freelancer with a small child. How fortunate to be married to Jack. How great that he was ambitious and still climbing the ranks when so many others were laid off. The renters' insurance, though, wouldn't come close to covering everything. They were down to one car, its survival due to a bit of good luck, since Jack's Volkswagen had been at the shop on the night of the fire. Caroline's old Volvo, a hand-me-down from her mother, had perished in the garage of the duplex. Perished was the word she used because it really was like losing an old friend or family member, and she wasn't in a rush to replace it. In the meantime, they were renting a car so that she wouldn't be stranded on the edge of the metropolis with Devon.

"This can't go on forever," Jack told her one morning before he left for work, and though his comment made her angry, she didn't really know what he was talking about.

What couldn't go on forever? The new house? The owners would someday come back from Holland or Denmark or wherever they were living. Caroline liked to picture them in some clean, Nordic city where life was easier, more reasonable. There were no fires in that city, with the possible exception of bonfires at pagan festivals, celebrations far from any human dwellings. The chalet did not have a fireplace, a detail Caroline found reassuring.

This can't go on forever. Well, nothing lasted forever. Nothing lasted in LA, but that was what made the place so exciting. Maybe Jack was referring to Devon, who would be starting preschool soon, moving on in her own way? Or was he waiting for her to go out and buy more clothes? She used to be so stylish. For the longest time she wore the dress she had worn on the night of the fire, until one weekend, when Jack took her and Devon to The Grove and gave them permission to go wild. Devon had no problem running around and grabbing every cute thing she saw, but Caroline bought only underwear and a nightgown. She still wondered how Jack was planning to pay for that shopping spree.

Jack put down his coffee cup and moved closer to her. "Caroline? Are you listening? You seem really distant."

"I guess I'm still in shock. I can't believe you aren't."

"It's helpful to leave here every day. Work is good."

"I work," she lied. "And I have Devon all day."

"I'm not saying you don't work. Nobody ever said that."

Jack left for work, at last, but the same conversation started again after dinner. All their discussions happened around breakfast or dinner. At breakfast, Devon stayed with them at the table, where she often turned the pages of one of her books, but after dinner she always wanted to go play in the little yard. They let her, as the days were getting longer. It was good for a child to be outside so much, and her absence gave them a chance to be alone.

"Do you want to help me with these dishes, or did you bring your work home with you again?" Caroline asked.

Jack laid one warm hand on her wrist. "I was thinking, do you want to talk to someone?"

There. A little flare of anger, a flame leaping up. She had been like this when she was pregnant with Devon, often angry, sometimes frighteningly so, but only in the first trimester. She hated to admit it though. It was like self-misogyny. What about the man who got her pregnant? Why was nobody monitoring his moods?

"Caroline?"

"I find your question very condescending. Besides, a good therapist costs a fortune."

"Come on."

"How about this: I'll go if you go?"

Jack looked around as if he were seeing the chalet for the first time and didn't know where he was. She knew what he was doing. He was struggling to figure out how he would fit therapy into his busy schedule. He couldn't miss work. And what would they do with Devon? They didn't have a babysitter yet. They didn't know a soul out here in their new neighborhood.

Caroline loaded the new dishes she had bought in a hurry into the chalet's old dishwasher. She would try to find a movie to watch on the new television Jack had chosen. Everything in her life was strange and new, from the setting to the objects. She asked Jack to bring Devon back inside.

When she was alone, she grabbed a loaf of sourdough, fell to her knees so that she would be hidden from view, and began the act of predation. She was hungry, hungry, hungry, and the sourdough helped settle her stomach. She chased it with a chunk of Monterey Jack. There. This too had happened when she was pregnant with Devon. She felt better.

She stood up when Devon and Jack came back inside. Devon was crying about having to abandon her play while Jack consoled her with the promise of a bubble bath. She loved the chalet's claw foot tub and the blue tile bathroom floor. Instead of helping with the bath, Caroline melted into the new couch and put her feet up. She closed her eyes.

What if none of this was real? There never was a fire. There never was a pregnancy. She had no obligations. Would that be so terrible?

What if she never got up from the couch? Jack and Devon would have to fend for themselves. Worse things had happened. She could turn to stone on the couch, or maybe bone, a tribute and a warning. But that would never work. It would not happen. She found herself rising, still exhausted, from the couch. The chalet was dark. She went to the bathroom and opened the door.

"You guys! Let's go explore the neighborhood this weekend. There's a funky old general store where we might be able to find lunch. And there's a library in Calabasas. Or," and here her voice sounded too high, too loud, "we can go on a real hike. See where these woods take us."

She was met with a beat of silence that made her want to burst out laughing. Then Devon went back to playing with her squadron of rubber duckies, so new they still smelled like plastic.

"Sounds like a great idea," Jack said without turning around.

Caroline walked upstairs to the loft they never really used. It was supposed to be her office, but she hadn't set it up yet. Devon liked it though, and played here when she wasn't playing outside. It had one big window with no blinds. Caroline would have to get some curtains for it, or maybe she could use an old sheet?

Right. There were no old sheets.

She stared out the window and tried to see into the woods. There was nothing but trees swaying in the darkness. Who was that woman planning for the weekend in the bathroom downstairs? Someone she didn't know. Someone who had nothing to do with the woman who would rise in the middle of the night and consume what remained of the bread, later telling Jack she had thrown it away because it was covered in mold.

* * *

Devon has Bear and Henry. The three of them sit at the little plastic table with the matching benches Daddy's work friend gave them. They're using the fancy tea set Grandma Carol sent. Normally her mother wouldn't let her take porcelain dishes outside, but everything has changed since the Horrible Night. Besides, she and Bear are careful with nice things.

It's the rabbit she has to watch out for.

He is not bad. He is impulsive, always running away when something captures his attention. Henry is fast, the fastest animal Devon has ever seen. Ever since they moved to the chalet, Devon can barely keep track of him. She'll turn her head and he's gone. She has had to search all over the chalet and the yard for him. Once she found him stuck to a thorny bush along the picket fence. Once he was in the laundry basket. And once he was in her bed, waiting for her.

She can't tell her mother about this. Mommy has a problem with Henry. She hasn't trusted him since the Horrible Night.

Henry did not start the fire at her old home. Daddy explained it was an issue with the neighbors' refrigerator. An electrical malfunction, the firemen said. Still, Henry must have got out first, leaving everyone else behind, and then he ran all the way to the chalet. His fur is still perfect. He does not smell like smoke. When Devon presses her little nose into his fur, when he lets her, he smells like flowers and some other musky scent she knows comes from the wild.

She has no idea where Henry goes at night. Often, in the morning, he is missing from her bed, even though she goes to sleep every night with one arm around each of her friends.

Mommy's not happy. Devon thinks it's because she lost all her pretty clothes on the Horrible Night, but when they went to the mall, Mommy didn't want to try on anything.

There he goes! Henry has left the tea party and is running up the hill. He knows they're not supposed to go past the picket fence. Devon and Bear look at each other in alarm. Bear is so sweet, so smart. He always does the right thing. He doesn't need to say a word. Devon knows he would tell her to stay in the yard. First she shouts after Henry. Then she stands on top of the table (not allowed) to see how far he goes, but he is already disappearing into the woods. Devon looks back at the chalet. She can't see her mother in any of the windows. She's probably working in the upstairs room.

For a second Devon considers calling out to her mother or running into the house and up the always-creaking stairs. She could ask for help and then they would be a team like they used to be, but something has changed between them, and Devon must now take the first step of what will become a long journey. She will not ask for what she needs because it is easier this way. It is easier for her whole family if she doesn't call out to her mother.

Devon cannot possibly let Henry go into the woods by himself. He is too little. He is not a real rabbit and does not have a true sense of the woods. Devon's reasons for protecting Henry are somewhat selfish, for she does not want to lose one more precious thing. It is easy to climb over the picket fence, although for one second she feels the old wood cracking under her weight. The soil on the other side of the fence is hard, baked by the California sun. She sees Bear standing on the picnic table, waving his arms in the air.

"You stay there. I will be right back," Devon says. Then she turns and begins the long walk up the hill. She never looks back.

She is not afraid of the woods. She is afraid of her mother.

By the time she is high enough up the hill to see the view of the ocean, Devon is panting. The path ends and she does not know what to do, but then there is Henry, standing and waiting for her. "You come back here right now," she says in her mother's voice.

All at once the Lady is there. This is the first time Devon sees her.

The Lady is tall and thin, with long white hair that covers her body like a shroud. Devon cannot see her face. She must be cautious and quiet. It's like the time her family saw a deer when they were hiking. If anything, the deer was afraid, and if they weren't careful, the animal would run away. Devon knows she is being bad. She is on the wrong side of the fence and the Lady is a stranger. At the same time, she knows the Lady is not like anyone else, not a real person, and so maybe the household rules don't apply.

Devon doesn't know what the Lady will do to Henry, and in any case, she doesn't know if Henry will be able to find his way home.

She follows them up the hill, but it's like watching herself in a dream or a movie, where she is the little girl in the foreground. She wants so badly to see the Lady's face. Henry is ahead of her, of course. His fur is now white, the same color as the Lady's hair.

Devon cannot let them get away from her.

The climb further up the hill is somehow effortless. Her legs are light yet strong. She knows if she turns her head she could gaze at the ocean. That is her old life, near the beach in the city, but if she turns to look at it now, this new world might disappear. The Lady and Henry veer to the left, leaving what remains of the path, and are soon under the branches of scraggly old oaks. Devon has to walk quickly because Henry is moving so fast that she occasionally loses track of him. During those moments when he disappears entirely, Devon's heart hurts. It's a chilling reminder that she has no idea where she is. If Henry abandons her, she will become that terrible yet familiar thing from all the stories: a lost child.

For one second she has a flash of Bear, his eyes huge with concern, standing and waiting on the plastic picnic table.

All at once the heat of the day surrounds her. It's summer, so almost everything on the hill has turned brown, but Devon finds a single patch of earth that is still alive, still green. And rising from this patch is a hut.

The hut looks like it is growing out of the refreshingly green grass. It is made of reddish wood and has a pointed roof, and there is a splash of blue flowers in bloom around its base. Ivy trails up one side. Devon sees the Lady disappear around the left side of the hut to what must be the front door. There are no doors or windows visible from where Devon is standing.

Henry is busy in the blue flowers. Now he looks like a real bunny, complete with power haunches and a twitching nose. Still, Devon knows this is her Henry. He's going to be really fast now, faster than ever. To her surprise, he turns his head and looks right at her with one brown eye. There is a sharp creak as the door of the hut opens, and Henry's left ear tilts, like a little antenna, to take it in. His whole body stiffens, and Devon knows she is about to lose him. She will both lose and be lost.

What happens next is another great shock in her little life. Henry launches himself into her chest and knocks her to the ground, and then he is in her arms, back to being her soft stuffed animal.

She hears footsteps approaching.

Like a superhero from a cartoon, Devon rises and turns in the same motion. It is crucial that she not see the Lady's face. She knows this now. She runs as fast as she ever has, remembering where to turn, and finds her way back. She is on the path to the chalet, still running, carrying Henry. His plush fur has returned to its usual color.

Talk about close. Talk about lucky. Devon's feet touch the soil of the yard just as her mother comes out the back door. Devon is really panting now. She knows she may have to lie. She is ready for it. Bear, facing the chalet with a teacup balanced on one knee, is prepared to help her. Devon takes her position at the table, but then things get stranger.

Her mother says nothing. She is not even paying attention to her. Her mind is somewhere else entirely.

Lying in bed that night, Devon senses a great change. She can feel Henry's heart pounding in the darkness. Bear growls in a low, plaintive tone. Devon knows there is no way she can keep Henry away from the hut on the hill. He wants those flowers.

Maybe Bear can go with them next time.

* * *

Sunday morning and all Caroline wanted was a certain pie pan. Diane had sent her off with a few kitchen things, but none of them worked for the berry cobbler she was making. She sank to the kitchen floor in defeat. The whole weekend had been a wash.

They had gone on a little excursion Saturday, but it left her even more unsettled. Devon acted dazed and grouchy all morning, which usually meant she was coming down with something. Every time Caroline reached to check for a temperature, her daughter tried to evade her. All Devon wanted to do was play with that stupid rabbit. She was constantly having one-way conversations with him.

"Aren't you worried?" Caroline asked Jack on Saturday night after Devon had gone to sleep, stiff and straight in her little bed, where she clung to Bear and Henry. "She's acting really strange. I wonder if there's something wrong."

"It's probably her way of dealing with the fire," Jack said without looking at her. He was tired too.

They had started the day at the library, where there was a Saturday morning storytime for preschoolers. Right away Caroline saw how Devon stood out from the other kids. For one thing, she was literally standing up and refusing to join the circle. She had Henry in her arms but had agreed to let Bear stay in the car.

"It's okay," Jack whispered. "She's going to be great in the fall. Everything will click into place when school starts. Devon's ready."

"She doesn't look ready."

All the other parents turned to stare at her, but Caroline refused to smile or apologize. She was about to take her daughter by the shoulders and march her outside when the reader persuaded Devon to sit down. There were three different books about animal characters, but Caroline could not for the life of her follow the plot of any of them.

"How about that store?" Jack said when it was over.

They drove out to the little general store and got sandwiches at the deli. Caroline could tell Jack didn't like the place. He was put off by the weird locals who were clustered in the parking lot. This is never going to work, she thought. Why are we out here? To save a little on rent? Devon was enjoying herself, checking out the store, and for a second Caroline could pretend her family was like every other, made of hardworking people who were mostly happy.

She had a strange thought for one split second: What would everyone do if she ran around screaming fire? She shook her head and tried to focus on minding her child.

"You're putting that sandwich away really fast," Jack said when they were back in the car. "I thought we were going to try to find a park."

Caroline froze. "I'm hungry, Jack. And I'm sure Devon's starving." She looked in the back seat. "Devon, do you want to eat now? Then we can go home and take another walk."

Jack told her to relax. Caroline's jaw clenched.

At home, things got worse. For the first time ever, Devon didn't want to play outside.

"She's tired. Maybe a nap?" Jack said. Devon had always resisted naps and she was more stubborn than ever after the fire. "Or we could snuggle on the couch and watch movies."

"No," Devon said. She had run to put Bear back in her bedroom right when they got home but she was still clutching Henry. "I want to play upstairs by myself."

"That's supposed to be my office." Caroline wanted to get a few minutes of work in while Jack was home to watch Devon.

Devon's voice rose. "I get to use it sometimes." She sounded genuinely hurt.

"If you want to play, we should all go outside like we planned. Then you'll be tired."

"I will not be tired."

Devon was so adorable it was hard to get mad at her. Caroline and Jack smiled at each other, which made their daughter even more angry.

"How about you, me, and the rabbit go on a little hike and let your mother get some work done?" Jack asked.

"I don't want to go outside with you guys."

"Devon," Caroline said, "you can't have it both ways. You can take a nap or you can go outside with your father. You cannot use my office as your playroom."

"I have an idea. Me and Mr. Rabbit will go on a hike by ourselves. When we get back, we'll tell you about all the fun we had." And with that Jack grabbed Henry and held him high in the air.

Caroline knew from the expression on Devon's face that all was lost. She was feeling a little nauseated, and she found herself on Devon's side, not wanting to venture out. She covered her ears when the screaming started. Devon outdid herself with this tantrum, throwing herself at Jack and trying to climb his body. Jack yelled at his daughter and then Caroline yelled at Jack and all the while Devon kept on screaming, and somewhere in the mixture Caroline heard another voice.

Jack and Devon heard it too. They all fell silent. "What was that?" Caroline asked.

"I don't know," Jack said, walking over to the window to check the back yard.

Usually when Devon had a tantrum it escalated into red-faced screaming and then came down in slow waves, the tears falling while she choked and gasped. One of her parents would have to rock her. Then she would need a glass of water and a nap. This time, Devon regained control quickly. She raised one hand, marched over to her father, and took Henry back. She was still weeping, but only occasionally hiccupped. She consoled Henry the way Jack and Caroline wanted to console her, and then she looked up and said, "You cannot ever treat Henry this way. He's sensitive and vulnerable. You have to listen to me. This is very serious."

Caroline and Jack exchanged incredulous looks.

Devon tossed her head and sighed. "Well. I don't want him anywhere near her. Come on, Henry, let's go discuss this with Bear. We'll see what he says." And then, with perfect posture, she walked off to her bedroom.

"Jack. *He's sensitive and vulnerable?* What the hell?"

"It's probably something she heard you say. About her."

"What in the world are you talking about? I never said that."

"You don't need to get mad."

"Stop. I mean it. And who did she mean by *her?* Is that supposed to be me?"

For a long time Jack didn't answer. "Probably some imaginary friend. Or, I don't know. Go ask her."

They didn't speak for the rest of the day. Caroline went up to her office and did nothing, as usual. Devon stayed in her room, her voice rising and falling as she conferenced with Henry and Bear. Jack went out to the back yard and mowed the uneven grass with the little push mower that belonged to the house. Then he got into the Volkswagen and disappeared.

He returned with two baskets of berries, a peace offering. That was when Caroline promised him a cobbler, but even a simple dessert was something she couldn't deliver.

* * *

There is somebody new. The Lady in the hut is like preschool starting in August, a fact of life, something Devon has to deal with. Her parents cannot help her with this. She has two families now, the one where she is the child, and the other one, with Bear and Henry, where she is the parent.

What can she do? Staying inside is not an option. The sun calls to her every day, reliably, a good friend. It is so much better outside than in the chalet with her mother, who has taken over Devon's favorite room upstairs. Devon likes her little bedroom, but it looks out on the yard as if to say, *This is where you belong. Come outside.* Outside is hard work. Outside she has to argue with Henry, who has become more talkative than ever.

His voice has changed. He used to have a baby voice but now it's deeper, more like her father's. He constantly fights with her and Bear.

All this conflict is making Devon tired. One day she falls asleep with her head on the picnic table and her mom has to carry her inside.

And by then Henry has disappeared again. Devon isn't upset, as she needs a break from Henry. Mommy notices his absence though, and asks where he is.

"Playing."

"Where?"

"He's hiding from me."

"Did you hide him somewhere? Is that what you mean?"

She can't say yes, but she can't say no either, because then her mother will know how bad Henry is becoming. Maybe Mommy will make him disappear into the donation pile, which is worse than the woods. In the woods, Devon feels like she has a fighting chance, no matter how scary it is. "Don't worry. I will find him," she tells her mother.

It's almost impossible. She has to search the woods and so she must wait until night. There is no other time when her mother isn't lurking upstairs. At any moment Mommy's head could appear in the window, and then they will start waving to each other.

The first visit to the hut was a rare event, both lucky and unlucky. It will never be so simple again.

On the next full moon night, Devon opens her eyes. She gets up and grabs the hoodie and shoes she hid under her bed. Slips them on. Bear is standing up but does not speak. Lately he has been talking less and less, as if he knows Devon's path has taken her beyond reason. Beyond safety. She is moving further and further away from him.

She kisses Bear on the forehead the way Daddy kisses her when he leaves for work. "I'm going to get Henry," she whispers. "I will bring him back."

He says nothing but he is crying.

She opens the back door. Goes down the steps. Walks through the yard. Climbs over the picket fence. Only when she marches up the hill does she get scared. Her feet know where to go. There is a left turn shortly after she starts to pant, exactly like the first time. Her eyes have adjusted to the darkness, but it does not matter anyway because the hut is glowing, as if lit from inside. It calls to her.

Devon can see Henry's form through the reddish walls of the hut. He is like a shadow puppet, as is the Lady, who towers over the little rabbit as she stirs a large pot.

Bile coats the back of Devon's throat but she chokes it down. What is there to do but charge into the hut? She knows who the Lady is. Everybody knows.

There are so many stories about women like her.

The walk around the hut to the front door is incredibly long, as if the structure were the size of a castle. Devon knows this can't be right, but there is no fighting it. When she gets to the entrance, she finds a door of black metal. It is radiating heat. Devon knows the big black door knocker will burn her, but she reaches up and grabs it. Her flesh sizzles. How will she get inside now?

The door opens slowly, with that piercing creak she heard once before.

Henry is a real rabbit again, his fur white. His nose twitches as he looks at her.

Devon expects the Lady to be an old woman but she is not. The Lady is the age of Devon's mother, and in fact, she looks so much like Mommy that Devon assumes this is her sister, a mystery aunt. Her mother doesn't have any siblings though, unlike her daddy, who has a brother in New York.

Devon is spinning. Her head, especially, is light, like it might detach and float away, leaving her unable to deal with the situation in the hut. Her limbs are tingling. A certain numbness, which she has experienced once before, at the dentist's, descends over her body, starting at her head and making its way to her shoes. She is about to address the Lady as *Auntie*, the way children do sometimes in the old stories, when the Lady pulls out a knife. This has its own sound, sharp and menacing, different from the creak of the door. It has a color too, silver, before it turns to a reflective surface and Devon sees herself.

Her eyes are enormous, exaggerated, like the walk around the hut. This can't be right.

The Lady never speaks or smiles. Her face never changes but it does come closer and closer.

Henry thumps so hard he rocks the hut. Devon wants to cover her ears but her arms are so heavy she cannot move them. She opens her mouth and closes her eyes. She has to scream now. It is the only way. She has no other ideas.

There is no sound. Her whole face is contorted with the effort of screaming, but there is only silence.

Everything goes red.

When Devon wakes, she is back in her own bed. The sky is dark blue outside, which could mean either dawn or dusk. She is alone in her room in the silent chalet. If she moves, she is afraid she will ruin everything.

Two things are wrong with her friends. Bear is not in bed but sitting on a chair and staring at her. She cannot read his expression. Henry is there, tucked under her arm, but his body is cold and flat.

Someone has ripped out all his stuffing.

* * *

Caroline woke up twice on the night Devon walked in her sleep. The first time, she heard the back door open, but she incorporated the sound into a dream she was having. A few minutes later she woke with a start, her heart racing toward disaster. Was someone in the house? She ran out to the main room, which was weirdly illuminated by the moon, and her mouth went dry. The nausea that was part of every morning was already starting.

She checked the back door. It wasn't locked, wasn't even shut all the way, and then she found herself in Devon's room, where she tore the sheets off the bed in a pointless attempt to find her daughter's little body. Then she was back in her own bedroom, struggling with her phone, wondering if she should call 911. Jack woke when she dropped it on the floor. "Wake up! Devon's gone!" she screamed. "She's not in her bed." Her husband was a second too slow to respond, but then he jumped straight up, swayed, and ran to check the upstairs room. He came back downstairs and paused in the kitchen.

"What are you doing?"

Jack opened the cupboards, then the refrigerator. The door to the little pantry.

"You don't honestly think she's in there, do you?"

Jack didn't answer. He grabbed a flashlight, put on his shoes, and went outside as Caroline ran after him on her bare feet. "Shouldn't we call the police? Jack!"

"Let's check the hill first," he said when she caught up to him.

The flashlight made everything worse. Scary. Caroline imagined animal eyes staring back at her. Coyotes. Mountain lions. What about snakes? Jack ploughed forward like a determined Boy Scout. Caroline needed water; the nausea would not stop. She gave up and stopped on the steep hillside. They were almost at the end of the path and she didn't want to tackle the weeds and branches. She turned around and looked down at the chalet, illuminated by the lights they had left on. The bright, empty house made her sad and frightened. Disoriented.

The unnamable clawed at the edges of her mind. *Taken from her bed. Kidnapped while her parents slept.* While this other one was growing inside of her. No. She didn't want this baby; she wanted Devon and only Devon. Her eyes were adjusting to the moonlight, but she could no longer tell where Jack was in the darkness.

She didn't want to call the police, yet she knew time was of the essence. Who could say how long Devon had been missing already? As soon as she dialed 911, her old life would be gone forever. She would become one of those mothers, defined by loss. Questioned. Blamed. She began the descent to the chalet, but she had to go slowly without the flashlight. The rocks cut into her feet with each step. She gasped when she saw a small figure standing in the weeds to her right.

"Devon?" she called. "Jack!"

Her husband ran back down the hill so fast she was sure he would fall, and then he had Devon in his arms. "I'm going to take her home."

Home. Was the chalet their home?

Caroline did her best to get back down without falling. The hill was steeper than she remembered. Adrenaline had helped her over the picket fence on the way up. If it was so hard for her, then how had Devon managed it? She had been right to worry about Devon playing in the yard. There was something about that creepy fence, with its peeling paint, that bothered Caroline.

Things were worse inside the chalet. Jack was holding Devon, trying to wake her up.

"Do you want some water, baby?" Caroline asked. Devon's eyes were open, staring at nothing. "Why isn't she responding? Jack, what's wrong with her?"

"I think she's still asleep."

"She's never done this before."

"No, but she's had nightmares."

"Everybody has nightmares."

The three of them sat on Devon's little bed. Jack rocked Devon, who was still clutching her rabbit. Caroline found Bear, propped him up on a chair, and then reached for Henry.

"Leave it," Jack said. "Let her hold him."

Too late. Caroline had the floppy rabbit in her hands before she realized he was empty, like a hand puppet. There was a neat gash down his center. "How did this happen?"

"Keep your voice down," Jack whispered. "She probably did it in her sleep. A nightmare, like I said."

"No way. This would have taken scissors. Look. There is no seam on his stomach. She could never have opened him so cleanly."

"What are you, a surgeon? Give Henry back to her, please. We'll fix him in the morning."

"You mean I'll fix him," Caroline muttered, too tired to start a real fight.

"And I'll call the pediatrician. See if they want us to bring her in. I'll take the day off." He tucked Devon into bed and then they went back to their room.

"You'll really take the day off?" Caroline asked.

"Of course. I can take the morning, at least. You're so pale. I want you to sleep."

But Caroline could not go back to sleep. It was four in the morning. She peeked out the window. It was still dark outside. She rehearsed the inevitable phone call to her mother. *Devon had a little adventure last night. She gave us quite a scare.* Caroline saw herself fielding her mother's guarded, judgmental comments. There was always so much she was doing wrong where Devon was concerned.

She went to Devon's room to watch over her sleeping daughter. The beauty of Devon's face, the immaculate skin, made her cry. She imagined a giant snow globe enclosing the chalet and keeping all three of them safe forever. She took Bear on her lap and sat in the little chair by Devon's bed. When she woke up hours later with a screaming pain in her lower back, Devon was gone.

Caroline sat forward. The nightmare on the hill replayed in her head, but then the sounds of Jack and Devon having breakfast together filled in and guided her forward. It was morning. They had all survived, even Henry. The pain in her back intensified. She reached around and put her hand on the spot that ached. Please let this be it, she prayed.

Let it be over so I can go back to work and Devon can start school. I'll get out of the house forever. She went to the bathroom and peed.

When she wiped, the tissue stayed as white as snow, with no trace of blood.

* * *

The doctor smiles too much and this makes Devon nervous. She is weighed and measured, her temperature and blood pressure taken, but she can tell this is not a routine visit. She has been bad, she knows, but she cannot explain it to anyone. She thought she would be in so much trouble, but when morning came, her parents were nicer than ever. So nice it scared her.

Now, at the doctor's office, she is once again spared. She does not even have to talk, not about the night on the hill, not about the Lady, not about the hut. Not about Henry. Her mother does all the talking for her. Yes, there has been a lot of stress lately. A housefire. And there will be preschool in August. They are in a lovely new house now. "Lots of big changes," her mother says in the controlled voice Devon knows is dishonest.

She is sent out of the room. Maybe now they will talk about how bad she has been. Maybe she has been so bad they can't even discuss it in front of her.

The waiting room is empty. Devon puts Henry on the little table and examines his scar. You can barely tell it's there because Mommy is so good at sewing. Everything she does is perfect. "She's detail-oriented," Daddy always says. "Nothing gets past her." During the operation, Devon had to hold Henry's paw as he was re-stuffed and stitched back together. At the last minute, Mommy put a tiny blue bead inside him for luck. "I found it in the pocket of the jeans Diane lent me. So now we're going to keep it."

Devon has to make Henry promise not to run away again. She must get through to him. Unfortunately, he has fallen silent in the adult world of the clinic and looks like an ordinary stuffed animal. You would never imagine the kind of rabbit he is at night. Devon knows there's no point in talking now. He can't even hear her. She makes the painful, terrible decision to leave him behind. He might be safer at the hospital.

Her mother and the doctor come out before Devon can hide Henry in the big toybox in the corner of the waiting room. She has to pretend she has forgotten Henry, so she turns her back on him. Another mother and daughter come in and Devon fears that all is lost. This new little girl will notice Henry and make a big deal out of him. Any child can tell that Henry belongs to somebody. He is cherished. The doctor, still smiling, says something about skipping dessert and going to bed at the same time every night. Then she says goodbye.

Devon is spiraling downward, already mourning. What will she tell Bear? She can't lie to him, not ever. This is for the best, but it is so painful. She cannot let her parents know what has happened or they will call the doctor to see if Henry is still there. Please, Devon prays, let that little girl steal Henry. Don't let her mother notice.

Then she has a terrifying thought. What if the little girl gets hurt somehow? You have to know how to handle Henry.

Before they leave the parking lot, as Mommy is backing out, they are stopped. Henry glides through her mother's window and is soon sitting comfortably in the back seat. "Don't forget your friend!" the other mother says.

Mommy is so grateful. "Thank you so much. She hasn't been sleeping well lately. Please say thank you, Devon."

Devon can only manage to wave goodbye; her throat is scratchy when she tries to speak. As they drive off, Devon sees the other little girl's face, her brow furrowed, lingering somewhere between anger and suspicion. Maybe she wanted to keep Henry.

This is for the best. She is glad to have Henry back even though she knows it will be harder for all of them. Henry is hers. She loves him. She folds him in her arms and strokes his fur.

At home she takes Henry and Bear out to the picnic table for a reunion. There is already a new lock on the back door—you can't get in or out without a key—and Daddy has made it so that her bedroom window does not open anymore. The words "nice and safe" float around the chalet all day. Mommy joins them in the yard with her laptop. Daddy comes and goes making jokes. Sometimes he puts a hand on Henry's forehead to check for fever or makes Bear say funny things.

It's okay though. Bear, Henry, and Devon pretend to play. They know they are being watched, from both sides of the picket fence.

* * *

Caroline got a job offer to work at an arts organization in Culver City. Very part time, an embarrassing wage, but still. It was exactly what she needed to get herself back out there, and she got it through Drake, an old friend from grad school. It was how everybody got everything in this city. You had to have a connection. They sat down to have lunch together so Drake could fill her in on the details.

"I heard about what happened, Caroline. Are you guys all right?"

She had dressed very carefully. It wasn't an interview exactly, but she had to make the right impression. She had not been able to sleep the night before. Her face was already puffy, and she couldn't manage the top button of her new jeans. "It's fine, really. We're starting from scratch. It feels good. Cathartic."

"I can't imagine how it must be with a little kid. Is Devon all right?"

"She's adapting."

"And you like where you are now?"

"It's a great house. There's nature all around us. A bit of a drive, but it's worth it." She shouldn't have said that! "Oh, it's no problem getting to this part of the city if I leave early. I wouldn't want to go all the way downtown though. And Devon is starting preschool in the fall. We just got into a great program."

"You can work from home when you need to. I do a lot remotely myself. I remember you worked on grant writing in the past?"

Panic. "A little." He was referring to a small project she had been involved with in grad school, but it was so long ago she could barely remember it. The whole field would have changed by now, leaving her in the dust. She was going to have to start making phone calls and taking classes. There would certainly be more business lunches.

"Don't worry. We'll have time to go over the details later. When can you start?"

The question was like a hatchet, splitting her in two and requiring a new self to step forward. The working mother. Who was she? The freelancer didn't count. The freelancer was a sellout who dropped her work whenever her child needed her. The freelancer was a primitive website. A fantasy of sorts.

"As soon as you need me," Caroline lied.

"We were thinking August first." Drake was all business now, almost unfriendly, and Caroline felt the power of money slam her in the face. Money was a tyrant. It controlled everything and made her ridiculous. She was flailing, a pregnant working mother, her secret hidden in her body. Her feet ached in the high heels she had worn to appear hip and relevant. Sexy.

Rage took over. She faked a smile. "August first. Perfect."

The old Drake came back and shook her hand, and then he was off, of course, because this was LA and he was busy. It was Saturday, otherwise she would have had to bring Devon with her, and everybody had things to do. Besides, she and Drake had never been close friends. They didn't hang out. They weren't having an affair. He left her some papers to look over, which was odd. They could have done all this by phone or email.

He had obviously needed to see how she looked. I must still be hot, Caroline thought with a wry smile. She considered staying at the café, popping another button on her jeans, and eating more. Or she could go for a walk in her high heels. There were a few little shops on this street. It would be a treat to stroll along without Devon. Sans Jack. And did she really need to eat more?

Who was she eating for?

She rose and tucked the papers in the big purse, almost a briefcase, she had brought with her. She eyed an oatmeal cookie, oversized and salted, on her way out, but she didn't buy anything. Outside it was hot.

She wished she had worn a little dress instead, but she didn't have one. The first thing she had to do was rebuild her wardrobe, but probably not on a street like this. She walked along, trying to keep her mind off her main problem, but it wasn't long before she came to an expensive store called Little Things.

No. She would not stop, but she did allow herself to turn her head and stare at the impossibly fine crocheted items, the white satin, the tiny shoes and hats. Adorable. Precious. Pink and blue everywhere. None of it was serious though. These were gifts for rich people to give each other at baby showers. Outfits to wear in those important pictures before the baby left the hospital, or for the birth announcement.

Caroline forced herself to press on, though she knew what was going to happen. The car, a used Subaru Jack had bought for her, was parked around the corner. There was nowhere to be discreet. No trees or thick bushes. She couldn't even find a stupid flowerbed and she didn't make it to the corner.

Caroline had to bend at the waist and throw up in the gutter. One mouthful of whatever weird juice she had swallowed at the café, but it contained all her angst. Nobody said anything to her. Nobody offered help. At moments like these, when she wanted to be invisible, she loved LA. Please don't see me. Don't acknowledge the trouble I'm in. She stood up straight and wiped her mouth with her hand. Her ears were ringing. This was all because she had let herself get too hungry. She should have ordered a pricey, decadent omelet at the café.

She saw the Subaru. The meter had run out and Caroline, sweaty and angry, galloped up to it. She put in another quarter to give herself a little time to sit and recover before the sharks started closing in on her parking spot. Now she knew what she should have said to Drake. "I'm done. We're done."

Meaning done having children. Drake hadn't asked, but he didn't need to. "I'm dying to get back to work. So glad Devon's starting at a great school." This would further the illusion that school took care of everything. As if some mythical school could take care of little Devon for the whole day.

She had two phone calls to make. One to set up childcare for August first. The second to the clinic.

* * *

Devon knows there won't be animals at her school. She knows but looks for them anyway, in everything green: the landscaping, the trees that border the south side of the property, the little vegetable garden the head of school is so proud of. Mommy is tense and quiet, keeping an eye on Devon like she doesn't trust her.

"She's very observant," says a woman in clicking heels as she walks them around the building. Devon's teacher is away for summer vacation, but they will visit the classroom anyway. This is a small school, only for little children, and Mommy says this is good. There are several different classrooms, and then two big rooms for art and music. A small playground. The vegetable garden. In each space Devon looks around to see if Henry could possibly have followed her. She even searches under tables and along the windowsill.

In the bright space that will be Devon's classroom, the woman sits down with Mommy and asks some questions. There is nothing to worry about. Devon knows her parents have already signed the papers and paid. It is very hard to get into a good preschool in this part of LA. Devon both knows this and knows she is not supposed to worry about this, as if worry is something she can control. She is already learning to accommodate her parents' fears, making room for them in her life.

She sits at a little table on the other side of the room, close to a big window, from which she can see two squirrels rushing around, either playing or working, Devon cannot tell. She hears Mommy's voice drop to a low hush and knows this means she is talking about the Horrible Night. Her parents never talk about it around her and this only makes the flames grow larger. Do they think she doesn't remember? She remembers everything, but most of all the smell and the black smoke against the city sky at night. Grown-ups always expect her to draw, so she draws a picture of the flames, red and yellow and orange, all by themselves, without her old home in it. This way she won't upset Mommy, who is upset all the time now.

Devon remembers all her old books and gets up to see if any of them are on the bookshelf in this classroom. She finds a copy of *Little Fur Family* and is tempted to hide it under her shirt. Her parents have not been very good about replacing her collection of books, mistakenly assuming she has outgrown them now that she can read on her own. She remembers a little wooden dollhouse and wonders if she should ask for a bigger, better one. She remembers the plastic barn, the same one everyone has, but hers was special. Those animals were hers and they all had names. She also lost a set of underpants with the days of the week written in French and she suspects it would be hard to find those again.

So many things are gone. She forgets herself and sighs audibly, causing her mother to turn her head ever so slightly in Devon's direction. Then she goes back to drawing the flames, red and orange, big and angry.

She is getting hungry and bored. She knows she will be bored in this classroom everyone is so happy about.

Before long, her mother and the woman in heels are calling to her. It is time to leave. Devon picks up the picture to take it home, but when she sees the woman's raised eyebrows and her mother's destroyed face, she regrets it. She should not have drawn anything.

The drive to the chalet is quick but Mommy warns her it won't always be this way. "We have to wake up early so we can be there on time in the morning. It's very important. Sometimes it's going to take a while to get home because of traffic. I'm going to be working nearby so you don't have to worry about anything."

Devon is surprised. Does this mean she can have the upstairs room now that Mommy has a new job?

Her mother laughs. "I'm keeping the room. I don't have to go in every day, but when I do, I can't be late. And it's not like I have a big office to myself like Daddy does."

"How come you get two rooms in the chalet?"

Another laugh. "Because I gave up so many other things."

Devon doesn't see how this is funny.

"Look, you have a bedroom and a back yard. I have to share a bedroom with Daddy. The back yard is yours. Everyone knows the yard belongs to the kid."

When they get home, the first thing Devon does is check on Bear and Henry. Bear is all big eyes, which means he is worried. Devon can guess why. Henry is gone again. His bad experience has not made him more cautious. If anything, he is more frantic. He can't sit still, and Devon knows his mind is often somewhere else. It's like he doesn't want to play anymore. He can't play.

Devon takes Bear out to the yard. Henry is already there, napping in the sun on the picnic table. He looks so peaceful, like his old self before all the bad things happened.

He looks like any other plush rabbit.

* * *

Caroline was looking for a fight, no two ways about it. She hadn't realized how much anger she was carrying around, and once she started giving it voice, it grew like a wildfire.

They were in the kitchen. It was late. Devon had gone to bed, but Caroline doubted she was asleep. Lately, whenever she went into Devon's bedroom at night, her daughter was lying there with her eyes wide open, looking like a frightened animal. Caroline was terrified of another sleepwalking incident.

"Why the hell should I have to learn from my daughter that you're going back to work?"

"Whoa. Listen to yourself. Do I have to ask for your permission?"

"Caroline, this is crazy. You discuss these things with me first, not with the kid."

"The kid. Listen, Jack, you're never home."

"Because I'm at work. So that you can take care of her."

Time stopped and the little kitchen filled with Jack's words. That was her job, her function, her life. To take care of Devon. For free. To sit upstairs and pretend to work. And Jack was fine with it. "You expect it to go on like this forever?" she said.

"What do you mean?"

"Seriously? You want me to be the babysitter and the maid?"

"You're her mother, Caroline."

There. Something about Jack's tone was so familiar. *You're her mother, Caroline.* Where had she heard that before? It was insidious. Yes, sure, she was Devon's mother, but there was much more to it. He was saying, you need to accept your lot in life. I am sentencing you. You can't get out of it. And why couldn't she turn things around and say the same to him? These words were supposed to be joyous, *Congratulations on your new baby girl!* but instead they were disempowering. Denigrating.

Look at his face, she thought. He's mocking me.

"What?" Jack said. "Isn't this what you wanted?"

The strength left her body. She was torn between silence and screaming. Maybe she should grab a bottle and go upstairs to her so-called office. Was this the feeling of a marriage ending? How would she know when they had reached the final stage? "Look," she began, "I'm going back to work while I still can. I can't lose this opportunity. This isn't going to happen again. Nobody else is going to offer me a way back in like this."

More silence, this time from Jack. And then he said, "Sorry, but I never wanted to have an only child."

Jack had one brother he didn't see much. Caroline was an only child, and she was tired of being pathologized for it. Too many people assumed she was selfish or maladjusted, or that she had an unhealthy relationship with her parents. She and Jack had had this argument about family size before. "You know what, Jack? I never wanted you to disappear into your work and leave me all alone with a kid."

"We're lucky, actually. You know that, Caroline?"

"Lucky."

Nothing was resolved. They did not discuss the logistics of childcare. Everything would be on her, as usual. She made popcorn and started looking for a movie on cable. They had watched a lot of movies when they were younger, pre-Devon. It was hard to find one that didn't have to do with coupling, and it was impossible to avoid the ubiquitous male-gaze problem. She tried and tried to come up with something in between girly and sexist, something they both could watch.

"I'm going to bed," Jack said.

"Good night."

She wanted to sleep. Pretending there wasn't something growing inside of her didn't help relieve her exhaustion. The life was being sucked out of her. That was the problem with babies. They went after your body to get what they needed, and now she was hungry again. The popcorn was gone. Maybe bread and cheese? She gave up on finding a movie and started flipping between channels. Before long she was dozing.

She saw someone in the window. She knew it wasn't a dream, even as it happened. Someone was outside. There had to be. Somebody must have been out there all along. Who else had ripped the stuffing out of that rabbit? This would explain why she felt Devon slipping away from her into imaginative play. It wasn't because of the fire. It wasn't only because she, Caroline, was such a bad mother.

And it wasn't because she and Jack were falling apart.

It was the weirdest thing. Caroline was half-asleep, but she knew someone was staring at her from the back door, which had a tiny window at the top. There were two big picture windows on either side of the back door, but she sensed the figure, a female, peering at her through the little window. Caroline was sure she was female. A woman. An old woman? Long hair. Long white hair flowed out behind her, as if buoyed by a breeze.

Instead of jumping up off the couch, Caroline squeezed her eyes shut. She was a little kid again, waiting for the monster to go away. At the same time, she was afraid the figure would evade her. As soon as she woke up fully and went to investigate, the figure, the specter, would disappear.

Caroline drifted for a few moments longer and then woke with a jolt, her heart pounding. She ran to the door. She checked each window. They were old, divided into six panes each by strips of black metal; charming, but impossible to keep clean. They were not airtight. And there were no draperies or blinds. She and Jack had discussed ordering some kind of window covering, but it was too expensive, and they could never agree on what to buy. Since the chalet bordered the woods, they left the windows as they had found them when they moved in. Uncovered. It was a little creepy at night, but not as bad as having neighbors staring at you in the city.

She darted back to Devon's bedroom. Her heart was racing but there was nothing to be afraid of. Devon was deep in the sleep of an angel, and Bear and Henry were on either side of her.

She went back to the main room and looked out each window again. There was nobody outside. Nothing was there. Caroline unlocked the back door and stepped down into the yard. She could hear the trees rustling in the breeze and other little sounds that came from animals or insects or her own imagination. Again, she thought of coyotes and mountain lions. Foxes? She wasn't sure. She kept meaning to go on the internet to look up some facts about the local habitat. Now she went forward and took a seat at Devon's little picnic table, facing the woods.

She kept staring at the trees, vaguely expecting something to pop out at her. She had been so scared when she first woke up, but now it seemed silly. It wasn't even day yet, but already her nightmare was slipping away from her. How could something be so real and then disappear? It was a dream. That's what Jack would say when she told him. It was all a dream.

And then she remembered why that phrase, *You're her mother, Caroline*, had bothered her so much. It was the way Jack said it, shaming her. Now she knew where she had heard it first, but it was different.

I'm your mother, Caroline. It was her own mother who had said it, whenever she wanted to control her.

* * *

Bear thinks he can save her. He talks to her more now than he ever has.

After she told him how the Lady on the hill hurt Henry, Bear was quiet for a whole day. He studied Henry's scar and bowed his brown head. They both know there's no keeping Henry away from that hut. He can't help himself. The new locks won't stop him. Daddy once told Devon that certain animals can get through any space big enough to fit their head. Henry is one of those animals. She has tried restricting him to the new toy box or the bottom of a drawer. She has asked Daddy to take him to work.

It's no use. He always gets out.

Bear tells her they will make a journey up the hill, just the two of them, to see the Lady for the very last time.

"Without Henry?"

"Without Henry."

"But he will find us."

"We'll play with him," Bear says. "We'll make him run around until he has to take a nap. Up and down the stairs. You'll see. He'll fall asleep and then we'll leave."

They devote the afternoon to wearing Henry out by playing hide and seek around the chalet. It takes time, but eventually even Devon is exhausted. Her mother never leaves the upstairs room even though they are making so much noise. Lately Mommy has been unavailable. This is because she needs to prepare for her new job.

Devon knows many things are wrong: in the upstairs room, on the hill, in both her little families. Going along with Bear's plan is a way to make something right.

It's dusk and Daddy still is not home. This is because of the traffic and it is also a sign. Bear turns to her and says, "Let's go."

Devon can tell he's afraid. Still, he pulls a key from his fur and unlocks the back door. It is not the same as the key her parents use. It probably opens all doors, Devon thinks. This is called a skeleton key, and she is not surprised Bear has one.

She lets him take the lead. It's funny watching him scale the picket fence with his moveable limbs, so undignified. Bear is such an old man for these little kid games, but Devon doesn't want to laugh at him, not when he's doing everything for her. She should have asked more questions. She doesn't even know what the plan is. What can Bear do to make the Lady stop? Devon knows what the Lady wants but she dares not speak it. She saw the knife. She saw the pot. She heard Henry thumping.

She has known a fear so great it takes over every cell of her body.

Nobody can help her. Her parents don't know who Bear and Henry really are. They pretend to understand, they play along, but they are faking it. And Bear belonged to Daddy first. They must have played together when Daddy was little, just as Devon plays with him now.

What happened to her father to make him forget his own Bear so completely?

Now they are going up the hill. Devon wishes they could burn down the Lady's hut, but that would start a huge fire, destroying acres and acres. The first time she heard the word *acre* was in relation to destruction by fire. This kind of fire goes on and on for days, a monster in search of food. Innocent people will die. Devon knows how painful it is to lose everything to fire and would not wish this on anyone else.

Devon is afraid to use the w-word. The Lady does not wear a pointy hat, but Devon knows who she is. Even saying the word aloud is dangerous. Looking at the Lady's face is also dangerous. Devon knows how this must end; she has heard the stories. The best thing would be to push the Lady into her own pot, or to do to her what she did to Henry. Devon is worried Bear isn't strong enough to do this, or perhaps he's too kindhearted. She has never even seen him get mad or raise his voice. Still, she knows about bears in the wild. She has seen them growling and fighting on television. Mommy says there is nothing more frightening than a Mama Bear protecting her cubs. *The way I protect you, Devon.*

If her sweet Bear turned into a Papa Bear, would he be strong enough to kill the Lady?

Watching Bear scale the hill like a sturdy little soldier, Devon loves him more than ever. He really is fearless. He loves his family and would do anything for them. He is better than all the heroes in the books Mommy reads to her. Devon wants to be like him when she grows up. Devon wants to be like him now.

How does he know where to go? He leaves the path and veers to the left, where there isn't even a place to walk, only a slight separation in the undergrowth. Devon is glad she is not alone this time.

There. The hut is beginning to light up inside. Devon can see the Lady standing near her pot. Chills cover Devon's body, running all the way up to her scalp. Her hands and feet turn to ice. Bear is more alive than ever, more certain of himself. He turns around, for the first time, and speaks to her.

"If she asks, tell her we want to marry."

Then he disappears around the corner of the hut. Devon is confused.

Marry? Devon has never considered this possibility.

* * *

Caroline got off the phone after scheduling the appointment. They would do an ultrasound and consultation first, and then she would come back on Thursday. This would all be over before the end of the week. In the meantime, though, the nausea was getting worse. She had to run to the bathroom, where she leaned over the toilet bowl for a long time, waiting. Thank God Devon was playing outside.

Closing her eyes made her dizzy; it was worse than staring at the old, stained porcelain. She needed to eat more. It was the only way to stop the nausea. She was supposed to go to the clinic on an empty stomach on Thursday, but how would she manage? She didn't even have a babysitter for Devon.

And where was Jack? He wouldn't be home for hours. She needed to start dinner soon, or start thinking about it at least. What could she serve that wouldn't make her sick? She didn't want to ask Jack to pick up pizza or Chinese. She couldn't bear his silent disapproval leaking through the cell phone. *You mean you do nothing all day and you can't even get dinner started?*

Water. Sparkling water. She needed to slam a glass of water and then she would be able to think straight. But first she had to check on Devon, who was being strangely quiet. Normally Caroline could hear Devon's little voice rising and falling as she played with Bear and Henry. She had been playing inside all day, in fact, running up and down the stairs, but now she was gone.

Caroline pushed open the back door and saw Henry lying on the picnic table, his stitches exposed to the evening air. And then she knew.

The world really did tilt and spin, almost as if the chalet were falling down the hillside. The dreaded earthquake, right here, in her heart. Her mouth filled with saliva as she stumbled down the three little steps and onto the dying grass, where she almost threw up. She forced herself forward, across the lawn, over the picket fence, and up the hill. She was all adrenaline.

No way was she calling Jack. No time for that anyway. She had to get to her daughter before it was too late. She had to find her. Who knew how long she had been gone? She tried calling out, but her voice fell flat. She made herself run though she was soon panting, her ears ringing. In no time the path ended and she was surrounded by trees.

Couldn't Devon simply be playing somewhere? Maybe she had already mastered these woods the way kids used to. Maybe they had left her alone enough times that she had found a new place to play. But Caroline knew this wasn't true. Her daughter hadn't even turned four yet.

Devon was lost. Again. Caroline stopped and tried to think. Why had Devon left Henry behind? She was always so wrapped up in that rabbit, protecting him, monitoring him. Where was Bear? Caroline hadn't seen him in the yard. If Bear was gone, then this must be a game. Devon and Bear had run off somewhere without Henry. They had left him behind on purpose. Was it hide and seek? Yes! Devon had been playing hide and seek all day while Caroline was trying to work.

She stared into the tangle of trees and took a deep breath. "Devon!" she cried, and the force required to call out made her mouth water all over again.

Wait. What about that night when she had found her daughter sleepwalking? Where was she standing? It wasn't too far from this path. It was farther down, she realized. Though she was reluctant to turn her back on the trees, which were guarding some dark secret, Caroline whirled around and started walking down the hill. The sea flashed in the distance, an old friend, a reminder of her life before the fire. She kept walking, looking for the spot from that night, saying her daughter's name over and over again. How she hated going downhill.

What about Bear? Should she call his name? Would he bring her closer to Devon?

Then she felt the first vile cramp. Could it be? She gritted her teeth but smiled. Would everything turn out all right? This would be ideal. It would give her more time. It would even give her and Jack more time, though she knew they had already gone too far down a certain road leading away from a healthy family life. The thing was, they were starting to lose respect for each other. She had read somewhere that losing respect in a marriage was worse than losing love. This was true, but when had it started? Before the fire, for sure. Sometimes she wished they could go away to an island together, just the two of them, and straighten things out, but life would not stop coming at them. There was no way to find that island.

Now her legs felt funny. Heavy. She was looking for something like a meadow. That had to be it. Devon was standing in a clearing or a meadow. In her memory, her daughter rose like an angel out of the grass, but there was no meadow up here, only scraggly trees and brush, weeds so dry they invited fire. Was she even in the right spot? And where was the path? Caroline didn't know if she could find her way again.

The best thing would be to sit down for a few seconds. If only Devon would do the same. Caroline stopped, sat, and said a silent prayer. *Devon, don't be afraid. Wherever you are, I will find you. Please wait and I will come.* Another cramp. Her lower back was really hurting now. She needed an Advil. She could not stay calm. She was spaced-out from the pain, almost high.

What was she doing, sitting here? She had to get up and find Devon before the night got much darker, before Jack came home. Caroline rose and felt something thick and warm rush between her legs.

* * *

Devon hates to wait and waiting outside the Lady's hut is the worst. Children are always told to be patient, Devon has noticed, but this is different. It is a test. Should she go after Bear? Or should she prove her loyalty by waiting?

Bear didn't tell her to follow him and he didn't tell her to wait either. He said something about getting married and stopped Devon in her tracks. As to how long she has been waiting, she cannot say. It's like a dream, in that it may have been a few minutes, or it may have been an hour.

The hut is illuminated again. Inside, the shadow puppet show is playing before her, and Devon can see the Lady with her long knife and her big pot. Devon knows this story. It is like the fairy tales or certain songs her mother sings: she cannot remember a time when she didn't know the words. At some point she will be inside the hut too, she is sure of it.

And then what will she do?

In the distance she can hear her name. The trees are calling to her.

She waits and waits and when Bear finally appears in the scene—an unmistakable figure, her beloved—it happens so fast it takes her breath away. She realizes she is late for the show. She is supposed to be there, in the scene, in the hut, saying her lines. Answering the Lady's questions. She is late and it is the worst feeling ever, worse even than the time they were late to a preschool interview because of traffic.

If she asks, tell her we want to marry.

Devon tries to run but her legs are frozen. The hut is filled with rapid action, an animated conversation between the Lady and Bear, but Devon is painfully slow. She drags her little body around the corner of the hut, and when she reaches the black metal door, Bear disappears inside. Which can't be right. She knows he is already inside, talking to the Lady. Devon understands that if she doesn't enter the hut, she will be forever watching Bear leave her behind. He will be inside while she will be stuck outside. She can't let this happen, so she grabs onto the hot metal door before it closes. She still has some little scabs from the last time the door burned her. She has been careful not to let anyone else see these marks.

No time to scream. Everything has changed. The Lady is dressed as a bride. She is beautiful. And Bear is wearing a suit.

Devon starts crying like the little girl she is. Her clothes, a pair of denim shorts and a little blue t-shirt, are dirty. If she had known it would be like this, she would have worn the fancy dress Grandma Carol sent her, and because she has no Mary Janes that fit, she could have gone barefoot. All of her jewelry was lost on the Horrible Night, but she would have brushed her hair at least.

It is too late now.

The Lady's gown is long and loose, covered in embroidery. What captures Devon's attention is her magnificent headdress, a tight headband that rises into a tiara. It is made of lace. The pearls and diamonds sewn into it cast their own pure white light. Devon wants to wear it. Desperately.

Devon was wrong about the Lady. She is not the age of Devon's mother. She is young, like a babysitter, a girl in high school. Devon understands this girl is her competition, a rival on the playground, but much worse because the game is so serious, and her mother is not coming to get her. She looks at Bear to see if he understands. Has the fancy suit gone to his head? Is he in love with this beautiful girl even though she is holding a sharp knife?

"Do you wish to marry?"

The question comes from the smiling Lady.

"Yes. I wish to marry Bear," Devon says.

"As do I. Now we must drink tea together to see who will be the bride."

A small circular table appears with two beautiful little chairs. There is a pot in the center of the table and two teacups. It looks a lot like Devon's set, but this one must be hundreds of years old, a real grown-up tea set, white with blue flowers. The flowers, Devon can see, are exactly like the ones that captivated Henry on his first visit to the hut.

"This is how we play," the Lady says. "I will pour the tea and then we drink. If the tea turns to blood in your mouth, you are the winner and Bear is yours."

They all sit down. Devon looks at Bear and sees the two most worried eyes in the world. She knows she cannot speak to him in front of the Lady. There is nothing left but to go forward, even though this does not sound fair. The dread grows within Devon's heart and will soon be big enough to make her burst, but surely Bear is meant to remain hers.

The Lady pours a cup of black tea for Devon and then one for herself. She gives Devon her cup. She never stops smiling.

"Are you ready?"

"What if I lose?" Devon asks. She knows she will lose Bear but she has to ask.

"Don't worry." The Lady smiles. "We will find someone else for you to marry. The forest is filled with bridegrooms. I will get you ready for your bridegroom."

Devon does not like the sound of this, but she nods. She does not know what blood tastes like. She can't imagine it. The Lady looks right into Devon's eyes as they each raise a cup and take a sip. Devon waits. She recognizes the disagreeable taste of strong black tea, and at that moment, blood gushes from the Lady's mouth in a river.

It goes everywhere, even on the headdress. On the table. On the walls. It begins bubbling in the big black pot. The Lady, now ancient, rises from the table as her clothing falls from her. Bear loses his suit. Devon has blood all over her t-shirt and shorts.

The Lady raises the knife.

Devon wants to scream that the Lady does not play fair. She wants her mom. The only word she can manage is the name of the one who is hers, and the voice that comes out of her is so huge it surprises the universe.

Her bear is gone in a flash of light, and what stands in his place does not have the same eyes. He is so tall he knocks the roof off the hut and lets in the mournful light of early evening. He has long teeth and his growl is a deep, low river of power.

He goes straight for the Lady.

* * *

The cramps were so bad that Caroline had to sit down after every few steps. The blood was really coming. She knew she would have to go to the hospital. She would have to lie to Jack about losing track of her period.

She did not have her phone with her.

She was hemorrhaging. Would she lose her uterus? She remembered hearing about a friend of a friend who had lost hers when she started hemorrhaging after her baby was born. Maybe she was dying? Shit. She sat up.

Devon.

Where was Jack? Was he making his way home yet? What time was it? Evening. It was too bad they were not getting along. Jack called her less and less these days, whereas in the past he would call her before leaving work and at least once on the long drive home. If he had tried to call, he probably thought she was blowing him off. If he only knew. In the distance she heard what sounded like an animal growling. It had to be a mountain lion. Did anything else make such a terrifying, violent noise? Oh God. Now her ears were filled with ringing and she could no longer be sure of what she was hearing.

She needed to find Devon. She did not have the strength to call her daughter's name, so she said it over and over again before stumbling on a tree root. Caroline fell to her knees as everything went black. Her pants were drenched in blood and her whole body shook. The cramps came in ocean waves.

At one point she came to in the darkness. Damn. What was happening? She wasn't worried for herself, but for Devon. And where was Jack? She heard animals moving around her. She remembered the night of the fire, the first time she had despaired in darkness, but everything had been so much louder, with the blaring of sirens and human distress.

Then, sometime later, she was being lifted onto a stretcher and reaching for Jack, but the reach was a question. Where was Devon? She heard Jack reassuring her. Afterward, either from exhaustion or something they had given her, she slept for a long time.

She was in the hospital, in a small room with a single bed. Jack was asleep in a chair next to the window. She tried to rise but she had no strength. Jack's eyes opened and he sat up, abruptly alert.

"Devon!" she said.

"It's all right. She's all right. I've seen her."

"What happened?"

"You had a miscarriage. When I found you, I thought someone had murdered you. Killed you and taken Devon."

"Jack."

"I'm sorry." He covered his face with his hands. "I've never been so tired."

"How did you find Devon?"

"I came home late and you guys were gone. The Subaru was out front, so I was worried. I saw your purse. Your phone. I got the big flashlight and went outside. Henry was on the table and I grabbed him. Don't know why."

"What about Devon?"

"Wait. Let me explain."

"Is she injured, Jack? Did something happen to her?"

"No. They don't know. She was in shock. She's on an IV, like you, but she hasn't lost any blood. No visible wounds. She's asleep now."

"Why can't I have her with me?"

"I don't know."

They fell silent. The room filled with the weight of everything they couldn't talk about. Caroline went on nervously, "So you haven't spoken to her? Asked her what happened?"

"No. Listen. I didn't know what to do after I found you. My cell wasn't working on that hill. I guess I should have carried you down right away and called the paramedics sooner, but I had to press on and find her. You could have bled to death. I'm sorry. I'm so sorry about everything."

Jack started crying and Caroline remembered how he had not cried on the night of the fire. Neither of them had. Could she manage tears now? Maybe the drugs were making her unnaturally calm. "It's okay, Jack. I would have done the same thing. Where was she?"

"I found her in this pile of wood."

"Wood?"

"Lumber. Old boards, a metal slab, but it was all overgrown with vines. Someone must have built a shed at one point and then nature took over."

"So she was playing in that mess and didn't know it was dangerous."

"She was really far away, Caroline." Now he was looking at her in accusation.

"Far away?"

"Pretty far off the path for a little kid. I can't understand how she got there. I didn't know she would go up the hill all by herself. I thought she always stayed in the yard."

"She does. I check on her constantly. This is the first time she's done this, aside from that one night."

"Anyway, I carried her back down and put a blanket over her. Called the paramedics. I didn't know what'd happened to you. I didn't even know you were pregnant."

"I'm sorry. You must have been so afraid." If the nurse hadn't come in to check her vitals, Caroline would have called for her. She was too tired for this conversation. She could feel Jack looking at her. He knew how regular her periods were. It was unlikely she wouldn't notice a late one. "Where's Henry now?" she asked, to change the subject.

"At home."

"You should go get him. I want him to be here when she wakes up. And Bear too."

"But I don't want her to be alone when she wakes up. I can't risk that."

"Then you should go to her now."

Jack left without another word. Caroline could see the judgment in the nurse's face. She was sure she wasn't imagining it. That nurse saw countless families in crisis. She probably knew exactly where they were headed.

$* * *$

When Devon sees Henry again, they fall into a deep family embrace. It pains her to tell him about Bear, but she sees in his tear-covered face that he already knows and blames himself. She sits with him on the bed in her lonely room. "I think we should stay inside today," she says. One arm is bruised from where they took blood, and she is still wearing the hospital ID bracelet. She knows she is not sick, only tired and sad. Bear's absence in her bedroom, in her life, is huge.

It is not long before her father realizes Bear is missing. This is his childhood teddy bear, a valuable Steiff, and Daddy spends the better part of an afternoon searching the hillside, but finding nothing. He gently questions Devon about Bear, who was his toy first, and though he does not show his disappointment, Devon knows she has hurt him.

She has lost something that is worth money. Her father hates losing money.

Mommy is back. She is more like her old self. She was in the hospital too, though Devon does not quite understand why, but she assumes it has to do with the violence in the hut. Bear attacked the Lady, but Devon knows he would never hurt Mommy. Still, she knows her mother lost consciousness, which is like dreaming. And she knows, though nobody ever says so, that there was blood. A lot of blood. Blood is a big part of the last night on the hill.

Mommy won't let Daddy pester her, but he does question her about where she plays. She says the picnic table. It is the truth. The episodes on the hill are not play. They are work. When he asks her about a pile of wood, some kind of abandoned structure, she only shakes her head. The Lady's hut was nothing like that, and now it is gone. Bear destroyed it.

She can tell Daddy thinks she is lying, or maybe he thinks she's bad. He does not know how brave she is, but telling him would be impossible. Dangerous.

Her mother's voice works like a spell. "Leave her alone, Jack."

Everything is different now. There are two teams, Mommy and her against Daddy. Daddy is going to lose, Devon can sense it. She loves him, she knows he's a good man, but there is something else, something she will never be able to articulate, that makes him the loser here. It may be simply that he can never spend enough time with her.

For now, she has to learn how to get through the days before school starts. This is grief, and it makes time slow down and speed up. It makes her refuse dinner and then wake up starving when her parents are asleep. It makes her birthday party in the back yard, with only Grandma Carol and her parents, a strange experience, all melting ice cream cake and gifts that don't hold her interest. They crowd around the little picnic table, the adults standing, as Devon blows out the candles. When she goes to make her wish, she sees Henry watching from the bedroom window.

Instead of a wish, she receives knowledge: This will all be over soon.

Slowly, and almost imperceptibly, so that she barely notices, she stops playing with Henry. Their conversations become less frequent, less urgent. She goes to school with other children who have all kinds of stories. All kinds of secrets. She and her mother move their few possessions into a little house in Culver City. Grandma Carol helps them to buy it and gives them their first piece of new furniture, a small sectional. Daddy finds his own place, fancy, but as tiny as a hotel room, in Century City, before eventually moving back to New York for his dream job.

They start going to Venice Beach again. They never return to the chalet, and Devon can't even remember her last day there, or the feeling of driving away from it once and for all.

Henry stays with her always but remains a stuffed animal. It is hard to believe he was ever a real rabbit. Did that happen or was it all imaginative play? He never stops tugging at her heart. She knows she will keep him forever because he is the only thing that survived the fire, a word she learns to say without cringing, without starting to cry. She remembers the Horrible Night, but forever abandons the word *horrible*, preferring to say terrible or awful.

She is loyal to Henry because he was with her when her little family was intact.

Her family. She has so much to learn about her family, still, before it is too late.

Jack: 1981

"Boys, this is Pamela," Jack's dad said in a strange tone, without the goofy smile that usually accompanied treats and surprises. It was more like a command.

Pamela's face loomed above them and then took its place among Jack's bad memories, even more troubling than his parents' announcement of their divorce, when he was still in elementary school. Many lessons came with Pamela's face. People change. Your own dad could turn into a person you barely recognized. Home itself, that place where he and Josh were supposed to be safe, could become dangerous.

Everything changed with Pamela's arrival. Even in the dark disorientation of the immediate post-divorce period, Jack had held onto the hope that his parents would get back together. Somehow, someday, they would find their way back to each other and then everything could return to normal. Pamela's presence made this hope impossible. She was mean, but always with a smile on her face. She would say something cruel and then follow it up with a little laugh.

At the wedding reception, Pamela took Jack and Josh aside to remind them she had married their father, not the two of them. Ha-ha. Her teeth were already stained with the red wine that danced in her glass and threatened to splash all over her, like blood, but no matter how violent her gestures, the wine stayed in its place, as if by magic. Josh reached for Jack's hand. When their dad came up to join them, Pamela slipped on her angel wings. Josh looked to Jack for help. *Call Mom.* That was the conventional playground wisdom. *Tell your mom.* Everybody knew this. But Mom couldn't help with the Pamela situation.

A judge decided the boys were to live with their mother in New York during the school year. Six weeks of summer and every other Christmas were awarded to their dad, who moved to California for an executive-level job. Jack's favorite time of year, summer vacation, became torture, thanks to custody.

"We have our bikes," his brother would remind him. "Dad bought us those great bikes."

Josh was simple that way. Sweet and smart, but simple. Josh never went looking for trouble. Jack's mom was always gently suggesting he could learn a thing or two from Josh.

He hadn't learned in time, and Josh ended up in the hospital.

That was the summer when Jack went to hell.

* * *

Each day of those California summers spent at his dad's house, north of San Francisco, was a challenge, and not only because of Pamela. The place didn't feel right, especially his dad's neighborhood, which bordered a creek. There was water all over the county, in fact, creeks and marshes and wetlands, everything eventually running into the bay.

All that water, flowing. Jack couldn't let Josh know how much it bothered him. After all, it wasn't as if he couldn't swim. Pools didn't scare him. For some reason the ocean didn't bother him, not unless there was an undertow, but he hated not being able to see the bottom of lakes and creeks. Jack tried to bury his fear of these deceptive bodies of water with their own tricky tides and weird winds, water that threatened him. It would be so easy to sink, to drown, where the land gave way, without warning, into the water.

His dad and Pamela claimed to love their Marin lifestyle, though Jack never saw them row a boat or go for a hike, not once. All he ever saw them do was drink wine and watch TV. It was obvious that Pamela—who never got to enjoy a honeymoon!—didn't want them around.

"We'll stay out of the way," Josh promised. "You don't even have to cook. I know how to make grilled cheese."

"Oh, I'm not worried about you, sweetie, but I don't want Jack here embarrassing me in front of my friends."

Pamela liked having her girlfriends over, all of them old, creepy dolls, carefully dressed, their smooth faces erupting in wrinkles over crude jokes and dirty little stories. They loved to sit out on the deck drinking bottle after bottle of white wine and devouring plates of grown-up treats, but only after a ritual discussion of calories and fat grams. Once, when an unexpected heat wave made the usually cool nights into a hot ordeal, the ladies were still sitting outside in their bikinis after sundown. Pamela called for Jack and Josh, watching television with the volume so low they had to sit right in front of the screen, to bring them some chips and another bottle of wine.

Jack and Josh looked at each other. They knew they were straying into dangerous territory because Pamela, whose face was already red, became even meaner when she was drunk.

They were quick with the chips and wine. The women exclaimed over how darling Josh was, already in his pajamas, and Jack immediately became self-conscious. He was in the way. Out of place. He was only twelve, two years older than Josh, but everything was different for him. The female body was everywhere, for one thing. He wasn't obsessed with it yet (he'd only had a few wet dreams), and he didn't have serious crushes on the girls in his class back home. These women on the deck, however, were different, frightening. Old girls. He preferred not to look at them at all. He was looking down, in fact, when he handed the bottle of wine to the nearest of Pamela's lady friends. She leaned forward and he caught a glimpse of her cleavage. All the women were wearing bikinis, there was cleavage everywhere, but this particular angle featured something new. Something so deep as to be endless.

All at once he was in trouble, under the spotlight. The woman exclaimed, half-joking, that Jack was looking at her tits, and then Pamela's hand came crashing against his face. The chips went flying as his brother tried to protect him, and the bottle dropped. It did not shatter, thank God, but landed on the deck with a thud.

Then things got blurry, as they did whenever Jack entered crisis mode. His father wasn't home yet. He worked all day in the city and always came home after dark. This way he was spared the daily drama and only heard Pamela's accounts, with sparse footnotes in the morning, from Jack and Josh. On the night of the cleavage incident, Jack and Josh were sent upstairs to bed immediately, without dinner, where Josh fell into his usual easy slumber. Jack was awake with anxiety but eventually dropped off to the sound of continuous celebration, only to be jolted awake later by Pamela screaming at his father. He got out of bed to listen at his door. He did not dare open it.

He could hear the usual complaints: the boys were messy and lazy; all they did was watch TV; she couldn't have any fun with them around. Then Pamela got herself under control and started whispering. He knew she was describing the scene on the deck, twisting it so that she would appear as the victim. She insisted, loud and clear, that Jack return to New York. For his own good, of course. At this, his father's voice rose over Pamela's, but Jack couldn't quite hear what he said. Pamela grew quiet. Jack got back in bed and worried about leaving Josh alone in California.

In the morning he expected to be in big trouble, but when he saw his face in the mirror, he wondered if Pamela would get busted, at long last. He had a light violet bruise running along his left cheekbone. He and Josh dressed and went downstairs where they helped themselves to cereal and orange juice. Pamela always woke up late, and because she had been drinking, she would rise even later than usual, with a puffy face and punishing migraine. Morning was the boys' only chance to hang out with their father. What would he say to them today? Was he going to take away their upcoming day camp at the Marine Mammal Center? The movie theater? Their bicycles?

When he appeared, late for work, he ruffled Jack's hair and told him not to worry about anything. Then he put two twenties on the kitchen table. He did not mention the bruise.

* * *

In California you had to get in a car to go anywhere. People walked, but only for exercise. One thing Jack liked was riding his bike on dirt trails and hills, and Josh was almost big enough to keep up with him.

There was a path that started along the creek behind his dad's house. If they rode their bikes far enough, the creek led to a marsh bordered by cattails, not far from the highway. Nobody jogged or walked down there. It was hard to access the marsh, almost as though the land itself was warning them off. The cattails were evil arms that could pull a boy in and drown him before he knew what was happening. Jack and Josh stopped their bikes at the same point each time, and after staring for a while, they would turn around and go back. It was boring but better than staying inside.

Jack knew he owed his little brother this bike ride, but it was hard for him to stay long at the edge of the marsh.

"What's wrong?" Josh asked him one day. "Why do you always want to go back so fast?"

Jack stared at his brother. He could tell Josh anything and the little guy would believe him. His power as an older sibling was incredible, and he had only occasionally abused it, like the time he swore roly-polies tasted like mint. He considered telling Josh a scary story about a swamp monster to see how far it would go.

That was when the boy came along, and from the very first moment, Jack knew there was something wrong with him. His skin was like milk and his hair, shoulder-length, was so blond it was white. He wore a pair of pants made out of some fabric Jack had never seen before, rough and dark brown, splashed with mud. He was shirtless, and his skinny torso, dotted with nutmeg freckles, shot up like a reed. He was barefoot.

Nobody went barefoot around here.

Jack assumed the kid was poor. Why else would he dress like that? He had a weird way of talking, hesitant, with a strange accent. Before Jack could steer Josh away, the boy offered to teach them to skip rocks.

Josh was off his bike and down the muddy hill in seconds. Jack hung back in order to distinguish himself from the two younger kids. Besides, he had never been good at skipping rocks. It was all a matter of practice, he knew, like everything, but he didn't want to advertise his lack of skill.

The boy led them to a level spot looking out over the water. He spoke slowly, as if he didn't expect them to catch on. "First you need a good rock. Not too heavy, flat, like a plate. Then, when you throw it, you lean down toward the ground so that the rock is no more than a foot or two off the water. When you release, you put some spin on it so it will glide farther. Don't launch it flat. If it's nose-down, it's going straight in the water."

The boy demonstrated with a rock he pulled from his pocket and they all counted as it skipped nine times. Nine. Amazing. Josh tried a few times to no avail until, after more demonstrations and a rock selected by the boy, he managed to get a rock to skip twice. Then he turned around to smile at his brother.

The boy stared at Jack expectantly, and after a few costly seconds that threatened Jack's honor, offered him a rock from his own pocket.

Jack put everything into it, taking it as seriously as a pitch, which was why, when the rock careened into the marsh—a miscalculation, something to do with forcing the spin—the laughter stung. He shrugged as his face turned red. There was nothing worse than Josh laughing at him. The moment passed and soon all three boys were skipping rocks with varying degrees of success. Jack managed to get a rock to skip four times, with the fourth skip barely registering. Only then did he know it would be safe to move on, otherwise it would appear he was backing out of something he wasn't good at.

"You're getting better," the boy said, "but that was your twelfth try."

Jack turned to face him. The boy's pride was out of proportion to the event. Jack had seen this kind of behavior before and it always made him embarrassed for the other person. "You're keeping track of my tries?"

"I count everything. The world is mathematics. I can add any two numbers. Go ahead and test me."

"We need to go home. Come on, Josh." Jack turned and got on his bike without waiting for his little brother. He knew Josh would follow, especially if he was afraid of being left behind, but this time Josh lingered, throwing various sums at the stranger, who solved them so fast it was uncanny. Jack could barely keep up, but he had the deep, disconcerting feeling that the boy was correct each time.

When they were finally pedaling away, Josh turned around and shouted at the disappearing figure. "Wait! What's your name?"

There was no answer.

"Pay attention," Jack said. "Watch for cars."

Back on their dad's street, where they slowed down to delay going home to Pamela, Jack told Josh not to mention the boy.

"Why not?"

"We don't need to give her something else to get mad about."

"Why would she get mad? You mean we can't play with other kids?"

"She's a control freak." This was a term Jack had learned from his mother, though she tried hard not to judge others and never said unkind things about Jack's dad. She had no tolerance, however, when it came to someone hurting her boys. Jack hated looking at his mom's face at the airport whenever he and Josh had to leave her. At his dad's, he was uncomfortable talking on the phone, as Pamela was always lurking nearby. He would end up handing the phone to Josh, who filled the house with his hopeful chatter.

Jack did not want his dad and Pamela to know about the strange boy. He couldn't explain why. He did not want to imagine their reaction when faced with a barefoot child in dirty clothes. None of the kids around here looked like him. It was better to forget about the whole incident. At least they had learned to skip rocks.

Jack changed the subject and promised Josh they would play Space Invaders for the rest of the afternoon. They put their bikes in the garage and went inside the house.

* * *

The week of day camp at the Marine Mammal Center went by in a pleasant blur. Pamela had to drop them off because their dad couldn't fit them into his commute, but otherwise the days were smooth and fast. Jack and Josh got to stay together even though they weren't in the same grade. The counselors were relaxed and friendly, nonjudgmental, the perfect grown-ups. Jack liked the binoculars and the microscopes, loved everything about science, and Josh could not stop talking about the baby sea lion they saw one day, its giant black eyes filled with compassion.

"You can't make any money as a scientist," Pamela said when the three of them were alone in the car.

Jack was surprised. He had been so careful not to show her how much he was enjoying the camp, knowing, instinctively, she would tear it down. Maybe he should have convinced Josh to pretend they hated the place? Then Pamela might have signed them up for another week. It was hard to hide his pleasure though. His whole body would tense with anticipation as soon as they reached the magical one-way tunnel leading out to the Headlands, and he could not suppress a smile, especially when Pamela would start complaining about how ugly the area was, all scrub brush and pebbly sand. "You two don't know what a good beach is supposed to look like."

One time he challenged her. "Then you should take us to a good beach."

"Okay, maybe I will," she said, surprising him.

For a second he thought he saw another side of Pamela, the woman she could be when she didn't feel threatened, or when she wasn't drinking, but she was back to her old self by the time she picked them up at the end of the day. She never spoke of taking them to the beach again.

He was deliberately mysterious with his mother over the phone when she pumped him for details about the camp, but when he got home, he was going to tell her his plan: he would become a marine biologist. He had noticed that certain high school kids volunteered at the camp, and one day he would become one of those kids. By then his father would have divorced Pamela. He would be old enough to drive himself everywhere. Everything would be easier.

He had given up on the dream of his parents getting back together, but he still believed his father would see the light and drop Pamela.

Jack liked the lunch break almost as much as the scheduled activities. There was a trail they were allowed to walk on without supervision, as long as they went in pairs and didn't go too far. As he gazed at the ocean, he felt the only true calm of his summer break. The Pacific never scared him. He wasn't afraid of water per se, only water that didn't know where it belonged. The ocean featured an ongoing battle between land and sea. One of the head teachers had explained that the water was gradually eroding the coastline, and even showed them maps of the changes over time. To Jack, though, it seemed the sea was gently kissing the sand and then changing its mind, going away and coming back, over and over again.

Jack dreaded leaving the camp. He was ready to beg his dad to sign them up for another session. He even asked the counselors if there were any spaces left, but they told him to have his parents put him on the waiting list. Jack wanted his father to deal with this without any interference from Pamela. The four of them sat at the dinner table one Thursday night before the last day of camp while Jack tried to figure out how to get his dad alone.

"I saw that boy again," Josh said, out of the blue.

Dad and Pamela stared at Josh and waited for more. Jack was aware that something had gone off track. He wanted to kick his brother under the table or change the subject.

"What boy?" Pamela asked with a theatrical sigh. She was on her third glass of wine.

"The boy from the marsh. He was standing out front."

The hair on the back of Jack's neck stood up.

"The boy from the marsh?" Pamela said, mocking Josh's little voice. She laughed and looked around the table.

Jack prayed she would not ask for more details. He tried to make eye contact with his little brother but by the time the message got through, it was too late. "There's this boy. He showed us how to skip rocks one day. He told me he wants us to meet his mom," Josh said, looking down.

"You gave him our address?" Pamela asked, suddenly curious.

"No," Josh said. His eyes were huge.

"Then how could he possibly find our house? What do you think of this, Neil?"

Dad shrugged. "They're just kids, Pamela."

"I thought they were supposed to ask for permission before having their friends over."

Jack fought to control himself. He knew she was baiting them, but they hadn't done anything wrong. They didn't even know the kid's name.

"What do you know about this, Jack?" Dad asked.

"About what? We don't even know the guy." He was compelled to continue, to fill in the heavy silence. "I forgot we ever met him, to tell you the truth." That was a lie, but it wasn't the kind of lie you should get in trouble for.

"He's not from this neighborhood?" Pamela's voice rose with each word. "Well, I hope he's not some kind of drug dealer."

Jack and Josh burst out laughing. It was too absurd.

Inevitably they were in trouble and sent upstairs to bed. Pamela, angry at being laughed at, insisted they not attend the last day of camp. The fight went on for a long time, their dad's low voice rolling in to wash over Pamela's cries. Jack and Josh didn't say another word to each other. Josh was in tears, miserable, but there was no anger on Jack's side, no resentment toward his little brother. Jack knew it wasn't right for Josh to take this on. It was too much for a kid.

He held Josh until his brother fell asleep and then moved back to his own bed.

* * *

Pamela had won and now they were in prison.

They were stuck inside the stuffy house for the next week. The Atari had disappeared. If they were "good," they might be released in time for the Fourth of July, but it didn't look likely. That first weekend, when the four of them were stuck at home together, the space shrank and grew hotter, like a greenhouse for emotional torture.

Jack thought of his real home, the apartment in New York, where he and Josh had their own bedrooms and their old black cat, Bonz, waiting for them. Jack packed light for each summer at his dad's, leaving behind everything he really cared about. Josh had brought along one stuffed animal, a whale he liked to sleep with but didn't play with anymore. In the daytime he shoved the whale deep inside the dresser drawer and Jack knew why. They couldn't trust Pamela. Things would disappear.

Jack always left behind an old teddy bear with moveable arms and legs that had been his mom's and now sat on a bookshelf all day. Sometimes Jack would imagine Bear, resigned and loyal, when he was visualizing his real room back in the humidity of New York. Jack counted the days until they could go to the airport and escape.

During their week of confinement, Pamela found chores for them to do, so instead of reading or drawing in their little bedroom, the boys scrubbed the grout between the dated bathroom tiles and waxed the kitchen floor. "We're like Cinderella," Josh said, in an attempt to get his big brother to laugh. On Sunday, when they had their weekly call with their mom, Pamela insisted they talk in the kitchen while she stood nearby. Their father turned to stone.

Josh went first and said little. His eyes were watering when he handed Jack the phone.

"Jackson, what's going on out there?" His mother's voice was like cool water.

"Nothing much," Jack lied.

"Did something happen?"

"Yes." He tried to sound upbeat. Then, with meaning, "The usual."

His mother exhaled. "I see. Is Josh all right?"

"Sure. It's all taken care of." He couldn't say more without blowing his cover.

"I understand." His mom! She was so perfect. "Well, I can't wait until you boys come home. We're going to have so much fun together."

They went upstairs to bed after the phone call. It was like they were babies. Jack couldn't stand it any longer. When his dad stuck his head in the door to say goodnight, a high-speed gesture involving little eye contact and no physical affection, Jack could not restrain himself. It would have been better if he had burst into tears, but instead his voice was icy and perfect. Where had he learned this from? His mom? Not likely. The bullies at school? Maybe. Pamela herself? Maybe he was turning into her. It was the wicked stepmother's ultimate vengeance.

"Dad. How come you always take Pamela's side? Every. Single. Time."

His father shot him an angry look before shutting the door. The Fourth was lost. Josh stared at him in dismay. "Why did you say that?" he asked his big brother, because, despite his innocence, Josh understood the rules of their family. Jack didn't reply. The boys fell asleep in a fog of exhaustion.

Jack remembered this night his whole life. He vowed never to be like his father, never to parent like his father. This promise would turn out to be difficult to keep. Instinctively, when things were rocky in his first marriage, after his only child was born, he would turn into the man of stone, of silence, that his father had modeled for him. Emotional distance was his hometown.

Maybe genetics controlled everything. Maybe they were all at the mercy of a simple fairy tale curse.

* * *

The fireworks sounded like gunshots. Someone was setting them off in the neighborhood though they weren't supposed to. Normally the four of them would have driven to the Civic Center to see the display, but Dad and Pamela had gone off to a party in another town. "I'm leaving you two here on your honor," Dad said, sounding foolish. Jack was beginning to despise him. He knew they were being left alone because his dad was too cheap to find a babysitter and Pamela didn't care. He felt like calling his mother to tell her they were all alone on a holiday, but he couldn't because Pamela checked the phone bill every month. They weren't allowed to call long distance without permission.

Josh walked around, picking up Pamela's knickknacks and throwing them against the ugly carpet. He was kicking the furniture when Jack spoke up. "Hey, come on. It's not worth it. You don't want to get in trouble."

"I don't care about fucking trouble."

What a surprise. Josh rarely swore and he certainly didn't use the f-word. Anger flared in Jack's heart. That horrible woman was changing his good-natured little brother. "Let's go then," Jack said, faking the voice of a rebel kid. He knew it was wrong, but he didn't care.

Josh stared at him. "Are you serious?"

"Who cares? We won't go far. We'll walk around. Maybe we can see some fireworks from here."

They left the front door unlocked behind them, sin number one, and then they walked into the summer night, abandoning their bikes because they didn't have lights. It started off great, liberating, their first true transgression. The night was beautiful, dark and private. They couldn't see any fireworks, but they still had the stars. The neighborhood was friendlier than usual. People stood on balconies and driveways, and the boys could hear celebrations coming from different back yards as they walked along. Why had they never gone on a night walk in this neighborhood before? It was something their mother liked to do. Dad would probably say no if they asked, and Pamela would ridicule them.

The boy was standing under a streetlight when they saw him. He was still shirtless and barefoot, wearing only those dirty brown pants. Jack wanted to turn around and head back, but it was too late. Josh saw the kid and went running ahead.

"Hello," the boy said in that strange voice of his.

Jack said hi and tried to keep walking, but Josh announced that they were looking for fireworks.

"I know where we can see some. Come along with me."

Then they went walking in the direction of the marsh, fast, crossing against traffic lights. Jack reached for his brother's hand but it was too late. Josh and the boy flew so far ahead of him he felt like a tagalong. He called to his brother, "You need to watch out for cars! People are drunk. They can't see you." Now he sounded like Dad.

Down by the marsh it was really dark. Jack couldn't see anything at first. Fear crept up his spine, where it stayed. "Guys?" he called, and then, when the two figures came into view against the rustling cattails, he felt silly for panicking. They didn't respond to him. He stepped forward.

Now he was pissed. "There are no fireworks down here. There's nothing. Josh, you need to get away from the water."

"You're not the boss of me. Besides, you're scared."

The boy's laugh cut into the night, like the screech of an insect or a strange bird.

"Whatever. I'm going back. Let's see if you can find the way by yourself. Maybe you'll be the one who gets in trouble for a change." He regretted the last remark as soon as he said it. This was no time for a fight. His little brother was pulling away from him.

The strange boy took over. "You go on home now. I'm in charge here."

Who was this guy? What was up with his clothes, or lack thereof? His voice? Was he faking that accent? There was no shirt to grab, so Jack lunged for his chest, a cold marble slab he could not get hold of. He had never been in a real fight before, not like this. Jack ducked and lost his balance as the boy's fist cut through the air, leaving behind a weird white streak, like a comet. Jack got to his feet and went for the boy's jaw, but somehow the kid evaded him. It was too hard to see and so frustrating. This would have been completely different in the daylight. A summer's worth of rage powered Jack's fists, but they met only night air each time. At last, in a fit of desperation, he leapt on the boy.

Josh was pulling Jack off the boy when it happened. In a moment it went from a three-way scuffle, to Jack's elbow flying backward, to his brother falling away and disappearing. Josh vanished so fast it was eerie, as if something had lifted him off the ground, and because there was no splash, it took Jack a second to understand his brother was down in the muck and the cattails.

Now he was going to have to fight that goddamn marsh. He really should have grabbed a flashlight before they left, but it didn't matter anyway because he needed both his hands. One step and he sank to his knees in the muddy water. Terror. No way of telling how deep it went, or where the danger started. First he screamed his brother's name. Then he screamed without words.

No answer.

Josh was down there somewhere.

The strange boy was gone.

He trudged forward to find Josh. A shoe hit him, but when he grabbed it, the shoe came off in his hand, like something from a horrible dream. If he could only see. Fuck. What if Josh had hit his head? The seconds were ticking toward something unspeakable. Jack could not fail. If he failed, his life would be over at twelve.

He tripped and found mercy, falling against the lower half of his brother's body, and then it was an endless, nightmarish ordeal of dragging Josh by the legs up that little slope. They had been wrestling since babyhood, and he knew his brother's lanky body as well as he knew his own, but Josh had never before been so heavy. Deadweight. Oh God, please help. It was like a gag, a set-up, this impossible task of finding traction in the mud. He screamed for help, over and over again, until his voice died.

Later, at the hospital, they gave him a blanket. He was shaking but he didn't feel cold. He had turned numb after he entered the water. Everything blurred.

For years Jack saw himself in this night scene, pulling and calling for help, pulling and calling for help, and he was always so tired, exhausted, as if he had lost a lot of blood. He dreamed about this night until he was well into his thirties, whenever stress and pressure got the better of him. But what had happened, exactly? He pulled Josh out and then ran to flag down a car. There were flashing lights. A stretcher.

Nobody was proud of him.

Dad and Pamela gave him the silent treatment, but the police wanted to talk to him. They needed it for their report. He wasn't in trouble, they assured him, but he had to tell them everything, and so he told them about the boy. Even as he tried to be accurate, he knew it sounded made up. A ghost boy in strange clothes who disappeared. Someone they had seen before, played with before, but whose name they never learned.

The only other person who could verify Jack's story was still unconscious.

Jack looked over at his dad. How could he forget that Josh had talked about a boy standing outside the house? Surely he remembered the fight they'd had. It was Pamela, wearing bright red lipstick like a cartoon villainess, who jumped to her feet. "For God's sake, Jack, this is serious! Will you quit it with these lies?" Then she turned to the officers and sweetened her voice. "I think this is all a fantasy, about the boy. Maybe he can't face what really happened. Maybe he's still in shock."

Dad led Pamela away. They were both dressed in red, white, and blue for the holiday, but through the distorted lens of trauma, Jack always remembered them wrapped up in American flags.

"It's the truth," Jack insisted, his lips quivering. "Josh knows. He'll tell you when he wakes up."

He could not recall when the police went away or what they concluded, but he always remembered their faces, their eyes. They were sorry for him.

* * *

It was a miracle.

Josh woke up. He was okay; shaken, but okay. There was an MRI, which was scary in its own way, but it showed no brain damage. Jack sat in silence with his dad and Pamela while they waited for the results. He had to close his eyes, and somewhere in a quick succession of imagined worst-case scenarios, he fell asleep. He woke with a start and saw his father crying tears of relief. For some reason Pamela was erased from that part of the memory.

His dad never got mad at him. There was no talk, no punishment. No questions. It was as if the police had stepped in to take over Dad's role. And then, no eye contact. It seemed his dad could not stand the sight of him, could not overcome his disappointment. His father did not allow mistakes, and Jack had made the kind of mistake that left a scar.

Nobody wanted to talk about the boy, and Jack was afraid to bring him up again.

Mom came out the next day. It was disorienting to see her in California, and though Jack was glad, her presence served as proof of his badness. He and Josh were overwhelmed by emotion when they saw her standing in the living room of their dad's house. Both boys cried while their dad and Pamela stood to the side in tense disapproval. Jack feared they were giving Pamela ammunition with this display of vulnerability. They would be in even worse trouble when Mom left.

And then another miracle occurred, not to be matched until he was a father himself, worried for his own child's safety. "Pack your bags," Dad said.

Pack your bags! They were going home early, to New York. Their parents must have reached some kind of agreement over the phone. He and Josh rushed upstairs, elated, while their mom called to Josh to be careful, to take it easy, for God's sake. The boys threw their possessions into their suitcases without folding anything. Downstairs, Mom's voice was the only one doing the work of civility and kindness.

Dad ruffled Josh's hair and shook Jack's hand, and then it was over.

When they got in the rental car, the sun came back into their life. They went to their mother's hotel room, where she threw the kind of celebration two young boys would appreciate. It wasn't the impromptu pool party or the pizza and Coke, it was the natural ease with which the three of them fell back into the groove of their little family. Josh talked a lot, almost nonstop, and Mom could not stop smiling. It would have been wrong to complain about Pamela or to talk about the Fourth.

But Jack was haunted.

There was a copy of the local paper in the lobby. Jack smuggled it into their room, and then he hid in the bathroom reading it when the other two were asleep. Only after he went through the whole paper did he find a short article about their experience at the marsh. It mentioned a possible third party but there were no details. It made it sound like some kids got into trouble on the Fourth, and for once it didn't have to do with explosives. Jack knew it wasn't true at all, and he would have written a letter to the editor if he didn't already feel so lucky to be getting away unscathed.

They left early the next morning for the airport, but it was already late afternoon when they got home, all the way across the country, where it was always three hours ahead. Jack had never been so glad to see dirty, muggy New York. His building. His bedroom. Bonz rubbed his head against their suitcases. First Jack unpacked and gave his mom all his laundry, and then he took Bear off his shelf and put him in the closet because he didn't want to see those big wise eyes. That night his mom came into his bedroom to tell him what a wonderful boy he was. She called him a hero. She didn't require him to say anything. To explain anything. When he started to cry, she stroked his hair. "It's okay, baby. I understand. I know how horrible it must have been. You did the right thing."

When he tried to tell her about the boy, she pressed a finger to his lips. "Not now, Jack. Wait until you're not so upset."

It took a while for him to talk to Josh about the incident, and by then it was safely distant. Jack was hesitant to make his little brother remember anything too scary. He wanted Josh to stay his old self and, he realized later, not to grow up. He never even got to apologize, but he wasn't exactly sure what he was supposed to be sorry for. They didn't tell their friends why they had come home so early. Josh never spoke about being unconscious. He didn't bring up the hospital. Nothing really changed between the brothers, but Jack knew they had come home two new people. While this was true of every summer, there was something different about that particular Fourth of July.

Only much later, when Jack was in high school and Josh in middle school, did they talk about the details of that night, and of how they had ended up in the marsh. They remembered the incident differently. Josh could barely recall the boy, while Jack had never been able to forget him.

"You're kidding, right? You're saying I made him up?"

"No, man, I remember skipping rocks with this weird skinny dude one day, but I don't remember him being there that night."

"You can't be serious."

"I don't remember much. It's like we were watching fireworks and then I was in the hospital."

"Josh, there were no fireworks. We were looking for some but we never found any."

"Well, I can still see them, right in front of me."

"There's no way."

"And I can see that woman standing above me."

"What woman? What the hell are you talking about?"

"She had long blonde hair. She was smiling. I don't know. Who else was there? Didn't anybody help you?"

"Josh, nobody helped me! I pulled you out of the water by myself. There was no woman. You were hallucinating or something."

The dueling narratives would resume when they were older, and Josh's version would always be so different from Jack's that it wasn't worth arguing about. Their dad didn't like to talk about that summer, except to say he had never been so afraid before in all his life. He ended up divorcing Pamela, and later taking out a restraining order against her, but he never apologized to his sons for the abuse they suffered.

Only Jack's mother was willing to hear him out, and over the years they would revisit that terrible Fourth of July. "I didn't make up a story about a third party. Josh still remembers playing with that kid, but nobody else wanted to talk about him."

"I think everyone had other things on their mind," she would say in her gentle voice. "We were terrified for Josh."

"Pamela said I pushed my little brother into the marsh. I heard her tell someone on the phone that they were going to send me away. Wait. Hear me out. I didn't remember this until much later—I was in shock—but I know it happened."

"Enough about Pamela!" His mother rarely raised her voice, but any mention of Pamela could set her off. "You're forgetting something. Your dad should have been in big trouble for leaving the two of you alone. I could have involved my lawyer. Instead I told him I would overlook it if he let you boys come home early."

"I'm sorry, Mom, but don't you understand how scared I was? You think I don't know about brain damage? I did not push him in the water or start a fight with him. I would never do that! I always protected him, always. You don't know what it was like. It was hell, if you want to know. That Fourth of July was hell."

"I know all this, Jack. I always knew it. You got mixed up with a bad person. Two bad people. First your stepmother, and then a troubled kid. The world is full of people like this. It makes perfect sense that he would run off after the accident."

"There was something so strange about that boy. He must have been poor, lower class, but there was something else. It was like he was from a different time. Maybe he was abused, or in some weird cult. I'm serious. I'd never hung out with someone like that before. How could I have known?"

His mother would frown and bite her lip as she listened, which made things worse. Jack did not want to hurt her. Sometimes it was painful to be so close to her. "Jack, I've told you this before. You're exactly like me. We're too nice. I've had this problem all my life. We're easy prey for dangerous people." Then she would take his hands in hers and remind him that he had no need to defend himself, not to her. She wasn't accusing him of anything. She believed him. He had to stop punishing himself. He had to forgive everyone involved. She was the mom here, and she cherished her two boys, who were home with her, safe and sound. Their love was the most important thing. He would understand this himself one day, when he was a father.

Elaine: 1968

Elaine wanted something she was afraid to name, something she had to keep secret. She wanted, as she told her best friend, to be a woman of experience.

"How are you going to do that?" Linda looked up from the album she was holding, *Flowers*. Both girls had done the unthinkable by choosing the Stones over the Beatles.

"They live that way in France," Elaine said. "I'm sure of it."

"You've had three years of French and now you're an expert?"

"It will be different in college. Everything will be different."

Elaine told Linda everything, but she didn't tell her about the couple she had met, not right away. It took her almost a year, which made it a secret. She wanted privacy more than anything. Sometimes she wished she could move away to live in a cold-water flat in New York, whatever that meant, instead of a dorm across the bay. She craved anonymity almost as much as she craved an outlet for the electricity humming across her skin. She was born a little too late. If only she could be in college right now and away from her parents. Thank God she could hitchhike or take a bus down to the Haight. Thank God Linda was always up for adventure.

She went everywhere with Linda. The summer before, they'd caught the bus in Mill Valley and gone to the Fantasy Fair on Mount Tam, where they smoked a joint and saw The Doors. That was righteous. It took an outdoor concert to show her what church was supposed to feel like. Her face melted and floated away and then she was so aware, so lucky. There she was, a part of history, sitting on a mountain listening to these boys from LA. It was so beautiful to be at one with the universe. How could anyone hate? How could there still be wars?

And what was wrong with her parents? They were completely unaffected when King was shot back in April. They shook their heads, but they didn't cry and shake like she did, refusing dinner and locking herself in her bedroom. Didn't they understand what was happening? And then Bobby Kennedy, just a few weeks ago. Bobby was her favorite. They had all gone to mass together to grieve, but Elaine wasn't reassured. The system was broken. The world was on fire.

She wanted to pull her skin off.

Elaine didn't want to drop out, not in any sense. She wanted to taste more and more of the damaged world. Her hunger never stopped. College would not be enough, she could tell. She wanted to travel. She was right about New York, it turned out, and she did end up out there eventually, though too late for Woodstock. She was always late for the best parties.

"We need to play it cool until we're out of here," Linda warned her, bringing her back to earth. "No more dropping acid in the park like last summer."

Last summer.

They had dropped acid only once. They laughed about it now, but they had both been really scared, especially Elaine with her giant spider dreams. That same weekend, her mother, after reading alarming reports in the local papers and seeing all those lost kids on TV, threatened to send her away. "Where? To a convent?" Elaine had screamed. Afterward, her strategy was to avoid eye contact with her mother. She promised her parents she would apply to Berkeley in the fall. She grew her hair long but kept it smooth and free of tangles, as if to prove her integrity. She embroidered big white daisies and blood-red hearts on her jeans, and all the while her mother scowled at her.

She applied to Berkeley and was put on a waiting list. In late spring she got in.

The best way to follow Linda's plan and play it cool until they could move into the dorms was to find a job. At first Elaine pushed for a job in the city. She could take the bus there and find something working among the people she liked, waiting tables or selling books. Her mother cried that she was done worrying about her daughter running around San Francisco. Elaine could work in a little shop near home. "Why do you want to waste your time commuting back and forth?"

The question hung in the kitchen. *To get away from you*, was the silent, secret answer.

Her father got up from the table, pushed in his chair, and left for work.

Elaine got a job at an upscale consignment shop she could walk to. She lied and told them she was going to the community college and therefore would be around in the fall, at which point she would lie again, and announce that Berkeley had finally taken her. She lied to her mother as well, telling her the job was full-time. She spent most of her days off in Linda's gazebo while the family pet, an orange cat named Fox, napped on the cedar shingles of the roof.

Linda lived in a little vine-covered gazebo in her parents' back yard. They had converted it into a small cottage with faulty electricity and no plumbing, graced by four big windows that let in the light, plenty of insects, and once, a bat. It was hot in the summer and freezing cold in the winter, but all the kids loved it. Linda's older sister had lived there before she moved out, and Linda's mom still longed for what was supposed to be her art studio. There was enough room for a bed and a dresser. Linda had sewn some oversized, shapeless pillows and scattered them across a big rug that didn't exactly fit the space.

And there was the record player.

"Guess what," Linda said.

"What?"

"My parents are going to Tahoe next week."

The girls' eyes locked as they screamed in joy, and then Linda hushed Elaine. "Don't make a big deal out of it. I don't want them to get suspicious. I had to tell them I'd lose my job at the grocery store if I asked for time off."

"But we have to have a party!"

"A small one. I'm warning you. We're almost out of here and we have it play it cool."

"I have someone to bring. A couple, actually."

"A couple?"

"Is that so strange? The more the merrier."

"Who are they?"

"You'll see."

"No, Elaine. You have to tell me now."

"Well, they're a little bit older."

"Yeah? How did you meet them? Why haven't you told me about them before?"

Though Linda gave her an encouraging smile, Elaine looked down. There was a problem. Linda was going to be shocked when she saw how much older these people were, especially Robert. Her parents couldn't find out. He was so much older that Elaine hadn't even asked him his age. That one afternoon in their apartment she had felt like grabbing his wallet so she could see his driver's license and know for sure.

"You'll like them," Elaine said. "He's nice and she's, well, she's amazing." Elaine chose her words carefully, since Linda could get jealous in a flash. But if things were intense between her and Linda, what had happened between her and Verushka the previous summer was beyond intense. Beyond belief. It had raged like a wildfire.

Elaine met Robert and Verushka on a weekend when Linda was away. She hitchhiked into the city by herself, nervous the whole way, but when she got to the park it was the same as always, crowded and chaotic, a celebration, but with something else underneath it all, something Elaine couldn't name. A guy approached her and offered her a joint, and being well brought up, she told him no thank you and then immediately got embarrassed. She walked around on her own for a while, stopping to look in shop windows as she edged her way toward the Haight. It was a long walk, way better to hop on another bus, but she didn't remember which line to take. She hated admitting how scary San Francisco still was without Linda. Linda made everything legitimate somehow. With Linda, and only with Linda, she had overcome her great fear and dropped acid. She would never forget the truth about acid: the time commitment. Twelve hours, at least, and then time ceased to have meaning—except for people like her parents.

That day in the city, she stopped feeling nervous and actually got hungry for real food. She was tired of drugs and the kind of talk that happened with drugs. She needed a bathroom.

And, she had to admit, she saw terrible things on the streets. A girl out of her mind. A toddler peeing on the grass in the park while his parents stood nearby, unconcerned. People stumbling around, lost, despite the festive atmosphere. There were so many people, too many, like a city on Mardi Gras or the Fourth of July, but they couldn't tell you what they were celebrating, something to do with peace and love. She pressed on, pretending to have fun, telling herself everything was fine. Far out.

She found a coffee house. She wasn't sure if she could ever find the place again. It was somewhere on Castro Street, cool and quiet, and she was so relieved to sit that she didn't mind blowing all her money. At least she was out of her parents' house. At least she was doing something.

She noticed a couple in the corner booth when she came back from the dark little restroom. Or rather, she noticed a woman checking her out. Verushka.

Her hair was long and white, what Elaine's mother would call platinum blond, and her eyes were dark, nearly black. She was striking, another Mom-word. It was hard not to stare, but Verushka was looking at her as well. At first Elaine barely noticed Robert, sitting at Verushka's side. In Elaine's memory of that moment, it was like he was cut out of the frame.

"I love your jeans," Verushka said. She had an accent.

"Thank you. I embroidered them myself. I like your voice," Elaine said, impulsively, and then blushed. "Where are you from?"

Verushka made a gesture that meant everywhere or nowhere and Elaine was embarrassed. She had to stop being so predictable. Those people on the street were right. She needed to open her mind. "And where are you from?" Verushka asked, her accent like honey, like wine. Elaine wanted to kiss her, to see how her lips tasted. It was the first time she had felt that way about a woman.

"Larkspur," Elaine said. She had always liked the word, the flower. She had not minded being from a little town.

"Where is that? Is it north?"

Robert cut into their conversation with a laugh. "Way north. Across the bridge. They're about ten years behind."

Elaine died a little, but it didn't matter because Verushka told her to join them, and then they were all drinking tea from glasses that sat in little metal holders, the most delicious tea she had ever tasted. They had borscht with sour cream followed by vareniki, which were little raviolis stuffed with cherries. Elaine ate everything in front of her.

When they introduced themselves, Verushka was delighted by Elaine's name. "Someone very close to me had that name. This is a sign. We were destined to meet." She never said where she was from though. Verushka referenced cities Elaine only dreamed of—Minsk, Prague, Paris—but called herself baseless. "I never stay in one place for long. Once I feel the roots settling into the earth, I move on."

"She's a real gypsy," Robert said, reverence in his tone.

Elaine tried to figure out their relationship. Robert wasn't wearing a ring but Verushka had a ring on almost every finger. "Do you two travel together?"

They looked at each other and laughed. "Will I take you with me, my darling?" Verushka said, before kissing Robert on the lips.

Elaine's face was on fire. She hadn't blushed like this since she was a child.

"So, do you go to Cal?" Robert asked her.

"I'll go there eventually. At least that's what I told my parents."

"Is that what you really want to do?" Verushka asked.

"Yes," Elaine said, pausing. Verushka and Robert stared at her and waited. "I mean, I think so. What I really want is to move out."

They laughed then, but not unkindly. If she had spoken from her heart, she would have confessed everything. She wanted, most of all, to fall in love and become a woman of sexual experience. That was the truth, but she could not speak it, not yet. Something held her back. She would never be a woman like Verushka. People didn't usually ask Elaine what she wanted. They weren't even curious about her major. The whole world assumed it knew who she was, from her parents to the guys on the street offering her drugs.

"And what will happen when you move out?" Verushka asked with a smile.

"I will have a lot of men," Elaine said. Her heart pounded inside her chest until it drowned out all other sound. She had finally spoken her desire aloud to someone other than Linda.

Verushka applauded and called for a toast. They didn't have champagne at the coffee house, but Verushka settled for a bottle of something sweet with bubbles.

"To all your future men," Robert said, raising a glass.

Elaine felt a tiny bead of regret. Robert was taking her truth and making it about something else, maybe even about himself, but Verushka grabbed a glass and corrected him. "No, no, no. To Elaine and her great adventure. Her journey. May it never end. May it lead her to a prince like no other."

They drank to her. Elaine drank to herself, and in that fine moment she knew her adult life was beginning. She wished she could peel the label from the bottle and stick it in her back pocket, and then someday she would tape it to the wall of her dorm room, right above her bed.

Elaine wanted to freeze this afternoon forever and keep it like a charm. It really happened. It was good. Despite everything that followed, there was that one moment when she was toasted by a magical woman in a coffee house in San Francisco during the most important summer of all.

Pain and death and curses were waiting right around the corner.

When did it start to go wrong?

* * *

Verushka's apartment was one big room and a little kitchen in the Lower Haight. Dark floorboards and white walls. The darkness was refreshing on a summer day, but Elaine knew it would be depressing to live in a space like this, at least for her. If she hadn't had so much to drink, she would never have commanded Verushka to open the drapes.

There were a lot of things she would never have done if they hadn't kept drinking and smoking grass. Her face was numb. She sat on the couch, directly in the ray of light Verushka let in when she swept back the drapes.

"For God's sake," Robert said. "I didn't move to this city for sunshine."

"Then put on your sunglasses, darling. I want to see Elaine's beautiful face."

"Do you both live here?" Elaine asked.

The way they laughed at her question made her blush again. She was definitely getting paranoid from the grass. In any event, she never did learn whose apartment it was. She assumed it was Verushka's because it looked like a woman lived there. Old black and white pictures in silver frames sat on top of the fireplace and in the bookshelves. She wanted to get up and study them, but it was so much nicer to sit in the sun.

Robert put his hand on her thigh and said, "Just wait 'til you see the bathtub."

Elaine froze. What was happening now? Had she agreed to something by accepting Verushka's invitation to come home with them? Weren't they going to keep talking, maybe smoke a little more grass? All she wanted was to talk to these friends she'd been waiting for all her life. She sat up and walked over to the fireplace, where she focused her eyes on the largest photograph, a family portrait.

"Oh," she said. "Is this little girl you?"

It was a picture of another world, another century. A little blonde girl with braids stood at the center of a large group of people, next to a mother and baby. If that was Verushka, then her hair was naturally platinum, or pretty close. Everyone in the photograph was formally dressed and nobody smiled.

"It's a picture of someone I used to be," Verushka said, "but it was taken without my consent and I consider it a theft."

"Every photo is a theft," Robert said, looking up from the little pipe he held.

"I guess I never thought of it that way." Elaine was dizzy. Self-consciousness fell over her again like a heavy cloak.

"Anyway, you should check out the tub, Elaine. It's huge. Clawfoot. They must have done the laundry in it in the old days."

"In the old days? How do you think I wash my clothes now, Robert?" And with that, Verushka took off her velvet top. She was not wearing a bra.

Over the years Elaine would remember one thing from that sleepy afternoon, an abrupt realization: her own wetness sliding from between her legs, surprising her. Her own smell. She was alarmed. Would it seep through to her jeans? Would everyone on the street know what she had been doing, later, when she tried to go home?

The truth she took away from the day, so startling it was immediately locked in a secret vault in her heart, was that Robert was in the way. He saw himself as the star, the victor, but he was in the way. Elaine knew why she had followed Verushka home.

But she didn't know if she had imagined what Verushka said to her in the bathroom, after she, Elaine, had surrendered and let them undress her. A butterfly brushing up against her ear. Verushka's sweet breath. That accent.

Be patient, sweet. Wait for him to fall asleep and then we can be together.

It did not come to pass. Elaine had no complaints though. Her body was transformed that day. She had known nothing of sex before meeting Verushka and Robert. When she woke to a pleasant kind of soreness, it was pitch-black outside. The drapes were still open. She shot to her feet in a panic, searching for her clothes and planning her route out of the city. She needed to find a payphone and give her mom some cock and bull story. Or was it better to feign innocence until after she got home?

"Is something wrong?" Verushka asked. They had both been sleeping on cushions on the floor, while Robert took the couch. There was no proper bed, as far as Elaine could tell.

"I really need to go home right now," Elaine said. She wanted to be cool, but circumstances wouldn't let her. "I'm sorry. I'm on the wrong side of the bridge."

"Do you want me to walk with you?"

Elaine looked over at Robert, still asleep. She hesitated. She wanted nothing more than to walk and talk with Verushka, but now she was in such a hurry. She didn't want Verushka to remember her as a scared kid rushing home before she got in trouble.

"Here," Verushka said, rising naked from the floor. She grabbed a pen and paper. "Let's exchange numbers."

Elaine took the scrap of paper and tucked it into her back pocket. In the months that followed, she would study Verushka's elegant, looping cursive. She was afraid to make the call from her home phone for fear it would show up on the bill. She did call from a payphone, twice, but it rang and rang, and all the while Elaine closed her eyes, imagining Verushka in the dark space of her apartment.

Elaine's life was never the same again.

She hated the person she was required to be in her parents' house. At the dinner table Elaine wanted to scream across the void between the world she lived in and the planet where her parents were stuck. People were literally dying in a jungle on the other side of the world because her parents refused to get off their planet.

In the worst moments Linda would try to calm her, promising that once they got to college, everything would be better, but Elaine now yearned for something else, something carried in the butterfly whisper of Verushka's lips.

On New Year's Day, 1968, Elaine was home alone. Her parents had gone to mass while she was still asleep. Elaine jumped when the phone rang.

"Happy New Year, my beauty."

"Oh, hello." Elaine tried to sound casual. Her voice cracked.

"Did I wake you? Were you up until dawn?"

"No. Just celebrating with family." The connection dropped for a second and Elaine was dismayed. "Hello? Are you still there?"

"I'm still here, across the bay. I hope you haven't forgotten about us." Verushka's voice was like silk.

"I've tried to call you a few times but you're never there." Elaine waited, her heart pounding. "I think about you all the time."

"Do something for me, Elaine."

"Okay."

"Reach down and touch yourself."

It was easy. Her parents were gone, and she was still in her nightgown. Her underpants dropped to the floor. She closed her eyes. Verushka talked her into pleasure, and then she issued her command. "Let me hear you, Elaine."

The house filled with a sound Elaine had always stifled before, burying it behind closed lips or releasing it into her pillow. It was liberating, singing like this in the kitchen where the smell of her sex made an appearance among the spices and leftovers. She started to laugh.

"We will see each other again. Soon." And then Verushka hung up. She was gone. She didn't come back for so long that Elaine felt humiliated, taken advantage of somehow.

Elaine slowly gave up hope. She called the number one more time, late at night, but still there was no answer. She hid the scrap of paper in her lingerie drawer.

* * *

The following summer, sitting in Linda's gazebo, Elaine could almost believe she had made up Verushka and Robert. She kept them secret. Maybe she'd imagined that whole afternoon they spent together. But she hadn't. She was there. She was one of those kids in the pictures she saw in magazines, one of those kids the big stores were now courting with their peace signs and paisley prints.

When Linda told her they could have a party, everything changed. Now she had a reason to invite Verushka and Robert over. A party at her best friend's house would make them real again. This was the only safe meeting place on Elaine's side of the bridge. There was no way her parents could meet Verushka and Robert. Elaine could imagine Mother's face narrowing in judgment and suspicion, her eyebrows flying upward in alarm. How she hated her. They lived twenty minutes from such a boss city and yet her mother had rejected it. Unbelievable.

All she had to do now was get in touch with them. Maybe Verushka would call her again.

Linda and Elaine sat on the gazebo floor one afternoon, getting stoned. "I have some bad news," Linda said. "I have to go to Tahoe with my parents. My uncle has cancer and we're doing a family thing. But don't worry. I'll give you the keys. You can still have people over and you should definitely invite that couple."

"Oh." Elaine didn't know how to process this information. She was more afraid than excited. Her plans were ruined. She was too shy to throw a party without Linda.

"What?" Linda asked. "You're not going to back out, are you?"

"No, of course not. I wanted you to be here though."

"There'll be another time. Mom wants you to take care of the yard while we're gone. This is a serious assignment, Elaine."

"What about the cat?"

"Fox comes and goes. Make sure she has food and water."

"I'll take care of everything," Elaine said, rolling over on her side. She was in the sun now. She closed her eyes.

"Don't be boring." Linda got up and put *Aftermath* on. "You always get so morose when you're stoned. It's a drag. Listen to this, baby. It's your favorite." She lowered the needle at "Lady Jane."

"What? That is not my favorite song! Give me some crayons. I'll draw you something amazing." Elaine forced herself to sit up and engage, but in the back of her mind she was wondering how she would entertain Verushka and Robert by herself. How long would they stay?

She wished she could call Verushka and invite only her. Could she?

When the Tahoe weekend came, her mother was busy with a fundraiser at the church. Elaine told her she had to housesit for Linda's parents, and then, without any finessing on Elaine's part, her mother said, "I guess you'll be staying over there then?"

"I'm going over on Saturday after work. Her mom wants me to water the plants. And the lawn."

"Well, make sure you don't forget. It's been terribly hot lately. The rhododendrons along our back fence were already so dry by the time I got to them. It happens fast."

"Okay, Mom. I'll be careful."

"You're sure you know how to take care of their garden?"

"I'll call you if I have any questions."

It was settled. She was free. The most important weekend of her life would be starting soon. Still, she didn't know how to contact Verushka. She had already called on Monday and Tuesday, but the incessant ringing made her give up. Sometimes she wondered if it was the wrong number. Or maybe they'd moved?

Then, on Thursday night after she got off work and was watching TV with her parents, the phone rang.

"I wonder who that could be," her mom said.

"Elaine, get up. It's probably one of your friends anyway," her dad told her from behind his newspaper.

She ran to the phone, and when she put it to her ear, she heard Robert's voice. She turned around so that her back was to her parents.

"You're a hard woman to get hold of," he said.

"Really?" Elaine wondered when he had called before. There was almost always someone home. What if her mother had answered?

"Verushka misses you."

"Well, I miss her too." Elaine tried her best to sound casual, as if it was one of her schoolfriends on the line. She had important information to convey, and her mother could not hear it. "Write this number down, okay?" she whispered. Then she gave Robert Linda's number. "That's where I'll be this weekend."

To her relief, her parents started talking about someone on TV. It sounded like they were trying to remember the name of an actor, which could take a while.

"Can you get away? Come across the bridge and visit us?"

"No. I'm housesitting. You need to come to me."

"I can barely hear you."

"Well," Elaine said in a louder voice, "call the number I gave you and you'll get what you need." She imagined herself in Linda's kitchen waiting for the phone to ring. After watering the plants, of course.

"Okay. Saturday then?"

"Saturday night. I get off work at seven."

"Where do you work?"

"New to Me."

After she hung up, she went straight to her bedroom because she knew she couldn't tell a convincing lie. She was all flushed and sweaty. The name her parents were trying to recall came to her in a flash, and she called from her bedroom, "That's Catherine Deneuve!"

* * *

Elaine wore a purple minidress with a matching headband to work on that historic Saturday. She knew Linda would tell her she was supposed to wear her white boots with that outfit, but it was much too hot, so she chose a pair of brown sandals that laced up to her knees. She waited until her mom left for the fundraiser so that she wouldn't have to explain why she was so dressed up for work. As she walked to New to Me, several cars honked at her and she swore at them under her breath.

She spent the first part of her shift putting clothes back on racks and replaying her conversation with Robert. She hadn't told him Linda's address because she was worried about her mom overhearing and interrogating her afterward. *Who were you talking to on the phone? You're not giving Linda's number out to strangers, are you?* God, she could die from the lack of privacy. But now she regretted everything she had not said. She'd told him where she worked, at least. She fantasized Verushka and Robert picking her up from work in a convertible sportscar, or waiting for her in Linda's driveway, but she didn't even know if they had a car. She shook her head to rid herself of the idea that they would take the bus. Maybe the ferry? And then a taxi?

By the time her shift ended, Elaine was dying to get to Linda's and sit by the phone. She knew it was pathetic and laughed at herself. It was still light out as she stepped outside the shop and looked up and down the street for the kind of car that might belong to her friends. No luck. It was over a mile to Linda's house and she regretted wearing the sandals, but she loved being on her own. She was leaving work to go to a place where her parents did not live. She was going to meet up with some interesting people. Soon every day would be like this.

It was weird to step inside Linda's empty house. Unsettling. "Hello?" she called, if only to hear her own voice. She walked through the house and checked all the rooms, even the bathrooms and closets. She opened the door to the detached garage and looked around. There. She had checked everything. Even her parents would be satisfied. Now for the plants.

Elaine left the sliding glass door open while she walked around the back yard with the hose; that way she could hear the phone when it rang. She put food and water in the cat's bowls on the patio. All she wanted was to go into the gazebo and take a hit, but they could never hear the phone from in there. Maybe that was because she and Linda always made too much noise laughing and listening to music. If she left the sliding glass door open as well as the gazebo windows, then she would probably hear the phone if it rang. *When* it rang. She wished she could rip the phone off the kitchen wall and drag it across the back yard.

She followed through on her plan and left everything wide open. Then she ran back inside and checked the lock on the front door. She could hear her dad's voice, booming at her from across town, telling her she was acting crazy. *Leaving everything wide open. Asking for trouble.* Her dad's voice, even in her imagination, angered her so much that she propped open the gazebo door with a brick she found in the yard, threw off her strappy sandals, and then lay down on her favorite cushion where she sparked up. She inhaled and held it for as long as she could. She wasn't planning to smoke very much in case Verushka showed up. Verushka and Robert. A glass of white wine would be nice, but she couldn't have one unless there was already an open bottle in the refrigerator.

A mean little voice in the back of her head told her she didn't have any friends, aside from Linda. Then it reminded her she had never had a real boyfriend.

She sat up. Something was odd. The cat. Fox usually turned up whenever someone was in the gazebo. Maybe Fox had a date.

Call them! she decided. Call the number she knew by heart. She didn't want to seem too desperate, but she could call and explain again that she was housesitting. Bored but available. All alone. They were invited. Never mind that nobody ever answered when she called. She would give it another chance. She had never called on a Saturday night because then they would have known how empty her life was. But first she had to get out of this dumb dress.

She had stripped down to her underwear when she heard someone open the side gate to the yard. Did she have time to run into the house and lock the sliding glass door behind her? There was nowhere to hide in the gazebo. The bed was a mattress on the floor and the dresser was pushed up against the wall. What if it was the police? What if one of the neighbors had called? Shit, she wasn't even playing loud music.

The joint sat in plain sight in a little leaf-shaped ashtray Linda had made in her ceramics class.

"*Bonsoir*," Verushka said, appearing in the doorway, her white hair like a blast of light. "Having a party?"

"I was getting changed. I just got back from work."

"I know. I dropped by and asked them where I could find you. Aren't you glad to see me?"

Elaine hesitated. She had told her boss she was housesitting, but nobody at work knew Linda's address. She must have included it on her list of references. She frowned as Verushka came forward and kissed her on both cheeks.

"May I?" Verushka asked, pointing to the ashtray.

"Of course." Elaine searched Linda's dresser for a pair of shorts, but all her favorites were gone. She found an old plaid romper she had never liked, but it was better than standing around in her underwear.

"Very stylish. You look like a little schoolgirl."

Elaine couldn't tell if Verushka was being serious. "These are my friend's clothes. She puts everything she doesn't care about out here. She has a real closet in the house."

"You act like you live here."

"I spend a lot of time here."

Verushka looked around at the gazebo. She was wearing a purple crochet halter top that almost matched Elaine's dress and a pair of lace-up jeans.

"You're staring at my body."

"Actually," Elaine said, her face blazing, "I'm staring at your top. I love it."

"Would it be so bad for you to stare at my body?"

On impulse, Elaine grabbed Verushka's hands and began stroking and kissing them. Then she noticed a set of tiny brown marks on the underside of Verushka's wrists. "What is this?" she asked. "Is it a tattoo, or henna? It's new, isn't it? I don't remember you having this."

"It is nothing," Verushka said, looking down. "I'll explain later."

"I don't know what I'm doing," Elaine confessed before they kissed. "I don't know what's happening to me." And then she slipped into a deep, dark sea. It was even better than what she had experienced in the San Francisco apartment. She wanted it to last forever, but by the time the summer sky had turned black, she was already weighed down by shame. Dread. She got up off the mattress and ran outside to close the sliding glass door to the house. She came back and shut the gazebo door behind her, and she would have closed the windows too if it hadn't been so hot. There were a few old sheets Linda used as curtains. Elaine did her best to cover every inch of the glass.

Verushka rolled over. "What are you doing?"

"You have to promise me you'll never tell anybody about this. My life would be over."

"Isn't that a bit dramatic, Elaine?"

"You don't understand. This is serious. I guess it's different where you're from."

"I don't believe love changes when you cross the ocean."

"Well, I'd have to cross the ocean if anybody ever found out about us."

"Then come traveling with me. University can wait." Verushka's accent sounded stronger than ever.

Silence. Elaine could hear crickets chirping and some small animal, probably Fox, walking around the yard.

"I can't. I have no money. It's all I can do to hang on until college starts."

"Your problem is that you are afraid of what you want."

The truth of the statement flooded Elaine's body, but it was quickly followed by the sting of injustice. None of this was her fault. She thought she knew what she wanted, but it hadn't yet come into complete focus. She was waiting but she wasn't passive. She felt powerless but she could still be strong.

"Are you angry?" Verushka asked.

"I don't know." After a few seconds Elaine asked, "What happened to Robert?"

"Do you want him too? He would be glad to hear that."

"He called me this week. I hadn't heard from you guys since New Year's. I've called before but you never answer."

"You should call at night."

"My parents are always around in the evening."

"Ah."

"Didn't you ever have parents?"

"No father. And I have not had a mother for a very long time."

"You mean she's dead?"

Verushka didn't answer her. Elaine got up and lit some candles. She didn't even know how old Verushka was. Maybe her family was killed by the Nazis?

"Do you want something to eat?" Elaine asked. "I haven't had dinner. Let's go inside."

It was strange standing with Verushka in Linda's kitchen, like putting the two different sides of her life next to each other. They did not fit together.

Even though they had just made love, Elaine was embarrassed, self-conscious. She wished she could study Verushka, wearing only her underwear, in secret. Impossible to guess her age, anywhere from sixteen to thirty. Her eyes. Elaine's mother always said the eyes showed a woman's true age. She turned Verushka around to face her. "My God, your pupils are huge."

"Are they?"

"Yes. It makes your eyes look so dark. Black."

"What are you doing, Elaine? Are you trying to tell my fortune?"

"How would I do that?"

"In my village, they say you can see the future in your lover's pupil. Go ahead. Come closer."

"Won't I see myself?"

Elaine peered into Verushka's left eye and saw herself. Up close she could see the finest of lines around Verushka's eyes.

"Satisfied?" Verushka asked.

"I don't understand."

"What did you see?"

"Me."

"And were you afraid?"

"I don't know."

"What are you going to make me for dinner?"

Elaine had never really played hostess before, but she opened the refrigerator and looked around. "I could make you some eggs. Or we could order a pizza."

"Let me prepare something for you, but you have to sit down over there. I can't have someone watching me if I'm going to cook."

Elaine tried to see the little kitchen through Verushka's eyes. Then she looked around and studied the house as if she had never seen it before, the wide floorboards, the white fireplace, the bookshelves. Linda and her parents lived close to downtown Larkspur and had huge old redwoods all around them. Elaine had always loved the place. It made her think of home, of childhood, as much as her own house did, but perhaps Verushka judged it as too suburban? Elaine had accepted the idea that she should be embarrassed about where she was from, that she had missed the best city in the world by a hair.

In mere minutes Verushka made a little cake and put it in the oven. "There. Soon you will taste the food of my village. I'm so happy your friends have sour cherries."

"I've never seen anyone cook like you. You didn't measure anything."

"I told you not to watch me, Elaine."

"I can't help it. You're so beautiful."

Elaine covered her face with her hands. She was not used to talking to another woman this way. Verushka led her out to the gazebo and they both lay down on the mattress. It was strange to be in this space with someone other than Linda.

"I just realized this is only the second time I've seen you," Elaine said.

"Doesn't it feel as though we've known each other forever?"

"Yes. Yes, and I think of you often. All the time. I always believed I would see you again."

"Soon you will understand I am never going to leave you."

Elaine must have been drifting off to sleep because the next thing she knew, Verushka was sitting above her, telling her to open up. A cherry burned the roof of her mouth, and for days she would remember this pain whenever she bit into something hot. She complained but sat up and ate the piece of cake Verushka had brought her, which was surprisingly tasty without being too sweet.

"Now it is done," Verushka said. "You've eaten from my hand."

"What does that mean?"

Verushka looked Elaine in the eye. "You will never be able to escape me or my descendants."

Elaine thought Verushka was joking. "Your descendants? You don't have children, do you?"

"Everybody has a family, somewhere."

"I've never met anyone like you," Elaine said. "This is delicious, by the way. My mother never bakes from scratch."

They smoked grass until Elaine passed out. In the morning Verushka was gone, leaving behind only her scent, which lingered on the sheets even after Elaine had washed them twice.

* * *

"Are you taking drugs?"

It was endless. Her mother would not stop bothering her about drugs and sex, so Elaine hid in her room. She counted the days until she could move to the East Bay. She could not wait to give notice at work. Everything was making her impatient, even hanging out in the gazebo with Linda.

"So why can't I meet your friends?" Linda asked. "This whole place smells like that girl's perfume and I don't even know what she looks like."

"I hadn't noticed." Elaine was embarrassed. What if she smelled like Verushka too? "Of course you can meet them, but they're not around. They must have gone on vacation."

The truth was she didn't know how to get in touch with Verushka again. She was afraid to dial the number. The endless ringing felt like rejection. Could she be in love with Verushka and afraid of her at the same time? She certainly didn't want to share her with Linda.

"Anyway," Linda went on, "this is weird but one of my mom's cake pans is missing. She keeps asking me about it. Do you know where it went?"

"No, sorry."

Elaine had made sure to leave Linda's house spick and span, but the kitchen was already clean when she went inside on Sunday morning. Verushka must have taken the cake with her, pan and all. She probably didn't consider it a theft.

Elaine had stayed at Linda's place longer than she needed to, and after cleaning the sheets, she dusted the whole gazebo. Filled the cat's bowls. Watered the lawn again, to be safe. Then she shut and locked the front door behind her and walked home. Home hadn't changed but she had. She'd left her parents' house as their little girl and come back as someone else.

Now she had to pretend she was still a little girl. Her mother was particularly hard to fool.

The battle started in earnest during the first week of August. Elaine came home one afternoon from work, stole away to her bedroom, and then heard the knock on her door. Always the same, three little taps. She breathed out and swung the door open.

Her mother stood there with what Elaine would later describe to Linda as a bullshit smile. She was holding the brochure for the local community college. "Good news," she said. "I called and you can still register for classes. You'll be living at home for the next two years. You're not ready for Berkeley."

Elaine exploded. She ran out of the room, grabbed the keys, jumped into her mom's car, and tore off without looking right or left. Without stopping. A bandit in a movie. Wanted. She sped all the way to her father's law office, where she parked sloppily and then got out of the car, leaving it unlocked, and thereby breaking another one of the family rules.

"I need to talk to my father," she told the startled secretary, Darlene, who had worked there for years. Darlene liked her.

"Okay, Elaine. Let me see if he's busy."

Darlene disappeared and Elaine sat in the little waiting room with her heart still hammering. Her father ran a small practice specializing in real estate law. The office was spartan and boring but always cool and clean and Elaine liked being there, especially on summer days. Nobody else was waiting, thank God. Of course her father was busy. He was always busy. Darlene had probably gone in there to warn him. How embarrassing.

Then her dad appeared, calm and smiling, and escorted her out the door and down to the diner where they often ate. It was as if they had an appointment. Was he expecting her? Had her mother already called to warn him?

"Don't you want something to eat?"

"I'm not hungry, Dad."

"You're not?"

"I ate on my break," she lied. She knew she was being judged, even for something as stupid as regular meals. As if everybody in the world hungered in the same way, for the same things.

"Elaine, let me tell you something about your mother. Once, right after we got married, we were invited to a barbecue out at Lake Merced. Your mother was supposed to bring a cake, and so she went all out and ordered one from Lady Baltimore. When we were almost at the lake, she realized she had forgotten the cake on the counter and made me drive all the way back. By the time we got to the barbecue, most of the guests had already left. I knew it was a mistake to go back for that cake, but there was no talking her out of it."

Elaine stared at her father. The story made her want to cry but she could not explain why. She knew she wanted nothing further to do with these people called her parents.

"What I'm saying is that your mother won't be talked out of these ideas she gets, but it doesn't matter. I've already paid Berkeley for the first semester. You're going, but on one condition: you have to keep your grades up. None of this craziness. No protests. No cutting class. All this chaos will resolve soon, and you'll have to get a good job one day, like everybody else."

"You don't see me getting married?" Elaine was almost afraid to ask him this. Marriage was not on her list, but she knew it was on her father's list for her.

He dismissed her question with a wave of his hand. "There are two kinds of women. Housekeepers, like your mother, and workers, like Darlene. You're a Darlene."

"You see me as a secretary?"

"I know you're not going to be content sitting at home. Look at you now," he said, smiling, as if he had paid her a great compliment.

Afterward they walked back to the office together. Elaine stayed until the end of the workday and then drove home, right behind her father. The family dinner was tense and terrible, as usual, but the green olive casserole was tasty, and Elaine imagined herself at Cal telling stories about her mother's weird recipes.

The next week she went through all her possessions and started packing. Every time she put something in the donation box, her mother would seize it and object.

"Mom! I'm clearing out my bedroom for you," Elaine said. "This way you can have a little studio."

"A studio?"

"Or a sewing room. Dad has his den. Why don't you have your own room?"

"Mothers don't have their own rooms. Unless you mean the kitchen."

Her mother wasn't doing a very good job of advertising a feminine future, and Elaine would remember this conversation for the rest of her life, but especially in the seventies, by which point she was in New York. Later she would feel sorry for her mother, but that summer she saw her as an evil force keeping her under house arrest.

After a few hours she was done packing. She could fit everything she cared about in two suitcases and three boxes. For a girl who worked at a clothing store, she didn't have very many clothes to pack, and all her makeup and jewelry fit into her little mint green Starline train case.

She was afraid to look up and declare that she was ready, afraid her mom might still change her mind. Her mother's eyes bored into her. "I'm going to get a glass of water," Elaine said, making an excuse to get out of the room. The phone rang right as she stepped into the kitchen and she grabbed it, knowing it was for her. She and Linda were calling each other a lot these days, talking about classes and their new dorm room.

It was Verushka. She gave Elaine a San Francisco address and told her to bring a suitcase and her passport.

"My passport?"

"Don't you have one?"

"Yes, I do," Elaine said, leaving her words hanging in the air. Her father had made her get one for a family trip to London, a trip that had never materialized because he was too busy with work. The picture was from only a few years ago, but it didn't even look like her anymore.

* * *

It was supposed to be the start of her new life, but Elaine was in a crisis, forced to choose, and not between two lovers, or between marriage and a career, but between Verushka and Berkeley.

The end arrived. Her last week at work. Her last week at home. Friday night she had dinner out with her parents at the Buckeye. Sunday was move-in day.

Saturday afternoon Verushka was expecting her to show up at an apartment at 73 Alpine Terrace with a suitcase and her passport. Every time Elaine closed her eyes the room would spin. It was worse than doing drugs in the park. Her mother kept taking her aside and telling her not to worry so much. "I know you're getting nervous, Elaine," she would say. "Everybody gets homesick at first."

It was unfair. Why wasn't this happening later? Verushka could have waited to see whether or not Elaine even liked Berkeley. But this was what choice was all about, wasn't it? There was always a loss involved.

Of course she was going to Berkeley. Her whole life up to this point had been about getting away from her parents, leaving home. It was the only, the obvious, thing to do. She had no other plans, no other future.

Of course she was running off with Verushka. She had no boyfriend. No lover. The boys in high school had left her cold. And who knew where Verushka would take her? It could make all the difference.

Saturday morning. Elaine opened her eyes and stared at the ceiling of her childhood bedroom. She didn't know what she was going to do but she couldn't imagine defying Verushka. She had to show up, at least, but she couldn't leave the house with a suitcase. What would her mom say? She put her favorite clothes in an old duffel bag and crammed her biggest purse with toiletries. Just in case. When her mom ran to the market to get three steaks, Elaine called Linda, who gave her a ride to the Mill Valley Depot, so that she would only have to transfer once. "I don't know what the big mystery is," Linda said.

"I need to say goodbye to a friend," Elaine explained, then immediately felt guilty. She was lying to everyone lately.

"I don't see why you need a duffel bag to say goodbye to somebody."

"It's hard to explain. Don't worry about it."

She still had not made her decision, not even when the bridge came into view. She wanted both worlds. She did not want to decide.

If she had a duffel bag and her passport, didn't that mean something? She tried to sit back and breathe. At the very least she would have one more day with Verushka. What was Verushka planning anyway? Elaine had imagined taking the bus from Berkeley to the city from time to time to visit Verushka. Not every weekend, no. Every so often. She would appear sophisticated and mysterious to her new classmates. "I'm going to see a friend in the city," she would say. "I'll be back on Monday morning."

When she got to San Francisco, she told herself she was a grown woman who had a serious, romantic rendezvous. She had been to the city alone before. She was about to move to the East Bay. People were staring at her now and she could imagine what she looked like. A little girl. A deer in headlights. She could already see the wide, slightly mocking smile Verushka would greet her with.

And then they would get down to business.

Elaine found herself walking up a steep San Francisco hill to get to the address on Alpine Terrace. She was glad she had worn her jeans because it was chilly. It was hard to believe it was so sunny at home on the other side of the bridge. Would Verushka offer her hot tea on this cold day? Would there be time?

She rang the bell at 73. The building was so nice that at first she thought she had the wrong address. Verushka, all in black, opened the door and squinted at her. "Is that all you're bringing?"

"You didn't give me much to go on," Elaine said. "Besides, I like to travel light."

"No coat?"

Elaine pictured her favorite suede coat, draped over her suitcase in her bedroom. Waiting for her. She didn't answer.

"You do have your passport, yes?"

Only when Elaine said yes did Verushka let her in. She led her up a staircase to the front door of her unit. The place was beautiful, much nicer and brighter than the first apartment Verushka had brought her to, where everything started. Elaine wandered around taking it all in. There was a living room with a fireplace, and a real kitchen with a big refrigerator and plenty of cabinets. A proper bedroom with a door. The biggest surprise was the dining room, graced by a bay window that presented, even under an overcast sky, a spectacular view of the city. Elaine stood in front of the window and dropped her duffel bag and purse.

"God, I wish I could live here."

"But we're leaving at eight," Verushka said.

"Where are we going?"

Verushka walked over to a little round table. There were two chairs on either side of it, but aside from the bed, there was no other furniture in the apartment. There were no pictures or souvenirs. No sign of Robert. Verushka took a folded paper off the table and came back to Elaine with a smile.

It was a ticket to Paris.

Elaine's mind filled with questions. She asked if Verushka was a French citizen.

"No. We will take a train to my village in the forest. It's a long trip but it is worth it, and we will be so, so happy. I can show you many great cities on the way."

Elaine took a step back and shook her head. "I'm really not prepared for this, Verushka."

"By the time we arrive, you won't remember anything of your old life. Trust me. Cross over with me. I will take care of everything."

"What are you talking about?"

"There is someone I want you to meet. He will change your life. And perhaps you will meet my son as well."

"You have a child? You're serious?" Elaine could not have been more surprised. She remembered Verushka's lithe little body. It seemed impossible that she had ever given birth. "I thought you were being dramatic when you talked about your descendants. How old were you when you had him?"

Verushka didn't answer. She stared at Elaine in disbelief. "Aren't you happy?"

"I need to sit for a second." Elaine walked over to the little table and sat in one of the chairs. Behind her back the city rose, a reminder of what was real. She took a good look at Verushka, whose eyes were black and glassy.

"You're not going to betray me, are you?"

"Betray you?"

Elaine thought about all the times she had dialed Verushka's number, only to listen to the endless ringing. She remembered how she had felt when Verushka disappeared for months on end. Now she was waking up. Everything came into focus. It was like being slapped in the face or jumping into the cold bay. She had let this woman she barely knew manipulate her. How she wished she had never come here! For once she agreed with her parents about where she belonged. She was tempted to make a break for it and run out of the apartment. There was a steep flight of stairs and she was tired and thirsty, but she could do it. She could find a coffee house to hide in while she planned her next move. She asked, "What happened to Robert?"

"Robert is a fool."

"Verushka," Elaine began, "you must realize I can't do this. I'm supposed to start school in a few days. I'm moving to Berkeley tomorrow. I would be glad to join you when I'm on vacation, but I can't drop everything and fly across the world. That's insane."

"You are so ungrateful. You are nothing but a spoiled, selfish little girl. You should join Robert. Do you want to see him? You won't recognize him, but I can take you to him. I can take you to a very dark place."

Elaine had enough time to grab her things with one hand and start running before Verushka, strong for such a petite woman, blocked her. Elaine had never fought anyone before, and now here she was, weighed down by her possessions. She couldn't jettison her favorite clothes. Why had she packed so much? What had she been thinking? The duffel bag and the passport were an attempt to spare Verushka's feelings, to go along with her plan or make it seem like she was considering it. No real friend would order you to get on a plane to Paris without warning. No real friend acted like their plans were more important than your life.

They slapped and kicked each other. Verushka grabbed Elaine by the waist to slow her down. They fell to the floor together. It was a challenge to get up and reach the front door, especially with her two bags, but Elaine managed it by kicking Verushka in the head. Everything stopped for a moment. It was the first act of physical violence Elaine had ever perpetrated on another person. Verushka was stunned; Elaine was scared. She rushed forward and struggled with the deadbolt for a few agonizing seconds. Then she stumbled onto the landing and started down the staircase.

Somehow her feet left the stairs. She was up in the air, suddenly on an amusement park ride, out of control. Then she rolled down the stairs as her purse and duffel bag tangled around her. Everything went black, punctuated by little flashes of light, like stars. Pain raged in her cheekbone and arm as Verushka approached. Elaine feared she would never make it outside, though she was so close. She could not get up.

Halfway down the stairs, Verushka stopped and said something in a foreign language. Then she spat three times. She was standing right above Elaine's head when she spoke to her for the last time. "This is your choice and you will live with it always. You ate from my hands. You pleasured yourself with my body. You loved me. You will live to regret it. Remember: time is on my side. If you cannot repay me, your descendants will. Be careful of your children, especially your daughters. The moment a girl is born, she is mine. I will return!"

And then it was over. Verushka disappeared upstairs, into the apartment. The deadbolt slid into place. Elaine knew she would never see Verushka again. Pain rushed in and replaced everything else. Her left arm was broken. It took her three tries to stand up and grab her things. She left the building and hobbled down the street, wincing, as she tried to keep hold of her purse and duffel bag. Her cheekbone was swelling. She had turned into the kind of San Francisco person her parents were always warning her about.

Going downhill was especially challenging, almost impossible. Now her back was hurting. She slowly lowered herself to the front steps of someone's home. What could she do? Was there a phone somewhere around here? She would never be able to manage the bus ride all the way home.

"Can I help you?"

It was a woman's voice. She sounded angry, but when she came down the steps and saw Elaine's face, she softened. "Did someone hurt you, honey?"

"Yes. I mean no. It's no big deal. A fight with a friend."

"A boyfriend?"

Elaine paused to consider the question. "Sort of."

"How old are you? Where do you live?"

"Far."

"How far? Do you want me to call the police?"

"No! I need to call my dad. I can give you the number."

The woman looked relieved. "Why don't you come inside and call him?"

She called home from the hallway of the woman's house. It was shabby and ordinary, somehow comforting. The woman dialed for her and held the phone to Elaine's ear as Elaine cradled her broken arm with her good hand. The phone rang seven times, shrill and excruciating.

"Dad?" He was home, thank God. She had expected him to be at the golf course. She knew it was best to give it to him straight. "Dad, I need you to come and get me."

"Where are you, Elaine?"

"In the city." Before he could react, she went on. "I'm hurt. My arm is broken. I can't get home by myself."

There was a long, punishing pause. "Give me the address."

The woman took over and finished the phone call for her. Then she brought Elaine a cup of tea with milk and sugar. In the bathroom, a little mirror showed Elaine her raised purple cheekbone. Great. She would be starting college looking like this. Her arm and torso had grown numb but could be roused to a shrieking pain with the slightest movement. When her father arrived, he thanked the woman profusely, made a quick call home, and then carried Elaine's things to the double-parked family car. Lowering herself into the passenger seat made everything go black again.

After they had pulled onto Divisadero, her father said, "Tell me exactly what happened."

"I went to say goodbye to a friend who's leaving the country. We had an argument. I had to leave in a hurry and I fell down a flight of stairs."

"Elaine, I know you're not telling me the truth."

"I am! I swear. It sounds crazy but it really happened."

"Except that you're leaving certain things out."

"Not really."

"Is this friend a boy or a girl?"

"A girl. A woman. I swear. There was no man involved."

"Were there any drugs involved?"

"Dad, no. Do I sound high to you? I had a stupid accident."

Her father sighed. Elaine was truly sorry for him. "How did you wind up at some complete stranger's house? Do you know what your mother is going to say about this?"

"Dad, please, help me out. Just one last time, and I promise this will never happen again."

They drove on in total silence until they got to Marin General Hospital, where Elaine's mother met them in the ER. In the parking lot of the hospital her father turned to her. "I'm going to say this only once, Elaine Rose. This is the end of your San Francisco adventures. I don't want to hear one word out of you. You're going over to Cal to see if you can stay enrolled. If you get one bad grade, or if I hear one negative report, one rumor, you're coming straight home. We'll find some other school. Dominican or something. Don't be stupid, Elaine. Don't destroy your future. Your life. You think it's really cool over there, don't you? It isn't. You have no idea how hard I worked to get out of that place. I grew up in the Mission in a little dump. You wouldn't be able to handle one week of it."

The rest of the day was the blur of her mother's tears, her own mumbled lies to the hospital staff, the cast, and a bottle of excellent pain killers. In her little bed at home she closed her eyes with only a vague idea about leaving the next day. When she woke in the early morning the pain was worse than ever, so she swallowed two more pills. Then she remembered what Verushka had said about Robert. Was he gone? Dead? Had that little woman actually killed him or was she only trying to scare her? Elaine wondered if she should call the police. She lay in the morning light and tried to picture herself telling this story to the authorities. Wouldn't they dismiss her as hysterical? Delusional? She didn't even know Verushka's last name. Or Robert's. And Verushka hadn't exactly confessed to a murder. But still. She had threatened her, hadn't she? Laid some kind of curse on her. Was there a law against cursing someone? Was it a form of assault? Her dad would know, but she didn't want to ask him anything. She didn't want to speak to him at all, except to say goodbye.

She decided to close the door on the Verushka chapter of her life.

She congratulated herself for packing early but wondered if the broken arm would sabotage her. What if she fell behind in her classes, doomed by the cast and all the new challenges?

Later that morning her mother came in with breakfast. She brushed Elaine's hair for her and then sat down on the bed.

"Mom, I can't talk right now. I really don't feel well. I'm going to sleep in the car on the way over."

"Honestly, Elaine, do you have to ruin everything? I wanted to give you something before you left."

Guilt overwhelmed her. She did not deserve a gift. Her mom left the room and Elaine wondered what it could be. Pearls? A pen? At graduation she got the watch she never wore, partly because it was too fancy but also because it simply wasn't her style. She wished it could be a lava lamp, or a record album, but that was impossible. Her mom came back with a forced smile on her face and a big box in her arms.

"Well, I'll open it since you can't." She took the lid off the box and pulled out an old-fashioned teddy bear with moveable arms and legs.

Elaine groaned, then apologized, then asked if it was an antique. Her mom liked to drive around the Bay Area looking for treasures.

"It's a Steiff," she said, as if that explained everything.

"Don't you think he should stay here, on my bed? I wouldn't want anything to happen to him."

"I only bought it to make you laugh, because you used to have so many stuffed animals, don't you remember? They covered your bed when you were little. You don't have to keep it."

"No! I want to, but they told us not to bring anything valuable. Thanks, Mom."

As much as she wanted to get away from her mother, she felt bad. She was grateful to her for not interrogating her about the events of the day before. Her dad must have interceded for her.

"Mom, don't cry and don't worry about me. I'm not going far."

"I'm not worried, Elaine. I know you've been leaving us for a long time."

Her dad, anxious to get on the road, interrupted them. Maybe it was the painkillers working too well, but Elaine experienced no nostalgia walking out the door and into her new life. She was ready. She didn't sleep in the car and instead kept her eyes wide open, feeling pleasantly stoned and hoping this was an introduction to life at Cal. Classes wouldn't start for a few more days. There would be parties and strangers, beautiful strangers, signing her cast.

Her face didn't look too bad once the swelling went down.

Elaine didn't return home until Thanksgiving, by which point she was getting one A and the rest B's, but better yet, she knew she could handle college. She could handle anything. She began to create her own life, imagining who she wanted to be and where she wanted to live. She was lucky, as these choices came easily to her generation. They were rewarded for their ambition, their daring, and even for their mistakes. Elaine loved to talk and she especially loved answering questions, even from professors, though that didn't happen often in her huge, introductory-level classes on the Berkeley campus. When she sat down with friends, she discovered a new self rising up out of the discussions they would have, a self made of words and choices and strong emotions. One question stumped her though, in the beginning, especially because she didn't like to lie.

"What happened to you?" everyone asked her. "How'd you get that cast?"

"I fell down a flight of stairs," she would say. And then she would add, after a dramatic pause, "I guess I had a little too much to drink one night." Wasn't that an expression, falling down drunk? She didn't like to fabricate further details but sometimes she would claim the lights had gone out in a stairwell. "It was one of those old San Francisco buildings," she would explain as her listeners nodded knowingly. She was able to appear mysterious for one second. At long last she was a young woman with stories to tell, and then everyone would tease her for her bad habits. Her wild behavior. Her decadence. At night, when she was about to fall asleep, she would sometimes see Verushka's dreadful face above her, but as the weeks and months passed, semester after semester, so many other faces entered her life. It was easy to forget about Verushka. Elaine even managed to forget the curse Verushka had put on her and on certain children who were not yet born.

Caroline: 2013

Caroline was relaxing in a hot bath when she got the phone call. "Melissa?"

"You need to come over here."

"Why? What happened?"

"Devon isn't herself and I think you should take her home."

The room spun for a second as Caroline tried to understand, but then she sat up. She hoped Melissa couldn't hear the water splashing.

"Oh, I think I've got it under control," Melissa said into the silence, "but you should take over."

"I'll be there right away."

She threw on a maxi dress that stuck to her wet skin. In the car she checked her face and smeared on lip balm. Melissa's family lived on a dreamy street on the other side of Overland and their house was huge for LA. It was only a few minutes away, but anxiety made the drive feel slow and surreal. Caroline parked in the driveway; there was more than enough room for her little Prius. She took a deep breath as she approached the front door.

Devon was at a birthday sleepover for Sierra and Samantha, mean-girl twins. The invitation had made Devon feel both relieved and anxious.

"If you're worried about it, Devon, you don't have to go. You can say no."

Devon had stared at her like she was hopeless. "I have no choice, Mom. These are my friends."

Thirteen was dangerous territory. Everyone knew this. Caroline had been warned. All parents were afraid of this age, and middle school was apparently more terrifying than high school. Caroline studied Devon for any changes, and sometimes she stared at her so hard that Devon would shout and storm out of the room. "What are you looking at? I'm not your science experiment, okay?" Her science experiment? What a strange thing to say, but smart too. All children were monsters their parents had created. Devon should explore that idea in an essay, Caroline thought, but Devon never wanted to pursue anything her mother suggested.

Devon was one of the youngest in her class because of her summer birthday. Her breasts were still small and she had a tight little waist. She hadn't had her period yet, but Caroline sensed it was coming. She couldn't help marveling at her daughter. Weren't all the other parents studying their kids, waiting for a sign? Caroline was alone in this project. She felt like she had full custody since Jack, chasing money and prestige, had moved back to New York when Devon was in elementary school. He saw his daughter only a few weeks each summer and every other Christmas.

Melissa and one of the twins (Sierra or Samantha—Caroline could never tell the difference) opened the door. Caroline was sure the girl was sneering at her. Melissa came forward and gave Caroline a one-armed hug. "Thanks for coming over."

"No problem. It's not far. What happened?"

"It was really weird, Mrs. Woodward. Devon's eyes started rolling back, like she was in a trance. Then she started talking, but not to us, so I went and got my mom."

Melissa led Caroline to the kitchen, where Devon was sitting at the table with her best friend, Reina, who held her hand. What a relief to see Devon wasn't alone. Caroline felt a big wave of love for Reina, and then she took her daughter's face in her hands and examined her pupils. "Are you okay?"

Devon didn't answer.

"What were you girls doing?" Caroline asked.

"We were raising a table and she started to freak out," Sierra-or-Samantha said.

Melissa stepped in. "They were playing around. You know that game? Everyone puts their hands on the table and chants, *Rise, table, rise?*"

"No, I don't know." Caroline faced the twin. "Please tell me exactly what happened."

"I'm trying to," Sierra-or-Samantha said. She was being disrespectful, in Caroline's opinion.

"You said her eyes rolled back?"

"She put her head up and her eyes rolled back, and all we could see were the whites. She said something in this weird voice. She wasn't even speaking English. Then the table dropped."

Melissa took over. "That got my attention. It's a heavy wood coffee table but nobody got hurt, thankfully."

Caroline had so many questions. "You don't mean the table was actually rising?"

"Yes! You can ask the other girls. Everybody's upstairs in our room."

"Oh, Sam, you need to stop this," Melissa said. "It's a silly game and you all got too excited. I'm sure Caroline wants to take Devon home now."

Samantha (mystery solved!) went charging up the stairs. The last thing Caroline wanted was to talk to a group of excited kids who had consumed too much sugar and now had their big story for Monday morning. No: for social media, and that meant immediately. Everything was different with this generation of kids, fast and merciless.

Devon stared at the table. She was sinking into herself, Caroline could tell. More than one therapist had explained this as her way of coping when things got to be too much. "Let's go, baby," Caroline said, steering Devon to the front door and away from the posse upstairs, which was gaining in volume. "Thank you," she said to Melissa. "I hope they have a nice birthday."

Devon had already made a beeline for the car, so Caroline turned back to Melissa and asked, "You don't think she had a seizure, do you?"

"I didn't see it happen, but she seems okay now, doesn't she? I would call your pediatrician on Monday."

In the car, Caroline resisted the urge to interrogate her daughter. Questioning Devon would only make her shut down more. Caroline followed her instincts and drove straight to the urgent care facility on Venice Boulevard. She expected her daughter to object, but instead she got the silent treatment. At the clinic they didn't have to wait long once Caroline said she was concerned about a possible seizure. They checked Devon's blood pressure, pulse, and pupils. They took blood.

Devon was forced to speak about her experience. She told the doctors about the party, the noisy atmosphere, the cake. She admitted to being anxious the whole time. She described the group of five girls raising a table in a dark room lit by one candle. "The table went up," she said, and "then everything went black."

"Did you fall?"

"I don't think so. Anyway, we were sitting down. The next thing I knew everyone was screaming and the lights were on, so bright it hurt. The other girls said I was, like, speaking in tongues or something, and my eyes were rolling back in my head. I don't remember any of that though. It was like waking up after my tonsillectomy, like I had been asleep for only one second."

"You never hit your head or injured yourself in any way?"

Devon looked like she was going to cry. "No. I was sitting on the floor and playing a game. With my friends."

Caroline was impressed by the ER staff and their gentle, objective questions. One of them asked Devon if she had ingested any substances, even something like Ritalin or Adderall.

"She's not on any medications," Caroline said, before realizing what the doctor was asking. Oh. Imagining the different kinds of trouble her daughter could get into was too hard and she was too slow.

"All I had was a Coke."

"That's all you consumed at the party?"

"I wasn't hungry."

Maybe hunger was the only problem? Low blood sugar?

They found nothing conclusive and advised Caroline to follow up with her pediatrician.

Devon dozed on the drive home. Caroline put her arm around her daughter as they walked through the front door, but Devon shrugged her away. "Do you want anything to eat?" Caroline asked. "I know you didn't have dinner. Or do you want a bath? I took one."

Devon went to her room, kicked off her shoes, and climbed into bed with her clothes on. Caroline stood in the doorway for a second. Then she grabbed Henry, Devon's rabbit from childhood, and put him on the bed. She stroked her daughter's hair. "Listen, Devon. I'm here. You can tell me anything you want. Anything. And you can sleep in my bed tonight."

She waited a few seconds. Devon was completely unresponsive. Was she already asleep, or was she faking it? Caroline was wide awake. She cleaned the kitchen and tried to watch television before giving up and lying in the dark, waiting for sleep. In the morning she found Devon beside her in bed and took this as an encouraging sign.

* * *

Monday afternoon came and Caroline was still not satisfied. She took Devon to the pediatrician, who ordered more bloodwork but did not see the need for an MRI.

"Maybe it was a problem with blood sugar. I really can't say at this point."

"Could they have missed something at the ER?" Caroline asked.

"I doubt it."

Caroline suspected Doctor Harrington was losing interest, but she couldn't help repeating, "They said her eyes rolled back. They said she was talking in a strange language."

The doctor smiled. "I remember slumber parties. Prank phone calls. Fortune telling."

"We weren't telling fortunes," Devon said.

Caroline left the doctor's visit feeling stranded. Scared. She hadn't felt this way since Devon was tiny, not since the fire. They lived in a nice little house now, but the threat of destruction still lurked in the corners. It didn't take much to stir up her old fears. Would her trauma scorecard ever fill up? An overused word, *trauma*. It meant wound in the original Greek, and Caroline often wondered if all she had to offer her daughter was a nice assortment of wounds.

"Don't be so hard on yourself," her mother had told her. "It's not like you caused the fire."

"What does that even mean, Mom? I know it's not my fault, but it seems like all our troubles started that summer, with the fire."

The list of misfortunes was long. The miscarriage. The divorce. That whole weird summer in the place they called the chalet. Devon was still an anxious child. She suffered from mild OCD and was highly secretive. "She's private, like me," Jack claimed. He never wanted to admit there could be anything wrong with his kid. Caroline and Jack were better friends now that they lived on opposite coasts. She still called him sometimes with her concerns, and he would try to reassure her. Their conversations often led nowhere useful, but they were going to have to talk again soon because of the slumber party incident. Jack would want to know all the details.

She hoped there was no fallout after the party at the twins' house, and to her surprise, nothing bad happened at school. If anything, the other kids were fascinated by the story of the slumber party. Devon said there was already a rumor going around that she was psychic, and it would probably gain speed now that the doctors had found nothing physically wrong with her.

Caroline still felt uneasy about those bitchy twins and their suspiciously perfect mother. She hated their enormous house that dwarfed all the other structures on an otherwise charming street near Carlson Park. Whatever. How could Caroline teach Devon to navigate the world? You needed an instinct for separating the people who were worth your time from the ones who weren't. You needed to be able to say no. The stakes were high in middle school where a kid really needed to learn all this, and fast.

Devon did not object to the attention the popular girls were giving her now. Instead she objected to her mom's concerns. "Sierra and Samantha are really nice, Mom."

"I guess I think of all twins as evil. They were when I was growing up."

"That's really messed up, Mom."

Another failed joke. Caroline glanced over at Devon, now deep in her phone, oblivious to everything else. This was her cue to bow out of the conversation, but she couldn't. "Have you been having any headaches? Blurred vision?"

"No, Mom."

End of discussion. For a while.

And then Devon started sleepwalking again.

* * *

The Thursday after the Twins of Evil slumber party, as she thought of it, Caroline found Devon standing in the kitchen at three o'clock in the morning. She needed a glass of water after a round of night sweats, and when she saw her daughter peering into the skylight, looking up, she gasped. "Devon, what are you doing?"

No response.

Caroline took Devon by the shoulders and gave her a little shake before she realized what was happening. She knew it was best to guide Devon gently back to bed without waking her, or so she had been told by the pediatrician when her daughter was little. She took Devon's hand and started walking, but Devon didn't follow.

"She's up there," Devon said. "I can see her."

Caroline stared up into the blackness of the skylight despite herself. "Who?" she asked.

"She's right there! She wants me to come with her."

"All right," Caroline said. "That's enough." She waited for a second and tried again. "Devon, can you hear me? Devon!" She clapped her hands.

Her daughter's eyes were wide open. She smiled and appeared completely lucid, but Caroline knew she was asleep. She had to get Devon back in bed and guard her all night.

"I have to go with her," Devon said.

"Who?" Caroline waited for an answer but there wasn't one. Against her better judgment, she asked, "Why do you have to go with her?"

"It's her turn again. She's come back. I shouldn't have opened the door."

"Shit," Caroline said. "Okay, Devon, you really need to wake up now."

The only light in the room came from the refrigerator, the dim glow of the water dispenser. Devon's face, in half-shadow, scared Caroline. They weren't having a real conversation, she knew. Devon wouldn't remember this in the morning.

"Devon, please."

"*Devon, please?* No! *Mom, please.* As in, Mom, why the hell did you let her take over? Why didn't you protect me, Mom?" Devon was screaming. "How the hell am I supposed to fight her now? You left me all alone. I've been alone my whole life."

She started pounding Caroline with her fists, and Caroline had to slap her daughter to wake her up. Devon doubled over and started sobbing, and only then could Caroline lead her back to bed. She spent the night lying next to her daughter and staring at the ceiling, and when the alarm rang at 6:45, it was as if they had slept for only five minutes before being wrenched awake. She was grateful when Devon appeared to remember nothing upon waking. "Mom, what are you doing in my bed?"

Caroline didn't know what to say. "You called out in the night, honey."

"I'm not a little kid. You know I can never sleep next to someone else. My neck is killing me."

"Sorry. I must have crashed here."

Unconsciousness was the theme for the whole day. Caroline fell asleep at her desk at work and didn't wake up until someone put a hand on her shoulder. It was Friday and the office had emptied early. She drove home alongside the other exhausted commuters to find Devon making cookies with Sierra and Samantha. The three teens looked at her like she was an intruder.

"Hello, girls," she said.

The twins didn't respond but Devon told her she looked cursed. It was one of the words her friend group liked to use.

"You will too when you're my age."

She wanted to pour herself a glass of wine, but not in front of the kids, so she went to her room and put her legs up on a pillow. It was obvious that Devon, never easy in the role of hostess, was trying hard to impress the twins. That was why she had criticized her mother's appearance. Ordinarily Caroline would have tried to kick them out, tactfully, after a pizza bribe, but she was relieved to have them in the kitchen after the events of the night before. Maybe the twins could work their own magic of affluence and normalcy.

She fell asleep with her legs still propped up. Devon woke her an hour later. "Mom, they're going."

"Who?"

"Sierra and Sam. Melissa is here."

"Should I come out?"

"You don't have to. And, Mom, can I order a pizza? I'm starving for real food."

"Yes, of course. Be my guest."

Caroline sat up and smoothed her hair. Now she had her daughter to herself. They could even have a movie night, though she would push for a non-horror film. Devon came back into the room with a giant chocolate chip cookie on a plate. Like a little girl she smiled at her mother, and Caroline wished she could press pause. Here was her Devon, the same as always. She knew this girl existed in private moments at home, but her child was also in the process of leaving her. Next year, by the time Devon started high school, everything would change again.

The episode under the skylight had featured a different girl, someone Caroline didn't know. That girl's voice was different and there was hatred in her eyes. Caroline had one faint bruise on her arm from where Devon had pummeled her. Her daughter would have to go back to therapy; there was no denying it. Devon had seen different doctors over the years but always ended up growing tired of the sessions and refusing to go back. Caroline would schedule an appointment with the doctor they had liked the best, the woman Devon saw after they moved out of the chalet. She needed to ask a professional about the sleepwalking, at least.

"Mom, can I go walking with the twins?"

"Right now?"

Devon rolled her eyes. "After school."

"Where?"

"Why do you have to know everything?"

"Be serious, Devon. I have to know where you go after school."

Her daughter looked down and broke the cookie into pieces. "It's not like there's a plan. We just walk around."

"Did you go somewhere today?"

More eyeroll. "Starbucks. We were starving."

"You went all the way up there?"

"Mom! It's not far."

"But doesn't Melissa pick the twins up after school?"

"Not every day. That would be ridiculous. We're in eighth grade now."

Caroline didn't know what to say. "I'd prefer you to come straight home. We can talk about it later."

Devon exhaled, her breath a great cloud of impatience and disgust. There was a touch of pity as well, Caroline discerned, aimed at her. "I'd like to have my own sleepover. Here."

"For your next birthday, sure."

"No, Mom. That's like a year from now. I need to do this as soon as possible."

Caroline knew what Devon was getting at. The kids at school were interested in her now because of her performance at the twins' house. The story of the table rising and the spooky trance was still flying through cyberspace. "Okay, honey. Maybe next weekend?"

"I was thinking tomorrow."

"Tomorrow?"

"Listen, it doesn't have to be a big deal. Just the twins and Madison and Reina. We'll get pizza. Or ramen. You don't have to do anything. No cake."

"But this place is such a mess." Caroline's muscles tensed in advance as she imagined waking early to clean her house.

"Nobody cares, Mom." Devon went back to her room.

Caroline didn't have the heart to stop her. The next morning, she woke before her alarm and started cleaning, first in the kitchen, still flour-dusted and filled with crumbs from the cookie session with the twins, and then she moved to the bathroom, with its walls of old tile. Next she swept the living room floor, dusted the bookshelves, and then attacked the little strip of hallway between the two bedrooms. She shut the door to her own bedroom and wished she could hide in there forever. Outside of Devon's room she paused. She did not want to disturb her daughter's precious rest, not before a sleepover.

Exhausted, she sat down on the couch. All her furniture was old and worn, from Devon's early childhood, and it looked like it. Walking into rich people's homes, always a hazard in LA, made her defensive and then depressed. She liked her space, a tiny house on a cute enough street that was walking distance from Devon's schools. That had been her big concern as a single mom: would her kid be able to walk home alone if she needed to? Caroline had tried to be there for Devon when she was in elementary school, but now that wasn't always possible.

Caroline would never have been able to get into the house without her mom's help with the down payment. It was just over a thousand square feet, built in 1947. It had big, pretty windows that were the opposite of energy efficient, but she liked them. There was even a fireplace. The previous owner had put a skylight in the kitchen to improve the light. She knew she should be grateful for what she had, but she had grown up in a roomy Craftsman house in San Diego. Her mom had been visibly disappointed the first time she visited and walked around saying things like, "You'll never get lost in a house like this."

"Mom, it's different here in LA, obviously. I can't afford anything bigger. I'm so lucky not to be stuck in an apartment."

"As long as you got what you wanted, dear."

That barb was a reference to Jack. Her mother still thought she was a fool for going through with the divorce. This was the same person who had given her only daughter a name so close to her own. Carol, Caroline. It was confusing. It made Caroline feel like she could never get away.

Caroline spent the rest of the day stocking snacks and trying to look more like Melissa. She even fixed her hair and put on expensive lipstick. Why was she so tired? Her face in the mirror was such a shocker. Everything was written on it.

Madison, a friend dating back to elementary school, was the first to arrive. Caroline was surprised at how much the girl had changed. Devon was still so small and skinny, but Madison looked like a woman already. Who were these kids? What was her daughter doing with them? The next to arrive was Reina, already too cool, unsmiling, wearing a hot pink minidress and Uggs. The twins descended as a Hollywood power duo. If she didn't know better, Caroline would have thought they were hosting.

Maybe they were.

The girls put their bags down in the middle of the living room, and immediately something was wrong. Everyone was silent after the initial blast of excited greetings. Caroline realized she was the problem, the damper, and she was about to beat a hasty retreat to her room when Sierra or Samantha announced they were going to get pizza right away. They moved to the door so fast it was all Caroline could do to grab Devon's arm.

"Wait! Let me give you some money at least."

"Mom, stop. I have money."

"Devon! You have to tell me where you're going."

The other girls were already on the sidewalk.

"I don't even know. I'll text you—I promise." Then Devon kissed her on the cheek, a sweet little lie. She was wearing a tight black top Caroline had never seen before.

Caroline walked back inside, stunned. Was this really happening? She was in charge of five feral girls who had abandoned her. She wished she knew the other parents better, but Madison's mom was the only one from the old days. They hadn't spoken in ages. There was no way she was texting Melissa to admit incompetence, and she had never even seen Reina's parents.

She put her phone down on the ottoman and waited for Devon to text with the details. Her lipstick had already worn off somehow. This was her life now.

She was pouring the glass of wine she had wanted since the night before when the text came through: "roma." What did that mean? She did a little research and figured out the girls were at a pizza place called Roma's. It was so far away, and it was still hot outside. Were they really planning to walk? "Do you need a ride?" she texted, though she knew there was one girl too many for her Prius. "no," Devon texted back. Naturally.

They didn't need anything except to get out from under adult supervision, and they weren't even in high school yet. Caroline vowed to lock them inside and limit the rest of their activities to the walls of her house. If she ever saw them again. She looked around. They were probably going to want to sleep out here, where the television was, and where they could distance themselves from her. She needed to pull out the air mattress and find more sheets. She finished her wine, washed the glass and even put it way, covering her tracks as if she were waiting for a real authority figure to arrive and bust her.

* * *

The evening began peacefully. The kids stayed in without an argument, as Caroline had hoped, and she did her best to keep out of the way, though it was impossible not to eavesdrop in the little house. Select phrases drifted into her bedroom, but before she could make sense of them, they were covered over by explosions of laughter or high-volume whispering. For a long time, Caroline lay awake, staring up at the ceiling.

Someone knocked on her door at three in the morning and Caroline sat straight up in bed. Devon. It had to be Devon. But what had happened?

It was Reina. "Mrs. Woodward, Devon's gone."

"What are you talking about?"

"She's not in her room. Or the bathroom. Is she sleeping with you?"

Caroline ran around turning on lights and searching the house. She even checked the hall closet. No sign of Devon. "All right," she told them, "don't any of you leave. I'm serious." Now that it was almost too late, her voice carried the authority she was entitled to. She grabbed her phone, slipped on her running shoes, and went outside in the sweatpants and tank top she had worn to bed.

Her mouth was bone dry.

There wasn't much traffic in their little neighborhood, but she worried about Overland. It was such a big street. Could Devon have wandered out there? Caroline remembered the different sleepwalking stories she had heard over the years: people found miles away from home, children falling out of windows. There were people who had complete conversations while they were unconscious. People who cooked meals. Should she call the police? Something caught her eye and she turned right.

Coombs Park, up the street. Of course. It would be lucky if Devon had only gone that far. It could be so much worse. Caroline flew up the sidewalk and then she saw something white in the darkness. There. She remembered Devon putting on a vintage white nightgown when all the other girls were changing for the night. She had probably wanted to look grown-up, but Caroline thought the nightgown made Devon look like a child. The other girls were wearing camisoles and yoga pants, on the borderline between casual and sexy. Caroline had kept her mouth shut while Devon drifted away to play hostess.

Devon was in the park. Thank God. Oh thank you, God. It wasn't much of a park, a simple rectangle of grass and trees, a place to walk your dog. I'll definitely have to get her on medication, Caroline thought. This is too dangerous. And then she saw someone else standing right next to Devon. Talking to her. Who hung around public parks at night? The answer was never good. Someone dangerous, but that didn't matter now. Caroline could have taken on a mountain lion. She charged forward, holding her breath. It was best not to startle her daughter. She would take her by the hand and lead her away.

It was a woman. She had long white hair and was wearing a white nightgown like Devon's. If she's wearing a nightgown, she must be another mom, Caroline reasoned, someone who lived in the neighborhood, taking her dog out in the middle of the night. Maybe. Caroline looked around to see if there was a dog nearby. She was about to say something when the woman whirled around and hissed at her. She saw the woman's face. She's a nut, or on drugs, a voice inside told her. Be careful. And then: No. There's something strange about her. She was pretty, with white hair, falling to mid-thigh. Caroline thought she recognized her.

She was reaching for Devon's hand when the woman's fist came at her from the left. Caroline had to duck so fast she almost fell over. It took her a few seconds to regain her balance, and by then the woman had led Devon away into the shadows. This was Caroline's last chance. She ran and launched herself into the woman's body, knocking her to the grass. It was like colliding with someone completely hollow, a detail from a dream. Had she crushed her?

"Mom, what are you doing?"

Devon was angry with her, furious, or perhaps she was still asleep and talking in that strange voice again. She was not her daughter.

"We have to get out of here," Caroline said, reaching for Devon, who had already turned in the direction of home. The woman on the ground wheezed, rolled over, and then got to her feet. She ran away so fast Caroline lost sight of her.

Devon bolted home without saying a word; Caroline had to jog to keep up with her. How she wished she could get rid of the other girls, who were still waiting at the door.

"We were about to call the police," Sierra or Samantha announced with the usual smug look.

Devon didn't respond. She dragged herself to her bedroom while her guests begged her to tell them what had happened. Before Caroline could explain that her daughter was sleepwalking, Devon turned around and shouted: "I. Don't. Want. To. Talk. About. It. Why the hell can't any of you understand?"

Silence. A few startled laughs. The end. Sierra or Samantha got busy and in ten minutes Melissa was there to pick up all the girls and take them to the twins' house. Caroline could not stop apologizing. And explaining. She even walked outside to say something to Melissa, who cut her off with a fake smile. "I hope she feels better. Tell her I said happy birthday."

And then the Porsche minivan disappeared.

"It's not her birthday," Caroline said to no one at all before walking back inside.

There was so much to process. The woman in the park. Caroline had seen her before, once. She could have sworn to it. She joined Devon in her bed and tucked an arm around her daughter. She wished she could surrender to the sweet darkness for a few hours of sleep, but her mind was racing.

She was afraid to call the police.

This was a real mess. The mean-girl texts were probably already flying, and the concerned mothers would join in come morning. So much drama for one little friend group. Devon needed to be on medication. No two ways about it. Caroline had a lot of phone calls to make now. She had to talk to Jack. Call both grandmothers to let them know something was up before they heard it from someone else. Get back in at that therapist.

* * *

It took a single phone call to the pediatrician's office to get a prescription for sleeping pills. No refills, only enough to get Devon through this rough patch, and Caroline also got a stern lecture from the nurse. "We don't normally recommend this for teenagers, Mrs. Woodward. She needs to cut all caffeine and sugar, and no screen time after eight." Caroline nodded and rolled her eyes, much like a teenager herself.

Unfortunately there was a six-week wait to get in to see the therapist Caroline liked. On Monday afternoon she called Jack and told him everything.

"Jesus. She's sleepwalking again? I was hoping she'd grown out of it."

"It's like when we were in the chalet."

"Meaning?"

"Jack, I need to tell you something. This is going to sound insane, so I'll just come out and say it. That woman in the park. I'm sure I've seen her before."

He paused for so long she got nervous. Even as she tried to steady her voice, she was aware of how she sounded. Unstable. Rattled. She was scaring herself.

"Do you think someone's stalking Devon?"

"No. I mean, I don't think so."

"Why didn't you call the police?"

"When? I ran outside to find her right away."

"I mean after the incident."

"What would I have said? She disappeared, Jack. There are lots of strange people around here, so many lost souls in LA. Maybe she's some kind of addict."

"You got in a scuffle with her, Caroline. The police might know who she is, or the people who work at the nearest shelter."

"I hadn't thought of that. Anyway, I wouldn't call it a scuffle." She remembered the sensation of knocking against that strange, hollow body. Was she supposed to tell this to the police?

"What did Devon say about her?"

"She said she didn't remember anything and I didn't want to push. She slept all day Sunday. She only got up in time to do some homework and wash her hair."

"I'm not happy about this situation. I really think you should have reported the incident, and I don't want Devon going out unsupervised."

"She never does, Jack. I made an exception for this sleepover. The girls went to get pizza. In daylight. They're in the eighth grade."

"Listen. Do you need me to come out there for a few days? I don't mind."

"Thank you, but no. Look, Jack, about that woman. I'm sure I've seen her once before. In the past."

"What are you talking about?"

"It was when we were living in the chalet. I was sleeping on the couch. Someone was at the window looking in at me. You remember the back door with that weird little window?"

"I remember."

"I saw someone one night. A woman with long white hair, looking in at me."

"You never told me this. Never. Why didn't you wake me up?"

"Jack, I was half-asleep. Dreaming, or almost dreaming, but I did get up and check. I checked on Devon too. I even went outside. By morning it was all gone. I would have felt silly telling you. So much was happening back then, a new crisis every day."

"Maybe you were dreaming, Caroline."

"But how is it I saw her again? Can you recognize people from your dreams?"

"I suppose it's possible. What I do know is that people can go into this hallucinatory state right before they lose consciousness. It's a real thing."

"I've never heard of it."

"Google it. You spend too much time alone, Caroline, and you never ask for help."

"I'm asking you now, Jack."

"I can come out there. I'm offering."

"That's kind. I really do appreciate it. I'll think about it."

"You know, you should call my mom."

"I will, of course. I haven't gotten around to it. The week just exploded on me and it's only Monday."

"I mean to tell her about this dream stuff. It's right up her alley."

"I guess you're right. I could share this with Elaine. She wouldn't laugh at me."

"I'm not laughing at you."

"No, but you're talking about getting on a plane. Calling the police. I know you're probably right, but I didn't want to get a lot of people involved. I didn't want to create some dumb Nextdoor scandal." She didn't tell Jack what she really thought: the woman in the park wasn't a threat to the neighborhood, only to her and Devon.

"Caroline, I think you're underestimating how hard it is to live with a teen. You're under a lot of stress."

Was he being condescending? She made an excuse and ended the call. If they stayed on the phone for too long, he would start talking about moving back to California and working as a consultant. Obviously he wasn't dating anyone right now. All his spare time would go to Devon.

And her. Through the years they had engaged in lengthy, intimate phone calls. They had definitely become better friends. The last therapist she had seen told her she wasn't emotionally divorced from Jack. She had bristled because it didn't seem fair. He was still Devon's father and sometimes she needed to talk to him. Besides, how could you dissolve a shared history? How could you ever get away from someone when you had a child together?

He was right about one thing. She needed to talk to Elaine. She put it off though, for days and days, held back by a slow trickle of dread.

She worked from home that week so that she could be there for Devon, but each time her daughter walked through the door she was lost in the world of her phone. Here we go again, Caroline thought. There was no point in trying to make conversation. She knew it was best to let Devon decompress, so she choked down her questions. The kid was worn out but didn't know it.

Devon took out her earbuds one afternoon and turned to her. "Mom, didn't I have a bear?"

"What?" Caroline couldn't help smiling.

"When I was little. Was there a teddy bear that was lost in the fire?"

"Oh, yes. You had this old bear. It belonged to your dad. Don't you remember?"

"Was he fancy?"

"It was a Steiff. Why?"

"I don't know. I've been thinking about him. I wish I could find him. Do you know what happened to him?"

"Well, you had him at the chalet and then he disappeared. You still have Henry though."

"Oh, Mom. I'll always have Henry." Devon opened the refrigerator and started the snack search.

"Have you looked on eBay? It was a Steiff. I'll bet they're pretty pricey." She watched as Devon scrolled and stared. Overwhelmed by love and fear, she wanted to buy her daughter a teddy bear, right there, on the spot. "I can get you a new one for graduation, if you like."

"If I make it to graduation."

"Devon, you'll have no problem graduating and moving on to high school. You have good grades."

Devon looked her in the eye. "I meant I don't know if I'll survive."

"What are you talking about?"

"I don't know, Mom!" The wall went up as Devon grabbed her backpack and fled to her bedroom, but Caroline couldn't let her go. She followed her daughter and stopped her from closing the door.

"How were things at school today? Are you still hanging out with those girls?"

"Those girls, Mom? *Those girls.* Who do you mean, exactly? You don't know anything about my life."

"No, because you won't tell me. Please."

Devon dropped her backpack on the floor and kicked off her shoes. "I feel like I'm going to die. Something is trying to get me."

Caroline sat down on the bed. "Do you remember anything from Saturday night? Anything at all? Do you remember the park?"

"Not really. I do remember walking outside but that's all. I was so tired."

"You weren't alone when I found you, Devon. There was a woman with you. You're sure you can't remember?"

Devon started to cry. She shook her head from side to side. "Mom, what did she look like, this woman?"

"She had long white hair. Something about her wasn't normal. I don't know how to say it. It was like she was deranged. She got away too fast." Caroline left out the detail of the white nightgown. She couldn't bear it.

"I'm sorry, Mom. It's like I wasn't there."

"You must have been dreaming, Dev. What did you see?"

"I was looking for someone. Waiting. No—I was expecting her."

"Her?"

"I think it's a her. I'm not sure of anything anymore. She's like a shadow. Mom, I don't know who she is but she's not good. It's like when you have to see a teacher after school. You're in trouble or there's some work you have to make up. Something you owe. And I know I've been with her before. Even while I was dreaming, I was sure I'd had that dream before."

If only this could all be a series of bad dreams. The person in the park was real though, wasn't she? She, Caroline, had been there, fully conscious. She had confronted a certain villain in the park. She didn't know how to interpret this for her daughter. She didn't want to do the wrong thing. She wasn't a girl at a slumber party telling scary stories. She was the mom now.

"Mom, I think I might be crazy. I'm really scared."

"Stress can make you see things that aren't there. You have those pills now. You can sleep in my bed. Take a few days off school—I don't even know why you went today."

"I'm afraid I'll die in my sleep. Or that someone will get me in my sleep."

"That's not going to happen, Devon," Caroline said as she rose to embrace her daughter. They were almost the same height now. How could she protect her child?

"I don't want to see her, Mom. I'm afraid if I look at her face, I'll die."

"Can you tell me anything about her? What she looks like?"

"No, not really, but I know she has long white hair, like you said."

"Let's go," Caroline said, as she grabbed Devon's hand.

* * *

Caroline had driven past the place on Lincoln Boulevard countless times over the years. It could not have been tackier but there was parking, and what was more, many of her friends had recommended Miss Amber, who was said to provide insight and a host of eerie details about the other side. Under ordinary circumstances this excursion would have been entertaining, but now it was serious. Dire.

"Why don't you let me talk to her alone first?" Caroline told Devon as they waited in the little shop.

"I saw an ice cream store down the block."

"Fine, but come right back."

Pink-haired Miss Amber, who looked surprisingly young to Caroline, sat her down at a little table and asked her if she had ever had any experience with the paranormal.

Caroline tried not to laugh. "I've never believed in this stuff. I mean, no offense."

"No offense taken."

"Once, in the past," Caroline began, but then she couldn't go on. It was embarrassing. She took a deep breath. "Once I thought I saw something. Someone."

Miss Amber waited.

"It was a long time ago, when my daughter, Devon, was little. I'm not comfortable saying this in front of her. I don't know why. I definitely saw someone. Devon was seeing things too, but she was so small, barely four. She was at the age of seeing things, if you know what I mean. The age of make-believe."

"I do."

"Well, we had been through so much trauma. I mean hardcore. There was a fire. Our whole duplex burned down but nobody died. It was a blessing and then horrible at the same time. I still sometimes remember the things we lost, and that was almost ten years ago." She bowed her head for a second, then looked up. "I was pregnant but I didn't want to be. Devon was sleepwalking. So many things were going on. I wish I had kept a journal because, even as I tell you this, I feel like it couldn't possibly be true. Like I'm making it all up."

"Why would you do that?"

Caroline laughed. "Indeed. Why would I? Anyway, what I remember was this face. This woman. Looking in at me through the window. And that's why I'm here."

"Were you at home when you saw the face?"

"Not at my current home, no. It was out where we were living at the time. We called it the chalet. Jack, my ex, had found this great place in Topanga. I was supposed to be working from home but nothing much was happening. I was looking for a school for Devon, and I found one, a good one. Something was off though. Our marriage was already falling apart and Devon knew it. You would think such a small child couldn't possibly understand what was going on, but I guess she did. Devon internalized everything."

Miss Amber stared at her and waited. She reminded Caroline of any other therapist: open, nonjudgmental.

"We're in so much trouble," Caroline said, the tears falling in big drops. "We're in so much trouble and nobody is helping us. I'm scared. I'm so scared."

"How can I help you?"

"Someone's coming after my daughter."

"Who?"

"I think it's a woman."

"Do you know her? In your heart? Who is she? Close your eyes and speak. Don't edit. Don't censor yourself."

Caroline closed her eyes and listened for Devon to return. There was so much she couldn't say to her or in front of her.

"This is unfinished business from the chalet. I left Devon unprotected and someone got to her. I didn't leave her alone, not really, but I was checked out. She had to play by herself a lot. She walked in her sleep. She must have crossed over somehow. I thought we were safe, but she must have opened some kind of door."

"Children of certain ages are especially vulnerable. Adolescence can be dangerous. All transitional phases are. It's during these in-between stages of life that the door can be opened, as you said."

"Is that what I said?" Caroline opened her eyes.

"Yes. And you also said she was at the age of seeing things. Can I ask what happened to the pregnancy?"

"I had a miscarriage."

"So there was a lot of blood."

"Yes. Does that mean something?"

"Everything means something."

"Please don't be so cryptic. Could Devon be tied up with an evil force? Some entity?"

A wise, sad smile covered Miss Amber's face. "This happens to people all the time, whether or not they cross over to the other side. I'm sure you could list the destructive people in your life. They are toxic and you need to protect yourself from them. But there is another class of dangerous beings. They exist all over the earth. Some are the dead. Some are malicious spirits."

"But why us? Why Devon? I've never willfully hurt anyone in my life, not like that."

"It's not always about retribution. Maybe you got this from your ancestors. Someone somewhere picked it up, like a virus. Or maybe you married into it."

"I'm divorced!"

"If only it could be so easy. You were married once and now you have a child. She has to learn to protect herself. Immediately. How old is she?"

"Thirteen."

"Has she had her period?"

"I don't think so. She would have told me. I'm sure she's really close. Her body is changing."

"You'll want to be careful when she has her first period." Miss Amber stood up and took something off the black bookshelf that towered behind her. "Give me your hand," she told Caroline.

She placed a brown, crystalline marble on Caroline's palm. "She'll want to keep this on her person at all times."

"What is it?"

"Smoky quartz. It will protect her from evil."

"How much is all this?"

"The basic consultation is fifty. There is no additional charge for people who are in real trouble."

"Am I in real trouble?"

Miss Amber didn't answer.

Caroline heard the bell jingle as Devon opened the door to the little shop.

"Don't you want to talk to her?" Caroline whispered to Miss Amber.

"I don't need to. I saw it when she first came in. She has the look. It's on her face, in her eyes. Now I'm going to ask you to respect my boundaries. I can't do anything else for you. Please don't come back here."

This was the first time in Caroline's life that someone had told her not to return to a business. LA people always wanted you to come back and spend more money. When Miss Amber gestured toward the door, Caroline tried to not cry.

She stood up, overwhelmed by nausea. She put a fifty on the table while Devon licked her ice cream cone like a carefree kid.

"You know everything you need to know. You carry all the answers in your body. The important thing is to not be afraid," Miss Amber said, speaking to both of them. She gave a solemn nod to Devon.

"Thank you," Caroline said.

It was hard to leave the shop. "I'm going to need to sit for a second," she told Devon when they got back in the car. "And here's this." She gave Devon the marble. "Put this in your pocket. It's smoky quartz."

"Cool, but I thought I was getting my fortune told."

"Not today. Don't lose that marble."

"This is dumb, Mom. What did she tell you?"

"You heard her. The usual mumbo-jumbo."

"I mean, what did she say when I was gone?"

"She said we were in real trouble. She said to be careful when you got your period."

"What did you tell her about me?"

Caroline took a deep breath and started the engine. Someone was waiting for her parking space. "I talked about that summer when we were living in the chalet. When you were little."

"Why?"

"All our troubles started back then."

"It's weird, but I can barely remember the chalet. It's like most of my memories start in preschool."

"But you asked about the bear. You remember him. Don't you remember the night of the fire?"

"I don't know if I remember the fire or if I learned about it from you. I can see myself in the scene. It's like watching a movie."

"How do you feel right now?" Caroline asked. For once she was grateful for the traffic. She didn't particularly want to go home, now that Miss Amber had destroyed the notion of safety.

Instead of rolling her eyes, Devon stared straight ahead. "Sometimes I can forget about it for a while. Sometimes I can be normal, like everyone else."

"What is it you're able to forget?"

"That I might die soon."

Everything went blurry as Caroline tried to blink back her tears. "Don't say that. Ever. Are you telling me you're suicidal?"

"Are you listening? That's not what I said. None of this is my fault. I'm afraid when it gets dark. Afraid I won't wake up."

"How long has this been going on? Since the twins' party?"

"No, Mom. Stop blaming the twins. I don't know. I'm not sure. It crept up on me slowly." Devon put her earbuds in.

Finally they were on their street, then in the driveway, then at their door. Caroline moved like a robot. "God, I can't wait for Friday."

"I know, and I have so much homework."

"You don't have to go to school tomorrow."

"Mom, don't you understand? It's better at school. Safer. Besides, missing school is the worst. You have to make up so much work."

"Well, we can do our work together at the kitchen table. I have a press kit to put together. And you can sleep in my bed tonight."

Caroline threw together a dinner of broccoli and Costco cod. It was easy to cook for two, like living with a roommate. If they could only get past this horrible phase and go back to having fun. The first thing she did when she opened her computer was buy two sets of smoky quartz necklaces with matching earrings. It couldn't hurt, and she was sure Devon would lose that marble.

She still needed to call Elaine. It was already so late in New York. Maybe she could do it on her break tomorrow.

Devon got up to go to bed at 11:30, but only after Caroline insisted. "You need your sleep now more than ever. Go, please. Take one of those pills in the bottle by the sink. Just one. And floss. You can sleep in my bed. I'll be there soon."

An hour later Devon reappeared in the hallway. "Devon, baby, you scared me. What's wrong?"

"Mom, I know you've been spending a lot of money on me lately."

"Devon, we can talk in the morning. Why are you still awake? Did you take your pill like I told you?"

"Yes, I took it. Listen. I can pay you back, or maybe it can count for all my gifts this year, but I really want my bear."

Caroline had to think for a second. "The Steiff?"

"It doesn't have to be big. And it doesn't have to be an antique. I found this one online."

"Sure. Send me the link. I'll look at it."

Devon blew her a kiss before she went back to bed. Caroline's heart ached.

* * *

"Elaine, I've got a problem."

"I know, honey. Jack told me about Devon's episode. You've been to the doctor, right?"

Caroline told her ex-mother-in-law everything. The difficulties of Devon's adolescence came pouring out, everything from the homework load to all the social stuff. "Something happened at that slumber party at the twins' house. Nothing has been the same since."

Elaine was silent for a second. "The doctors didn't find anything?"

"No. Listen, the sleepwalking episodes are really scary. Terrifying. She's not herself."

"Well, sleepwalking can be that way. Are the pills helping?"

"They knock her out. She did get up last night to talk to me, once, and I don't think she was sleepwalking. She was completely lucid. Coherent, and not angry, thank God."

"I'm sure everything will straighten itself out. Adolescence is the worst age, the hardest thing I ever did. I wouldn't wish it on my worst enemy."

Caroline wasn't sure if Elaine was talking about Jack or Josh. "It's different now, Elaine, with social media. You always say things were wild when you were a kid, but it's all changed now. Even Woodstock was innocent."

Elaine laughed. "Honey, I wasn't actually at Woodstock. I was still a kid, living in the Bay Area. I believe you though. This whole world took a dark turn and the kids are suffering because of it."

"Did Jack tell you about the woman in the park?"

When Elaine didn't answer, Caroline explained that she had seen her daughter with a strange woman one night in the park, but the story was losing force with each retelling. She confessed that she had not called the police. She was certain Elaine would judge her. Any other parent would. For a long time Elaine said nothing.

"Did she have an accent?"

"The woman? We never spoke."

"And how was she dressed? Tell me again."

"A long white gown. A nightgown, I guess. Really long white hair."

"How old would you say she was?"

"I have no idea. About my age? I couldn't see her well enough. It was dark. I haven't even told you the really crazy part. Are you ready? This is embarrassing, but Jack said you would understand."

"Go ahead, Caroline."

"I think I've seen her before. After the fire, when we were living in the chalet—you remember that place. This was right before the divorce when so many things were happening. I saw her one night."

"You saw who?"

"That same woman, from the park. Looking in at me. I was sleeping on the couch, but I wasn't dreaming, I swear to it. I even got up and looked around but I couldn't find her. Jack thinks I dreamed the whole thing. I'm sure I sound insane."

"No. No you don't. I believe you."

There. It was done. Caroline had crossed over to the groovy hippie camp. She had told a fantastical horror story to her ex-mother-in-law, a child of the sixties. She didn't feel any better though. If anything, she felt worse. She expected Elaine to tell her to burn sage or drink a certain kind of tea, but she didn't say anything. "Are you still there, Elaine?"

"Yes. Listen, I was thinking. Should I come out there?"

"Jack said the same thing, but I don't see how it will help to cram our little house with more people. That always ups the stress."

"I can stay with friends."

"Please don't feel like you have to come all the way out here. Maybe for the holidays?"

"December's a long way off. What about Halloween? There's still enough time left for me to get a cheap ticket. I'll start looking."

"Sure. I don't even know if Devon will want to trick-or-treat this year. Honestly, I don't know where she stands with her friend group. They might want to go out to Universal, but then some lucky parent has to drive them."

"Devon can go off and do whatever she wants, and we can stay home and watch monster movies. Or tell fortunes. Oh, I know, we should go to that cemetery in Hollywood."

By the time she got off the phone, Caroline's mood had improved. She always felt better after being in Elaine's presence, and now she had an extra rush of energy. She had woken up early to call New York, and coffee would have to help her get through the day. She knew she would crash by three, maybe even fall asleep. Fortunately she had no meetings. If only it were acceptable to put her head down at her desk.

It was easy to be a supermom when one woke up so early. Everything went off without a hitch: breakfast, clothes, teeth, backpack, and briefcase. There was even time to tidy the kitchen. Devon wanted to be dropped off at a donut shop before school to meet Reina and the twins. In the car Devon remembered her phone was still in Caroline's bed. Luckily they hadn't pulled out of the driveway.

"Let me go get it, okay?" Caroline said. "I like to be the one to lock the door when we leave, otherwise I'll worry all day."

Caroline rushed inside and went straight to the bedroom. When she lifted the blankets, she saw the blood. It was like an announcement or an omen. She ripped the sheets and the mattress cover off the bed, mechanically, as if the stain was her only concern.

In the car she said nothing at first and waited until they were stopped at a light. "Why didn't you tell me?" Devon didn't respond. "Come on, Dev. Your period?"

"Mom, I've got this. It's no big deal. All my friends have had it."

"Do you have everything you need?"

"You've got to stop, Mom. You're really embarrassing me."

"Well, congratulations." And right away, because she couldn't help herself, she added, "Did you remember your talisman?"

Without a word Devon held up the little ball of smoky quartz, which caught the rising sun.

* * *

Caroline was useless at work. She was useless everywhere. Why hadn't Devon told her about her period? How could she keep her daughter safe if there were constant secrets between them?

She started getting cramps around ten. Typical, she thought, but then she smiled. At least they were unified in this one respect. Maybe they could watch *Carrie* together, or *The Shining*. They could embrace the river of blood, have fun with it, as long as the splashing blood wasn't flowing from the female body.

But it was impossible to forget Miss Amber's warning.

Later in the day, Devon texted her one word: "dying."

"Me too," Caroline replied. "Go to the nurse."

All this talk of death. All teenage girls were dramatic, weren't they? It was hard to tell from texts alone. Caroline remembered her own youth, a nonstop rollercoaster, tears then joy then tears again. She wanted Devon to have a normal experience.

She went on the internet yet again to find a solution to their problem, but didn't know what to search. Something to do with evil spirits and adolescence. Possession? Poltergeist? Sleepwalking?

Jack called her at noon. "Are you at lunch?"

"I've been out to lunch all day. I'm useless, Jack. What's up?"

"Is Devon okay?"

"Yes. I don't know. I'm trying to handle it."

"My mother called me."

"Oh, she's coming out here for Halloween. Are you mad? It's less loaded if she comes. We can have a girls' night. Anyway, you're the one who told me to call her."

"I'm not mad but she was really worked up. She wanted to talk about the past. About that summer when Josh almost drowned. Do you remember?"

"How could I forget? It was the first thing you ever told me about your childhood." Caroline had heard the story of Josh falling into the marsh shortly after Jack introduced her to his brother. It was tangled up with memories of an evil stepmother and a horrible summer vacation.

"She asked me some questions about that night. I wish everyone had taken it more seriously back when it happened."

"I'm sorry," Caroline said. "Josh survived and nothing else matters. He's alive. Families always hang onto these scary stories. They like to retell them."

"Maybe I want to forget."

"I don't blame you."

"My mom's obsessed with that kid."

"What kid?"

"The boy. Remember, I told you? He was trying to drive a wedge between my brother and me, and we got in a fight. In the dark. Josh got shoved into the water. That's what happened."

"Don't get upset. It was such a long time ago. We need to focus on Devon now."

"I am, Caroline. I always am."

She was relieved to get off the phone. It was exhausting to revisit the same topics again and again. Now she remembered why she and Jack were divorced. He was too slow to catch up to her, even where Devon was concerned. Before she left work, she called the pediatrician's office one more time. They had never told her the results of the bloodwork. Maybe they'd found something after all. Maybe a crucial puzzle piece had fallen into place.

The receptionist told her they would have called if there had been anything new to report. Caroline hung up without saying thank you.

* * *

She left work early and went to meet Devon at school. It wasn't much of a walk, but her daughter's backpack was always too heavy. "I'm here," she texted. "On the corner."

No answer.

"I can carry your backpack. Since you have cramps." She looked through the emojis, trying to find something funny.

Still no answer. Was Devon already embarrassed to be seen with her? Caroline had such fond memories of walking home together when Devon was little.

A group of girls appeared on the other side of the street. Caroline saw the twins and Reina, all of whom looked taller and more mature since the last time she had seen them. Had it been that long? What was happening? Like girls in a music video, the twins shrugged off their plaid shirts to reveal the sexy black bustiers they wore underneath.

"Does your mom know how you dress for school?" Caroline said under her breath. She was tempted to shout.

The little pack of girls called out to someone and went running. Caroline turned to see what was going on.

Devon ran up to join the group. She didn't look anything like herself. She hadn't changed her clothes, but the difference was in her posture. Her attitude. What was she now, a mean girl? She was menstruating and it was having the opposite of the Carrie effect. Was this what Miss Amber had meant? *You'll want to be careful when she has her first period.* Devon was beautiful. Her hair was so long. Her skin was pale and clear. But if Caroline had seen her on the street, a random young girl walking by, she wouldn't have liked her. She wouldn't have trusted her.

Her phone chirped at her. A text. From Devon.

"don't ruin this for me mom"

Caroline fought the urge to scream. She didn't have the strength for this. What if she went running after Devon, dragged her back here, and grounded her? Or what if she took her out for a meal and gave her a tutorial? "A little politeness would go a long way, Devon. You have to be smarter about how you deceive me. You could have acknowledged me and told me your plans." Or, even more impossibly, "You could have chosen different friends."

A few seconds passed and there was another text. "I have to do this by myself. PLEASE.

Verushka: 2013

Verushka likes California. She is always happy to return to it. Of all the places she has lived over the decades, this state is one of her favorites. It is easy to remain anonymous because everyone, while aggressive about their happiness, is safely distant. She finds Californians self-assured yet strangely childlike. They are so fatally American they make her laugh out loud. They eat danger without knowing it. They breathe it in and call themselves lucky.

One family has what she needs. She has searched the globe but never found the right girl. A maiden. So much depends on a maiden.

She drinks the last of her golden matcha and grimaces. It is definitely the worst of the current café drinks, too sweet. Her taste buds have changed over the years and bitterness is all she can tolerate. She shakes the cup and studies the dregs to see where Davor is, and the news is not surprising. He is on the other side of the world, on the banks of a river, a stone's throw from his beloved water. He never stays with her for long.

She is a monster, after other people's children, but she is still a mother.

And she has work to do.

* * *

Verushka was always different. Her mother, Elena, hoped her daughter would be just like her, a born midwife, but she was forced to accept that Verushka was another kind of being entirely. Gifted. Cursed. Destined to lead a life Elena could only imagine.

Before Verushka could walk, when she could stand and speak no more than a few words, she saw her first ghost, a mother who died before she could see the infant Elena held in her hands. The mother dwelled for a moment, long enough to reach for her baby, and then she floated up through the roof of the hut. There were others, souls who clung to the river or the marsh, men who stood near the trees, old women who appeared at holiday tables. A single bride. An endless line of women who had died giving life. None of them spoke. All of them were distant. Verushka could see the dead, which Elena explained was unusual, a gift. She warned her daughter to keep it a secret. Even more remarkable was that Verushka could see sprites, but this she did not confess to her mother. Unlike the dead, the sprites spoke to her.

They appeared in the forest from time to time, like rare birds or stags, never staying for long. Verushka was five the first time a sprite spoke to her. She came upon what she thought was a wooden statue of a little girl, but then it moved, and all at once Verushka understood how ancient the world was. She felt the size of the forest, the depth of the roots, the distance the trees would spread if unchecked by men.

"Give me what you have in your pouch." The sprite spoke in the voice of an old woman.

Verushka was frightened. She took the bread her mother had given her and set it on the ground before the wood sprite, who then froze and became as motionless as a statue. Was she only wood after all? Did she not have fingers? Could she not bend at the waist? Verushka panicked and put the bread on the twigs that had just a second before resembled a hand.

Nothing. The statue, the sprite, began to look more and more like a tree.

"Come back," Verushka whispered. "Come back."

She knew it was wrong to take food or drink from a sprite. Everyone knew that eating their food would trap you in their realm, but was it wrong to feed a sprite? Was she being disobedient or selfish? Curiosity prompted her to put the bread in the hole that had been the sprite's mouth, curiosity and the desire to see the sprite again. She wanted to hear the sprite's voice. Then she would know the sprite was real, and not her imagination. It felt more like greed than curiosity, and when Verushka thought back over her life, she would understand that feeding the sprite was her first sin.

The bread brought the sprite back instantly. Her wooden face became flesh, her golden curls tossed in the breeze. She ate like she was famished. "Thank you, Verushka," she said. Then she laughed with cruel satisfaction before turning and speeding away, as if she had never been there.

She knows my name, Verushka said. Are there others? Do they all know my name? She turned and looked at the forest around her, examining everything, from the dirt to the treetops. This was her home, but she began to wonder if she knew it at all.

The forest wasn't dangerous, she believed, though you had to be careful not to get lost. There was a certain area she was allowed to explore by herself, usually to search for berries or mushrooms. It was work, not adventure. Her mother was always warning her to stay alert and not to daydream, to remember that life was never far from death, to understand that blessing and bounty could turn to blight and famine in the course of a year. She was raised to be generous and to respect her elders. She was taught a reverence for nature, a love of the land.

She was drawn to one special tree, which had what looked like the face of a man protruding from its trunk. All the villagers told stories about it. Everyone, young and old, whispered their wishes in front of the wooden face on full moon nights. The elders claimed, however, that one should never touch it, and children were warned not to look at it, never to speak to it. Verushka did not comply. She could not help reaching up to place her hands on the face. It would grow warm in response and the heat would spread to her whole body. Verushka kept her love for the tree a secret from her mother, just as she never spoke of the sprites she saw, especially not the one she had fed. She doubted her mother knew the hidden world of the forest. Elena, who delivered children and healed the sick, who believed in human bodies she could lay her hands on, would view Verushka's adventures as dangerous disobedience.

The seasons passed and Verushka grew taller. If she stood on her tiptoes, her face, young and pretty, almost reached the face in the tree. Her lips could almost touch those mysterious wooden lips. Her visits became more and more frequent, often late in the day when she was supposed to be gathering firewood. A terrible burning had started inside of her as her body changed. She had not yet begun to bleed but she was gaining the curves of a woman. She had no words for what she felt for the man in the tree.

Why don't you kiss me then?

Had he said it, or had she only imagined it? Did it matter? She could not resist.

Kissing the tree flooded her mouth with the sweetness of apples and honey. It was like tasting her homeland. At first she thought such pure sweetness could not be dangerous, but then, all at once, the wood turned to flesh. She could not breathe. A man emerged from the tree, picked her up, and carried her off, away from her home.

She feared she would never see her mother again.

It was not love; that much she knew. The longer she stayed in the realm of the sprites—for that was where he had carried her—the more she wanted to leave. She felt no love for the man or any of the sprites. The man, however, constantly pledged his love for her and spent hours trying to win her over. It was impossible to evade him.

One day she found a banquet spread before her across a wooden table which had grown from the forest floor, its base a sturdy trunk, its roots twisting up into a dozen chairs. The plates were piled with mushrooms, berries, and roots, then sprinkled with soil, accompanied by goblets of spring water. While the dirt repulsed her, she ached with hunger. She knew she could not eat anything or she would be lost. She could imagine how horrified the faces of the other villagers would be if they could see her at this banquet.

A dozen sprites appeared, one by one, all of them smiling. Verushka recognized the little female she had fed when she was a child, and a guilty shame washed over her. The sprites, grinning and golden-haired, took their places at the table. There were two ornate chairs, decorated with leaves and acorns, at the head of the table. She knew one of them was for her.

The man stepped out of a large tree. He was always surprising her, even here in his realm. She had lost track of time and no longer knew how long she had been gone. Sometimes, when she tried to escape, she would find herself wandering in a circle, her long hair snagging in the tree branches, always returning to this patch of enchanted forest. Was this what happened to all the missing village girls, this relentless stepping on a cursed path, instead of the rumored drownings or abductions? Her mother would never know her fate. She had to get away somehow. She had to go home. She was so very hungry.

He gestured to her to take her place at the table. *He.* She never knew his name. She thought of him as the man in the tree, or perhaps the king of the forest, yet she did not want to give him any authority, any power, by addressing him as majesty. How could she get out of this? When he had first carried her off, she had expected to die. He would strip her of her clothes and then a kind of murder would begin, the end of her maiden self, her human self.

But he never touched her. The seduction was to be drawn out, maddening.

As she sat at the table and gazed at the little assembly of wood sprites, she tried to think of all the ways one can kill a tree. Chop it down. Poison the roots. Deprive it of water. Burn it. Whenever the man assumed a more human form, his skin still covered in tiny wood splinters, his beard a stubble of twigs, Verushka wondered if transformation rendered him less powerful. Was he made vulnerable by the love he declared to her? Because her mother was a midwife, Verushka knew it was usually the other way around: women were the ones devastated by love, undone by it, more so than men. Their bodies forever carried the marks of the love stories that had swept them away. A man might go mad with love, or even hang himself because of a lost love, but it was the woman who could never escape the love story. There was no way out, especially if she turned into a mother. Love was written on her. Love lived alongside her, in the body of a child.

A mother. Verushka's heart grew heavy when she understood the man in the tree might require this of her. She looked again at the various wood sprites: tiny, misshapen, terrifying. Some of them were white like birch trees, and others had the golden glow of oak or maple. The man in the tree looked nothing like them. Who were his parents? Where did he come from? All she knew was that he needed her.

When the meal was over and all the sprites were sated, Verushka was so hungry she had to lie down. The man arose out of the ground beside her, as if he had been there all along, covered in leaves and dirt. He thanked her for joining him.

It was painful to speak. Her mouth and throat were parched. "If I give you a child, will you let me go?"

He did not answer her.

"This is why you brought me here, isn't it?"

He was silent as a stone.

The solution came to her in a flash. She would deplete him so that he could not chase her, and then she would run in the direction of her village. If she could still find it. She pulled up her skirts and straddled him. She was a virgin and knew nothing. The pain was so intense and there was so much blood that she thought she would surely die. Perhaps this whole scene, this entire interlude in the forest, was meant to be her death.

Perhaps she had been dead all along.

She couldn't find him when it was over, after he had ceased to give her his seed. Nothing remained but a pile of branches with a few dead leaves clinging to them. She rose and stumbled past the space where the banquet had been only to find the beautiful table had disappeared. The forest was silent, cold, abandoned. The very idea of wood sprites felt like a distant fairy tale. She was no longer lost and quickly found the path she had always taken to reach her home. She paused only once, to wash the blood from her legs in the cold river, before entering her mother's hut.

Her mother turned white and fell to her knees, and Verushka had to rush to her side to help her up. Elena had lost so much weight that Verushka could feel her ribs poking through her dress.

"Mama, what's wrong? Are you ill? Speak to me."

"I thought you were forever lost to me."

"I was lost in the forest for a few days. You must forgive me. It can happen to anyone."

"A few days, my daughter? A few days? Verushka, you have been missing for three months. I thought I would never see your face again."

Elena, who knew the ways of the female body, immediately suspected her daughter was pregnant. She could smell the difference in Verushka's scent, just as she could see the subtle change in the lines of her daughter's face. She never asked about the father, not once. Elena and Verushka had always stood apart from the other villagers, who came to them only when it was time to give birth or when they brushed up against death. Now Elena and Verushka stood apart from each other. Elena knew her daughter had crossed over, lived a different life, and then somehow returned.

* * *

This is the first time she has ever gone after someone repeatedly. Unwise, perhaps, but Devon is special. Verushka can get close, so painfully close, but each time the girl slips away. One never knows with children. They seem so vulnerable, but they can evade a monster at the last minute. There is a reason why escape is such a big part of the fairy tales.

And Devon had help. Verushka curses herself. She should have known better than to take on a bear. They are even more difficult than wolves.

Devon never leaves Verushka's mind. Verushka watches her constantly. She knows what she is doing. Children exist in a freefall between this world and the other side, but they don't know it. She herself was such a child once, in her little village. She remembers what it was like to walk along on beloved ground without suspecting that everything could be stolen from you. She remembers feeling doomed.

The maiden Devon is even more promising than the child Devon, infinitely more useful. She is exactly who Verushka has been searching for, hoping for, all these years.

This new world, especially California, has always been surprisingly helpful. Parents aren't able to be attentive, and there are so many ways into a child's mind. It is almost as if other evil forces are at work to help Verushka achieve her goal. Devon doesn't know how close Verushka is. They have not met face-to-face since Devon was little.

This girl is just within reach. Verushka can taste her. She smells like her grandmother. Her *grandmother!* That is how long Verushka has pursued this family, across three human generations. Verushka senses this is her last chance. Though she hates to admit it, she is getting tired.

The Woodwards are giving her so much trouble.

* * *

The battle was on. Rushing outside to be sick, only to expel bits of bark and leaves. The hunger, sporadic and insistent. Her clothing, tight, unable to drape as it once had. Her lower back, screaming. Her mother, an expert.

Her story, a secret.

Verushka could not endure life in the little hut. "Do you want me to leave you? To go and live in the forest?"

"Winter is coming. You will freeze."

"Soon I won't be able to live among our people."

"We could go to another village. We'll say your husband was killed, or that he never came back from the army."

"Mama, I will never be able to escape my husband."

Elena's face turned white as birch.

"I should leave here. I don't want to put you in danger."

"No, child. Please, we must stay together. We must." She placed her hands on Verushka's belly.

"You don't understand," Verushka said, covering Elena's hands with her own. "I am changing."

"I know you are changing. I can always tell."

"This is different. I am different now. Motherhood is only part of it. Please don't blame me. I didn't know. I didn't know about the forest."

"What do you mean?"

"I should not speak of this. There are certain trees—"

Elena covered Verushka's mouth with her hand.

Verushka wrenched herself free. "Let me go. Now. I don't want to destroy you."

"Whatever you've done can be forgiven! I forgive you."

"It's not what I've done, Mama. It's what was done to me. It's too late."

Elena saw that her daughter was serious. She rushed to bundle together linens, bread, a small portion of sausage, dried herbs, whatever she could find. She found her warmest wool shawl and wrapped it around her daughter's shoulders. "You're sure you must leave? This is madness, Verushka."

"I don't want to put you in danger. You should leave as well. You should leave soon."

"What have you heard? Is someone coming? Soldiers?"

"Mama, nothing burns faster than a village. It is all wood." Then she kissed her mother for the last time.

Before the birth, Verushka walked many miles, farther than she had ever gone, each step triggering the pain in her center, where a thousand tiny branches scratched and poked. When her feet were bleeding and she could not walk anymore, she would sit on a stump and close her eyes. She ate whatever she could find, but as the days grew colder, the trees offered nothing more than bare branches.

She knew she would return home for the birth and she feared her home would look nothing like the village she had left. She imagined a tiny wood sprite rushing out of her and running away, after which she expected to die. She would bleed to death—she, Verushka, who had never bled as a woman, not once. Perhaps this was some debt she owed, a payment to the forest. It made sense. People took so much from the trees. Everybody owed something to the forest. And she, the midwife's daughter, had communed with a tree.

When she arrived home, the village was as she had feared: Empty. Abandoned. Verushka had grown up with tales of villages being destroyed, of men, in uniform or not, riding in and putting fire to everything out of sheer hatred, often under orders. Her time with the wood sprites had made her more sensitive to the possibility of flames. She could smell fire from miles away. Her village had burned, and the smell of smoke still clung to her childhood hut, spared from the flames because it was set apart from the other dwellings. Smoke was in all the linens, the bedding, her clothes. She slept now, breathing in charred memories, in the windowless room where her mother had delivered so many babies. She was dry all over. When she put a hand to her face, it felt like parchment. Her hair was straw, her nails cracked. The thirst was painful. She lived for a while in her childhood hut, but she went to the marsh when the pain started.

Verushka knew about the water sprites. She had seen them once before, flickering yet undeniable, their eyes glowing in the darkness. All of them looked vaguely female. Maybe they could help her with the birth as her mother would have? She shook her head, knowing there was nothing good she could expect from a sprite. Still, the water was so inviting. She stumbled into the marsh as the sound of women's voices, high-pitched and not quite human, rose around her. She would have the baby here, straight into the water. She turned around, hiked up her skirts, and squatted into the reeds, her breasts pressing into the soil. All she cared about was expelling the creature before the pain got worse. She did not know if she would survive.

The birth was a murder. The blood gushed from her at last, in an explosion of red that tinted the water. The singing turned to screeching.

She opened her mouth to scream but she had no strength, no breath. Her insides were scraped clean as the creature, the child, came out of her and slid into the water. Verushka heard a soft splash as the sprites swam toward him.

A great wind descended and the trees swayed from side to side, nearly breaking in half. One large branch hit her on the head.

She had to decide.

She whirled around and snatched the baby, for it *was* a baby, from the water. The sprites fell silent and drew back, their eyes burning. Verushka climbed up the marsh bank and pressed her baby to her flesh.

The placenta came out as a tangle of branches and roots and mud. Verushka stamped it into the soil, where she was sure it belonged, though she did not know what would grow from it. Then she turned her attention to the naked child in her arms. It was a boy, human in appearance, though his skin was covered in mud and blood. She stepped into the water again to wash the blood off the baby and herself, and when she did, her son's skin began to match hers. He grew more and more pale.

All the while the sprites sang in victory.

Verushka breathed out. Was her son a child of the water or a child of the trees? Where would they live and what would become of them? She wrapped him up in the linens Elena had given her, in the same way Elena had wrapped so many children before. She raised her face to the blue sky.

"He is my child," she said.

The forest fell silent around her. The water was still, like a mirror. The trees stopped moving. Where had the man gone? Where was the tree where she had first met him? She worried he would appear and try to separate her from her son. She would have to leave and go to the city, like so many before her. When the village crumbled, when humans fell out of harmony with their surroundings, there was nowhere else but the city. Verushka knew a long struggle was before her. Every day would be a fight.

As she went to say goodbye to the hut, she knew she had changed in more than one way. She had become a mother, yes, but there was another important difference: when she pricked her finger on the gate on the way out, she did not bleed or feel pain. She stood and marveled at her changed flesh, her changed life. She named her child Davor, after the old god of war, because she knew he would always be engaged in battle.

Saying goodbye to the forest proved impossible. Every time she thought she could exit, a certain tree appeared before her. Here he was, at last. Her tree. She had strayed from the main path and now she was truly lost. In desperation she looked at the familiar face and said, "I am leaving now, with my child. You stole my body, but you cannot have my life."

He is my child. He belongs to the forest.

"I will die first."

You kissed me. You loved me.

"I was a child."

You fed us with your own hand. When you feed one of us, you feed all of us.

"I was a little girl then. I refuse." Verushka pulled the only threat she had left out of her heart. "Do you want me to give him to the water sprites? I'm sure they will take him."

The wind howled and the branches of every tree came alive like angry hands, pointing and reaching. Verushka held the baby tightly to her body and kept her feet planted on the earth.

You cannot take my son. You can try to leave, but you will never be free of the forest. A million footsteps will not provide enough distance. You will have to replace what you have stolen. There is no escape.

Verushka inhaled the scent of the place she had once loved. Her breasts ached with milk. She couldn't bear to join the man in the tree, and she couldn't surrender her baby to the water. She began the long process of inhabiting her fate. She tried to ignore the pregnant ghost girl she saw as she made her way down the road. Everything will be new, she promised herself. I am stepping into a new life and I am not alone.

In the filth of the city, Verushka and Davor often breathed in smoke. There were house fires, industrial pollution, tobacco. Chimneys. "Mama, the smoke is killing me." Those were his first words, a whole phrase. Verushka was not surprised. Davor was half wood sprite, born in the company of water sprites. He feared fire and craved water. There had to be a place where the two of them could thrive, a place between a forest and a river perhaps. Verushka had other reasons for living in the city. Cities were full of people, and some of those people were desperate. Starving. They could be manipulated. She wasn't the only one who had survived a nightmare before leaving a village. She wasn't the only one whose story was too terrible to speak.

She would have to learn to be more enterprising.

Survival was easy, at first. Verushka became a dressmaker, and then the wife of a rich man who believed she had lost her first husband to cholera. They lived in a grand house above a river. The days were good for their little family; the outside world was filled with both wonder and terror. Verushka did not age, which made her the envy of all who knew her, but she could never conceive again. Neither could she respond to her husband, Vadim, who lay on top of her and groaned while she stared at the ceiling. They did have one child, Davor, who loved to hunt and fish. He was a good son, but this was not enough to tie Vadim to them. He began to spend more and more time away from home, and Verushka knew he was seeking comfort with other women.

The years passed. She thought she was safe.

Verushka feared the forest would steal Davor from her, but it was the water that took his life, during a fishing expedition with his stepfather. She heard Vadim crying even before the carriage wheels rolled up to the gates of the house. Vadim tore his hair and refused to look her in the eye. Verushka told the servants to bring the boy inside but said nothing further. Then she waited for the sun to go down.

Returning to her home village took all night, even with a team of horses. She convinced Vadim that Davor had to be buried in the village of his birth.

"Then why not bring the servants with us? Why not invite our neighbors, our closest friends?"

"They are waiting for us in my village. They will help us, but we must hurry."

Verushka feared she would not be able to find her way once they left the main road, which was now paved. Out in the country, where the road turned to dirt and the trees took over, she found what she thought was the post where a sign had once been.

Vadim was hesitant. "Are you sure? The road is so poor."

"Will you deny me this one comfort?"

They rode on until they found the ruins of her old village. Everything was overgrown, the forest having conquered their tiny, vulnerable piece of civilization. Birds had taken over one of the biggest houses. Collapsed fences looked as though they were growing from the wild grass. The remnants of the old well were covered in mushrooms, surely inedible. The village still smelled of smoke, at least to Verushka.

Ghosts flickered everywhere, staring at her. Waiting. Judging.

"This place is empty. There is no priest here. There is no church here. My dear Verushka, you have let yourself be consumed by grief."

She lifted Davor's body out of the carriage but could not carry it. He was too heavy for her slim frame, which had never grown after the pregnancy. "Help me," she told her husband. "Help me take him to the marsh."

"The marsh? We must go back, my dear."

"To the water first, please. This is the last favor I will ask of you, I promise."

Verushka led the way as her miserable husband trudged behind her over dirt that soon became mud. "What is this accursed place? Verushka, why are we here?"

A red tree with red bark grew on the bank of the marsh, not three feet from the water. Verushka knew it had grown from her placenta, her body. She gave it a grim nod and stopped to lay a hand on it. Then she proceeded to the water's edge. "Come here, please, Vadim. Put him next to me." Verushka knelt in the dampness.

"I can't. I'm sinking." Sweat dripped down Vadim's face as he struggled to carry Davor's body.

"Bring him to me!" She turned to face the water and extended her arms.

Her husband did as she asked, stepping into the mud. "What is happening to you, my Verushka?"

"He must return to the water. Now. Do as I say, or you will never hear him speak again."

"Get back in the carriage, Verushka. We're going home." In response to those words, the water began to churn. Vadim sank to his knees.

Something raced through Verushka's blood; it felt almost like happiness. Her nostrils filled with the smell of smoke and her eyes burned. A sprite rose out of the water and approached Vadim, who gazed at her with terrified eyes as he clutched Davor to his chest. Dozens of other sprites, dripping and dark-eyed, rose behind the first one. Vadim opened his mouth to scream but was drowned out by the violent wailing of the water sprites. The wind picked up out of nowhere as the sprites rushed to the bank of the marsh, slithering on their bellies to capture Davor. They seized him and submerged his body in the water.

Verushka looked on in wonder. She felt gratitude. "The sprites were here when Davor was born," she said. "Now they are here for his death. It is right."

But was he dead? Could these sprites give her son back to her? Would he live on in a different form? The sprites turned transparent as Verushka stared at them. Before long they had disappeared completely. Her husband disappeared as well, running into the forest in fear.

Best of luck to you, Verushka thought. You don't know this forest like I do. She turned to leave. She knew she had done the right thing by coming here. Someone grabbed her ankle. Verushka looked down at the smallest wood sprite she had ever seen. Her little voice came from the bottom of a well: "You are beholden to so many, Verushka. If you take your son from us again, you will owe us forever." In response, Verushka hissed and stamped her foot. The little sprite slipped away. Verushka was angry now. There was no point in trying to defend herself, explain herself. She had never been like other people.

If she was going to survive, she would have to be ruthless. She stared at the water and searched for a sign of Davor. She wanted only to stay with him. Should she jump in and surrender? What did she have to return to without her son?

"Here I am, Mama."

Davor tugged at her hand. He was sopping wet but did not shiver. Still, Verushka took off her shawl and covered him with it. She kissed him on both cheeks, then on his mouth. "Where have you been, my child?"

"I have been swimming. Floating. Did you know that wood floats?"

"Yes, I know, Davor."

"I am so happy, and do you know why? The sprites have been whispering to me."

Verushka waited, her heart pounding. She was afraid to speak.

"We are going to live forever, Mama. I never have to leave you. We are going to live forever! Why aren't you happy?"

"Life is a gift, Davor, but this life of ours does not come without a payment. We are in debt."

"What is debt?"

"Something you owe. You will understand as you grow older," Verushka said. "The forest holds a deadly beauty."

She led her son to the carriage and drove off. The sun was already high in the sky. She would go home, pack all their valuables into three trunks, and then get on a train. She had to go west, as far away from this land as possible, maybe as far as the New World. As they turned onto the main road, she saw something out of the corner of her eye.

It was Vadim, hanging from a gnarled tree by a noose made of vines.

* * *

She bought a family picture of a group of strangers from a professional photographer, who was puzzled and urged her to sit for her own portrait. "A beautiful woman like you should be immortalized." And then, in a more discreet tone, "You'll be grateful later."

"When I'm old?"

He bowed his head in embarrassment as Verushka stared at his face. If he only knew, she thought, and then stopped herself. Nobody knew anything of her life. She had long become a stranger to this world, a woman of secrets. But was she a woman anymore? Sometimes she woke and found splinters poking through her skin, a sign that a payment was due. Sometimes she found Davor in his bed in the morning, drenched.

Davor, who never changed, who was always a boy, forever on the brink of adolescence. If it weren't for her child, she might have let herself live with the sprites forever. She might have stayed with the man in the tree, or the sprites of the marsh, but Davor tied her to the real world. Something about him made her think of Elena. Elena would have wanted her to fight.

But Elena had never seen ghosts, as Verushka had, all her life. Elena had never seen a sprite.

Over the years, as she became monstrous, committing every sin, every crime, doing things that consigned ordinary humans to hell, she told herself, I'm doing this for my child. What mother wouldn't kill for her child?

She would never grow old. Davor would never grow up. She did not even know if she could die. How would humans kill her if they were to seize her at a border crossing? Fire, she supposed. Flames would do it. And Davor? She did not know what would kill him. How he loved to swim though. Sometimes she thought, when he dove deep into a body of water, that he would never return. He could always stay under for longer than any other child, and when he did resurface, his eyes danced with mischief. He would refuse to tell her where he had been.

The decades passed in a series of high-ceilinged apartments across the continent. They survived revolutions and outran fascism by constantly moving, flying along railroad tracks, all their possessions reduced to three trunks, their contact with ordinary humans strategic and selective. Verushka enjoyed the freedom, the anonymity, of their vagabond lifestyle. Davor became shrewder and more loyal with every year. Verushka prepared tea and cakes like any other mother, and one of her greatest joys was sitting with Davor in the sunlight of whichever kitchen they had claimed as theirs, never mind that their true appetite was not for tea and cakes. Verushka's previous life, her village childhood of ghosts and sprites, felt far away. She rarely saw dead people. Other beings held her attention now. Her victims.

She learned the value of accumulated wealth, gold and jewels. She, who had to pay in human lives, sighed as ordinary people struggled to survive. If they only knew! Their souls held the greatest value, not the material wealth they coveted. They did not cherish their own lives, and that made it easier to despise them. Still, the young girls she sacrificed were hard for her at first, perhaps because she herself had been a young girl when she was taken. Davor seemed to feel nothing for the babies he drowned. I must truly be a monster then, she thought, if my child is so accomplished.

On the outside, Verushka had changed subtly. Her skin was flawless at a glance, but constantly dry, no matter how much oil she rubbed into it. Her hair stayed thick and platinum blond, but it, too, became as dry as sun-baked straw if she didn't oil it. She didn't need much food or drink and rarely felt true hunger. Eating was a novelty, a diversion, like going to the theater. Sleep could go on for hours, but only after days and days of empty, aimless consciousness. Time itself ceased to have meaning. The sun and the moon, those relentlessly showy astral players, felt like old lovers she had lost track of.

She learned to speak and read several languages. Davor's passion, by contrast, was for numbers. She bought him books of mathematics, and he showed her all the patterns that existed in nature. The Fibonacci sequence was everywhere: in flower petals and seeds, in the shell of the nautilus, in the spiral of pinecones. There was also the six-fold symmetry of snowflakes, the geometry of honeycombs and wasp nests, the structural perfection of the spider web. Symmetry meant more than beauty. It held the world together. Verushka smiled and nodded, marveling at her child, understanding only that she had created a being so different from herself.

It was obvious when her debt came due. Her skin would itch, and if she let it go on for too long, wood splinters, some of them as big as sticks, would break through.

She didn't have to seduce all the girls she captured. Some of them were simple abductions. Poor, starving girls. Seamstresses. Factory girls. Girls who sold themselves. Addicts. Verushka was human enough, charming enough, to convince others to come away with her. There were plenty of desperate young women who wanted to be complimented and invited to a picnic under the trees. They were happy to eat well in the company of an attractive and well-dressed woman. How lucky to sit beside someone as agreeable and wealthy as Verushka appeared to be. None of these girls objected when Verushka fed them with her own hand, then brushed off their quivering lips. After she had drugged them, Davor would help her carry them through the forest, and then they would begin their search. There was always an ideal tree. Verushka could feel it in her bones and Davor would nod in agreement. They would leave the body there, at the base of the trunk, and Verushka knew better than to look back as they walked away.

Kira was not the first girl to be sacrificed, but she haunted Verushka with a persistence rivalling that of any ghost. At first glance Kira's dark brown eyes reminded Verushka of Elena, and that was where the trouble began. She took things slowly, so slowly that Davor asked her to explain.

"Are we going to keep her with us, Mama?" He was worried.

She did not answer.

"I know you're not like other people," Kira told her one day. "You're very rich. And you've done something. You're running from someone."

"You're the one who ran away from home, Kira." This was true. She was a merchant's daughter who had left home because of an unwanted pregnancy, but the baby had died within days.

"All interesting people leave home. It's different in your case."

"Can you prove your theory?"

Kira frowned. "I'm not accusing you of a crime. I want to know you better. I love you."

They were living as a couple by this point. Davor stayed away from the apartment. Verushka spent the days sleeping and the nights wandering the streets, trying to outrun her emotions, while Kira grew more and more frantic.

"Where do you go? Where does a respectable woman go at night?"

"You are still attached to respectability?"

Kira grew flustered and her face turned red. Verushka knew that under her clothes, Kira's whole body was blushing. Sometimes she could calm this girl merely by leading her over to the bed. Kira, though intelligent and a survivor, was still a child. Verushka knew she could do anything she wanted to her.

"Why are you staring at me like that?"

"You worry too much, my dear. You tell yourself stories that upset the both of us."

"I don't like it when you leave me alone. Sometimes I think I don't belong here. Perhaps it would be better if I—"

"What? If you lived on the streets? Who would buy you such pretty gowns? Where would you rest your head?"

"You're being cruel."

"You don't know what you're saying, Kira. You're overwrought. Let me make you some tea."

"I do know what I'm saying. Your body is changing. I've seen it. You scratch your wrists and ankles in your sleep. Sometimes your skin looks different. Once I thought I saw the shape of a tree on your back. You must be ill." And then, with a touch of hope she asked, "Do you go to see a doctor in the evening? Are you hiding some terrible illness and you're afraid to tell me?"

At first Verushka was furious, but then she managed to control herself. She took Kira's face in her hands and promised her the tea would make everything better.

That was the end of Kira. Verushka's feelings changed even before Kira swallowed the last drop of poison. The mistake was obvious. She had allowed herself to love someone other than Davor. She would never be so careless again. She could not afford to fail.

After she and Davor laid Kira beneath a tree deep within the Bois de Boulogne, Verushka made the mistake of turning around. The man, her man, stepped out of the tree and took Kira's body, just as he had taken her body all those years ago. Verushka rushed off to a café where she could surround herself with ordinary humans. It was reassuring to blend into a large public group after she had completed her gruesome task. Davor bid her goodbye and went off on his own. He had the soul of a teenager and would appear again when it suited him.

In the café that evening something unprecedented happened. The waiter brought her a cognac and told her it was from the man in the corner. Verushka barely smiled. She was always getting unwanted attention, and this was yet another signal that she needed to move on and return to her apartment. Still, she turned her head and saw that it was the man in the tree, sitting there at a corner table like any other Parisian gentleman. Her mouth went dry. A terrible itching buzzed from her scalp to her toes and she had a moment of panic. What if she turned to splinters right here?

She rose and walked over to him.

He stood and bowed. "Good evening, my dear."

"How are you here, like this? Where did you get those clothes?"

"These questions are hardly ladylike."

Verushka realized she had never heard such a human voice from his lips. She shook her head in disbelief.

"Don't worry. This human form has taken everything from me. I will not be able to stay here long."

"Then why risk it?"

"To persuade you to come home."

"I have no home, thanks to you."

"You and Davor both have a home in the forest. You know this."

"I feed you. Davor feeds the water sprites. We give you everything you need."

"I need you. We need you. You have a family in the forest."

Verushka wanted to cry out. She kept her voice low and calm. She could already see the man changing before her, slowly revealing his true self. "Tell me," she said, "what I can do. I don't want to live this way forever."

"Come home. To the village of your birth."

"What if I never want to return? Is there no other way?"

"If you deliver me a maiden at the tree where we first met, then she can take your place. Choose carefully. Be vigilant. If you fail, you will live as my wife forever."

His forest self flashed before her for one horrible moment, and then he dissolved into the wooden chair where he was sitting. Verushka went back to her table and drank the cognac in one gulp. She left the café. Extreme fatigue overtook her, and after she arrived at her apartment, she slept for three dreamless days.

No more love, she reminded herself when her head cleared. No more wasting time. How she wished she could have delivered Kira to the tree in her village! She should have had more patience with that girl. She also wished she had learned something more about Davor's future, but that was his problem to solve. Maybe he would be content with a lifetime of tossing babies into various European rivers. She needed a change. She had lived long enough on this continent. It was time for a new place.

Davor agreed to come with her, at least for the time being. They packed their trunks again.

"We have to get you some proper clothes," Verushka said, as Davor filled his trunk with the usual rocks, sticks, and dried plants.

"It's better this way, Mama. Easier."

There was no use arguing. Her son was happy skipping around half-naked along the banks of rivers, swimming every day, no matter the weather. He didn't mind feeding the sprites. Perhaps he was more sprite than human, not only because of who his father was, but because he was born in the water. He had never known anything different.

But Verushka had lived an ordinary life once, and now it was time for her to convince someone new that she was like any other woman, only more desirable. She had to become the kind of person who could make a girl throw away everything she had ever known.

* * *

Verushka has never succeeded in the great project of trying to free herself.

She came so close with Elaine that it still hurts to think about it. Yes, she can be hurt. When she remembers Elaine attacking her, fighting her, she feels her body turning to wood deep inside, dragging her back to the forest. She remembers how the rage flared like her own private forest fire and how quickly she wanted to destroy Elaine. In a second she can turn from desire to destruction. This is what her lovers never understand until it is too late.

Where would she go if she could be free of the man in the tree? What would she do if she could regain the life that was stolen from her?

She does not know. She is willing to die to find out. She has been living in the shadows for so long she barely remembers anything else. She opens her mouth to speak, to persuade, to seduce the ordinary humans she encounters, and now she no longer knows what is true. Her childhood has turned into a collection of fairy tales suspended in time. Who is Elena? Who is Vadim? And whose is that face in the mirror, the one people stare at? There's something off about her but they cannot pinpoint it. Is she ill? How old is she? Did she suffer trauma, cancer, the horror of immigration? Unspeakable loss?

Yes, to all of these. Verushka masters the most important lesson of survival and learns to tell each person the story they want to hear. The story they need. Then, without their noticing, she turns the tables on them. Skillfully, carefully, by saying very little and answering few questions, Verushka tricks her listeners into telling her story for her. The tales, beautiful and implausible, come spilling out of their mouths. She never corrects them.

Now that she is in California once again, installed in a corner apartment by the immense Pacific, she is keeping to herself. No new people. No need for storytelling. She knows where Devon lives, where she goes to school, where she walks. She has seen the mother and senses she is not much of a threat. All mothers are dangerous though. Verushka has always thought of mothers as the animals that are most likely to kill. This one is absent much of the time and there is nobody else in the house.

All signs point to success, but because the mother has seen her in that park, she takes an extra step and dyes her hair black. Even if this buys her only a few seconds, someday in the near future it will be worth it. The process takes several hours but her always-dry hair soaks up the dye like a sponge.

Verushka has been refining her skills. She can visit her victims in their unconscious, while they dream or when they let their guard down. She did this first with Kira, one day when they were dozing. There is no other power like a direct visit to someone's unconscious mind. The intimacy is delicious yet horrifying. It makes Verushka feel like she has become a god, all-knowing, but when it is over she is fatigued to the point of oblivion. She rests for days.

Verushka still turns heads, but she would rather not have this attention. If too many people notice her, the authorities will begin to investigate, and then she will have no choice but to flee. She is pushing into dangerous territory. She must choose every word with the utmost care. No action can be taken until the right moment. She has always prided herself on her exquisite patience, but the hours are flying by, and she still has not made true progress.

Devon is her last chance. There is no time for a drawn-out seduction, no long beach days spent rolling under the sun. She mourns this loss in advance. She enjoys her lovers because they are her only link to real human experience. She, Verushka, never got to be a girl. She never knew naïve hope. There is something achingly beautiful about human innocence.

Devon embodies all of this. When Verushka sees Devon walking down the street, she becomes ecstatic. It is like she is watching her own child, and it is difficult to keep her silence. How she wishes she could call to her and wave! How she wants to claim her. After all, Devon is hers. Because of Verushka, Devon will have the most privileged, the most coveted, of all human experiences. Immortality.

The Woodwards should be grateful, but humans can never understand a true gift.

The girl is beautiful in the way of children, her skin like that of a baby. She is so fresh, so new. Untouched. Exquisite. It is hard to get her alone, but not impossible. On the night of the rising table, they had achieved an almost perfect union, but Devon woke up. Still, what a sacred moment! Devon's mind is a beautiful place, like a meadow. Verushka has never before tasted such sweetness. She herself was never so good, never so pure. It is tempting to dwell on the peacefulness of Devon's mind and abandon everything else, but when she reminisces for too long, the splinters appear on her skin, ringing her ankles and wrists. They are more pronounced than ever, reminding her that it is time to pay. How many other things will get worse for her, how many dangers will she face, before she has her chance?

Devon is the one. Verushka feels this truth in her whole body. The girl is hers.

She cannot fail.

Time is running out.

Here she comes.

Devon: 2013

They met in real life, not on a screen. That made all the difference.

One day after school, Devon, so hungry her mouth was watering, walked over to the Mini Mart to buy a Mrs. Fields milk chocolate chip cookie. Milk chocolate chip, not semi sweet. She felt someone looking at her and assumed it was another customer, rude and in a hurry, so she turned her head to look.

Everything stopped. Devon knew what this was, or at least she thought so. She knew all about sex trafficking. She knew about scams. From the time she was little, people had approached her in malls, even when she was with her mom, to tell her she should consider modeling. Now an attractive woman was staring right at her. Maybe she was working with some gross old man. Were there pretty pedophiles? No makeup, perfect features, silky black hair, wearing something amazing. The woman was a stranger, but Devon couldn't help herself. "Your dress."

"Do you like it?" She had an accent Devon couldn't place.

Devon stared at the dress, floor-length, in alternating panels of dark blue velvet and white lace. She wanted to touch it.

"I made it. Do you sew?"

"No. I want to learn. I have my grandmother's old sewing machine."

"Ah, well then, you must learn."

Devon took her cookie and they started walking together down Overland. It would take a little longer to get home, but Devon wanted to keep talking. The woman was carrying a black coffee, lidless, without spilling it. Devon didn't remember seeing her pay for it.

"You are a student?"

It was the first time a stranger had asked her that question. A student, as if she were in college already. "I start high school next year," Devon said, then immediately felt childish, since the school year had barely started. They hadn't even gotten to Halloween yet. She was an eighth-grader, only recently a teenager, but the woman didn't laugh at her.

"What is your most beloved subject?"

"Art. I like collages." There she went again, sounding like a little kid. She wanted to be interesting, worthy of this conversation.

"Now I must take my leave. I have enjoyed talking to you."

"Do you live around here?" Devon asked. She would have expected the woman to live somewhere more interesting.

"No. I live in Venice."

"Oh." She did look like a Venice person, from what Devon's mother referred to as the old Venice, but she certainly didn't sound like one. "I love Venice."

"Do you like to go to the beach?"

"Yes. I go there with my friends."

"Well then, perhaps I will see you around, as they say."

"See you!" Devon called. The chips in her cookie were melting.

She hadn't gone very far before the woman's voice was in her ear. Devon whirled around and saw the woman standing right behind her, holding out one hand. Devon's smoky quartz marble sat on her palm. "Did you lose something?" she asked.

"Where did you get that?"

"You dropped it."

"Thank you," Devon said, snatching the marble back. Now her heart was racing.

"It won't help, you know."

"What?"

The woman nodded at Devon's clenched fist. "Those old superstitions. They never help anyone. You should free yourself."

"From what?" Devon asked, even though the woman was crossing over into the category of adults to be avoided. It was hard, almost impossible, to wrench herself away. The woman was mesmerizing, and with each word, Devon wanted to spend more time with her, to be in her presence.

"From everything holding you back. From all that keeps you from your true self. Perhaps it is time for you to transform." With that she turned around and walked off in the opposite direction.

Devon opened her mouth to say something, but nothing came out, and then right away she drowned in self-consciousness. She wanted so badly to be cool. She knew she was, deep down inside, but other people couldn't see it yet. She had to learn not to overreact to things, not to jump out of her skin every time somebody said something to her. There were kids at school who could do it, who were like calm water all the time, no matter who was trying to set a fire near them.

Maybe it was time for a transformation.

Was the woman good or bad? Was she another one of the "untreated mentally ill" her mother was always talking about, or another LA con? Would a criminal be so attractive, so carefully dressed? She didn't try to make Devon do anything. She didn't ask Devon to come with her. And she certainly didn't take anything from Devon. In fact, she gave her back the marble.

A few more steps and she was covered in shame. Of course the woman was a bad person. Of course she was trying to get away with something. Devon looked all around her. What if someone from school had seen this go down?

And then, as she turned onto her street, no. Nothing bad happened. It was no big deal. Why did she have to freak out about every little thing? She, Devon, was a pretty, interesting girl, and other interesting people wanted to be around her. The world was opening up and she was going to have a wonderful life. She would be successful and happy, but what was more important, she would be real. Authentic. Not like her parents, running around and lying all the time, scared while pretending not to be scared. Pathetic. She was nothing like them.

Time to transform.

The house was empty. She grabbed her phone to text Reina but then put it away. Instead of going to her room and taking out all her homework, a ritual she performed every day, she sat on the living room couch and did nothing. She closed her eyes for a second, and when she heard her mom's key in the door, she rushed down the hall to her bedroom.

She didn't want to talk to her mother yet. Why can't I keep this afternoon for myself? she thought. She got out her sketchpad and some colored pencils and tried to draw the woman's dress. She wasn't going to tell anyone about her. Her friends wouldn't get it, or they would ask too many questions Devon couldn't answer.

Her mother would never understand. She would make it into something it wasn't.

* * *

It took two applications of L'Oréal Colorista Bleach to turn Devon's hair white.

"You're sure you want to do this?" Reina asked. "I'm afraid we're going to fry it."

"Are you on my side or not?"

"I'm always on your side, girl."

Reina's bathroom smelled like chemicals, even with the window wide open. Devon left the bleach on for so long that Reina had to scream at her to rinse it out. When it was over, Devon's hair was still too yellow to please her, but she didn't want to hurt Reina's feelings. "It looks good. I like it," she said.

"Your eyes look different now. So dark."

"Yeah?"

"Do you want to straighten it?"

"No. I'm going to tie it in a scarf in case my mom's home."

The girls embraced at Reina's front door and then Devon walked back home by herself. Nobody approached her on the street. Nobody made her doubt herself. The mystery woman was losing importance in Devon's memory. The next time a stranger approached her she would blow them off, no matter how they looked or sounded, no matter what they were wearing, no matter how nice their features were. She was safe now, for the moment. Safe-ish, but was she ever truly safe? From the time she was a little kid in preschool, Devon had been afraid of dying. She knew it would be sudden. Violent. A therapist once told her it was because of the fire.

"But I don't remember the fire."

"Your body remembers."

She felt the truth of that statement in her whole body, but she was still troubled by the vast blank spaces of her mind, a wasteland where memories should have been. There was some important place she wasn't allowed to go.

She was nothing like the other kids. All through elementary school, when she ran around the playground or sat in class, she would hear voices. They were everywhere, when a door creaked open or a tree branch groaned in the wind. Was that a noise or a word? The whole world spoke to her. It didn't speak to everyone else though, so she never mentioned it. As she grew older the voices quieted but she never forgot them. And she was still different. She remembered listening as one of her teachers spoke to her mom. "There's so much extra work to do if a child can't focus. I could get the whole class to move like a rocket if they could all stay on task."

She knew she was not on her teacher's rocket. Instead she was on a vessel that sometimes moved like a slow, suffocating cruise ship and sometimes tossed like a sailboat about to wreck. Both feelings were uncomfortable. She wasn't having trouble in school, no, but she had to work hard to keep her mind focused on what the teacher was saying, on worksheets and books, on various screens dancing with information. Her mind wanted to be somewhere else. She noticed everything in the room, and the effort of pretending otherwise was exhausting. When her mother met her at the end of each school day she could barely speak. It was all she could do to go to her bedroom and shut the door. Lie down.

It was best to play along, otherwise they would attach three initials to you or pull you out of class or give you medication. She hated words like crazy or pretty or stupid even though she used them herself. They were each so subjective. She didn't understand why ordinary events, like graduations and crushes and bleeding, were supposed to be such a big deal, but she did cry about the tiny broken eggs she sometimes found on the sidewalk and the toys other children lost at the beach.

Magic was another word she used cautiously because she knew Henry, her plush rabbit, had emerged from the fire on his own, and with Henry came the blank spot in her memory. It was not white, like a page, but more like a forest at night. She would be forever angry at the adults in her life for allowing her, encouraging her, to forget that place called the chalet. She was going to make her mother drive her out there one of these Saturdays. If she could only see it, maybe even walk around the property, she might begin to remember. Why couldn't they knock on the door? "Hi, we used to live here. Do you mind if we look around?" People did that in movies all the time. If she brought Henry with her, what would he do?

Her mom was wrong. The sleepover and raising the table hadn't caused all the trouble in her life. The mounting dread had been there all along, in the form of a gnawing sensation right beneath her ribcage. It wasn't low enough to be cramps, which would come later. It wasn't pain exactly. Anxiety, perhaps. What it was, Devon figured out, was something coming due, something her family had failed to deal with. It was on her now. Her turn. Everything clicked into place. She was going to die. She knew it. Her body knew it.

This was nothing special. Teenagers died all the time. Romeo and Juliet, of course, but they were out of control, especially Romeo. Her homeroom teacher had described adolescence as something not everyone survived, and that day in class Devon wrote THANK YOU in her notebook. If she was going into battle, she wanted credit for it. "If you're overwhelmed, you should talk to someone." How many times had she heard this? But who could she explain her fears to? She wasn't suicidal, she was marked. In middle school of all places she found someone who was able to listen. Reina.

"Oh, I love scary stuff."

"This is real. It's my life."

Was she exaggerating? Being a drama mama? No, it was all true. All the things she had never been able to talk about to any therapist: the fire, the one bad night she couldn't remember because her parents were still hiding it from her, her parents' divorce, her fears that something much bigger than her was still unresolved.

Reina was attentive and respectful. She never smirked once while Devon spoke, but instead listened, her brown eyes exuding warmth. Was this empathy, a word Devon had been hearing since she was little? Best of all, Reina believed in solutions. This was her gift, her power.

"You might have to dig, Devon."

"What do you mean?"

"You need to talk to every member of your family and all your old friends. That's what I had to do, or else I would never have figured out my family history. Like why we immigrated, and how we got here. I even learned my dad was married once before."

"Wow. Did he have other children?"

"No. Well, I don't know for sure. This is what I'm talking about. You have to ask and ask and ask."

One day, when Devon was looking for a copy of her mother's signature (to practice it, just in case), she found a picture of herself as a baby holding a big Steiff bear. There. He *was* real. This was evidence. If she closed her eyes she could see a forest. That bear belonged in a forest. Now she was getting somewhere.

She knew she had been right to ask about the bear!

She could tell she was getting somewhere whenever her mom fell silent. When her mom got quiet, it meant that she, Devon, was on to something, and something big had definitely happened that night at the chalet. Why did they live all the way out there, when it was so far from the rest of the city? Why did they leave after only a few months? Her parents always made it sound like a safety issue, as if she, Devon, was at risk somehow, in danger, but they would never say how. *You used to sleepwalk when you were little. It scared us.*

She used to sleepwalk. Why couldn't she remember this? When she googled it, lots of scary stories came up. People wandering along the side of the highway. People having sex with strangers. People hurting their family members, even killing them. Sleepwalking children were incredibly vulnerable. How did they get her to stop? And another thing: Devon and her mom had both wound up in the hospital that summer, but it's not like there was a car accident or an illness. So what happened?

"Why were we in the hospital?" she had asked her mom countless times.

"They were keeping us overnight for observation. You were fine, Devon. Probably dehydrated."

"But why were you there, Mom?"

"Same as you. I must have fallen."

"Where?"

"There was a hill behind the chalet. You don't remember any of this, do you? You were so little."

Whenever her mother lied, she looked at a space somewhere to the left of Devon's face.

A plan was forming in Devon's mind. She couldn't put it into words yet, but it was starting. She needed some protection. The smoky quartz was nice, but she wanted her bear back. Needed him. Even if he couldn't protect her, he would share the same memories. He would have answers. How could she ever find him again? What had become of him?

Her parents were useless. Even Grandma Elaine, who visited the most of all their relatives, never told her much of anything. She liked to talk about Dad and Uncle Josh when they were little. She liked to talk about how happy she had been as a kid and how worried she was for Devon's generation. At least Devon had friends she could rely on. They had hidden in the walk-in closet and made a blood vow at the twins' birthday party, the five of them slitting their palms and pressing their hands together. A drop of blood fell on the seagrass rug, but Sierra refused to clean it up. "That's our communal blood," she said. "Leave it."

Later that night, the table lifted off the floor like it was made of air. Devon would never forget the exhilaration of it, followed by a calm satisfaction. This was all because of her. This was real. She couldn't enjoy it for long. She lost control, falling though darkness though her body was still firmly planted on the floor. Devon felt cold hands around her waist and on her face, and then she came to. The other girls were screaming at her, but for what? They all fell silent and stared at her in confusion.

She'd had a few weeks to think about that night. At first she walked around in a daze and nobody—not her mom and dad, not the physician in the ER, not her pediatrician, not even the psychic—could help her. They told her to breathe. To sleep and stay hydrated. To stay away from screens. To clutch smoky quartz. But they were all missing something.

One detail edged its way back into her consciousness.

When she was falling into darkness at the twins' party, as she was entering a strange new place, somebody caught her. A veil of white hair enveloped her. Consumed her.

She had to fight.

* * *

Her mom's face went white when she saw her. Bloodless.

"Mom, come on. Don't be such a drama queen. It's only hair. I need it for my costume. This Halloween is special to me."

"Halloween is one night! I would have bought you a nice wig. You're not a little kid anymore." Her mother fingered Devon's new hair. "Devon, your hair is ruined. You've destroyed it."

"I have not!"

"What are you going to do if it falls out? The damage could be permanent."

Devon yanked on her long locks to show how strong they were. "Mom. It's just hair and it's not going to fall out. And anyway, you can already see the roots."

"Please, leave your roots alone. Let your hair grow. You can bob it and it will eventually go back to its natural color."

"I can bob it? *Bob it?*"

"What is wrong with you?"

"It's not your hair, Mom. I'm not going to *bob it*. I can do whatever I want with my own hair."

"You're acting like a silly child to defy me. Don't be so sure I won't take away Halloween."

"For having white hair? For having long white hair? Mom, I'm on the fucking honor roll!"

Out of fear Devon stormed off to her room. She had never sworn at her mother before and now she was shaking. She looked at herself in the mirror and was pleased by the wrongness of it. It shocked her. White hair. Well, almost white. And brown eyes. Reina was right. The white hair made her eyes look darker. People in school and on the street were going to stare at her now, and not in admiration.

The little house filled with the scary silence of two women's anger. Devon heard her mom pour a glass of wine, which meant she was really upset. Devon still hadn't told her about the costume. She opened her backpack and took out all her homework even though she knew she wouldn't be able to focus.

Round two started after dark. The doorbell rang and her mom went to the front door. Damn. The package. Devon had been hoping it would be delivered when her mother wasn't home. Why hadn't Reina texted her?

"Devon! Do you know what this is?"

She came out of her room and tried to take the box out of her mother's arms. It was heavier than she'd expected. "It's mine."

"Stop. What is it?"

"Can I have no privacy?"

"That's enough, Devon."

"It's for my costume. It's supposed to be a surprise."

Her mom stood right in front of her, blocking the hallway. "Open it, please."

"Mom."

"I need to see it."

"Why?"

"Don't start. We have to get some things clear. Yes, I still need to know what you're up to. You still need my permission for everything. Especially when you've had a health scare."

"I haven't had a health scare! The doctors couldn't find anything."

"Open the box, Devon."

"What are you afraid of?"

"I'm not afraid, but if I don't like your costume, you're not wearing it."

"Mom, I know what you're thinking, but this is not some sexy-girl costume. It's the opposite."

"Fine. Then there should be no problem." Without another word, her mom took the box away from her. Then she grabbed the scissors and sliced through the tape.

"You're going to damage it!"

"Stop screaming, Devon." Caroline lifted a large, plastic-wrapped object out of the box. Devon took it from her, ripped open the plastic, and freed two enormous white wings. "Help me put these on, Mom, please?"

Her mother helped her into the wings but said nothing. She went through the packing materials to find the invoice before Devon could stop her. "How did you pay for this?"

"Reina ordered them for me."

"Then how did she pay?"

"She has a Depop. Her shop, remember? I told you. She has an online business."

"I'm not sure how all that works, but you're saying she gifted these to you? Because it says here they cost a hundred and fifty dollars."

"I gave her something of mine to sell in her shop to pay for the wings. Something you wouldn't care about."

"Jesus, Devon." Her mother looked ugly when she got angry. This had always scared Devon, and now she worried she would have the same ugly face someday.

"You never even noticed it was missing. You would never have asked about it."

"Devon!"

"It was the coat Grandma Carol got me when I was really little."

Her mom sat down at the table and put her head in her hands.

"Mom. Please. I could have bought cheap wings but it's very important I don't look slutty in this costume. That's the whole point. Look. These wings are made of white feathers. They're real."

"Devon, the coat I'm thinking of cost way more than a hundred and fifty. It had a fur collar."

"Fur is disgusting, Mom. I can't believe you let a child wear that."

Her mother stayed silent for too long, which meant she was really angry. The wings grew heavy. "Go away, Devon," she said. "Go to your room. I need a break."

Devon went back down the hall in her wings and locked her bedroom door behind her. Typical. Her mom had a way of ruining everything, or at least spoiling her pleasure. She took the wings off carefully and set them on a shelf. Good thing they didn't have a cat. Reina couldn't keep them for her because her cat, Astro, would have taken apart those feathers.

She pulled the vintage white nightgown, a great find at Goodwill, from the bottom drawer of her dresser. She had to hang it so the wrinkles would fall out. Now all she needed was a little pink lipstick. The twins wanted her to wear full makeup but that wasn't the look she was after.

She wished she could put the whole costume on but knew she had to wait until Halloween night. Maybe when her mom saw her, she would stop being so angry. Her parents would never understand her. She was so alone, and it wasn't enough that her friends were on her side. Someone from her own family should be on her side, but she had been alone since she was a little kid.

How could anyone be mad at an angel?

* * *

Devon was at Venice Beach with her friends the second time she saw the woman. It was cold and windy, one of the last possible beach days of the year, but they weren't there to swim. The twins were busy taking selfies. Reina was focused on building a little sandcastle. "Join me!" she said, smiling up at Devon like a kid.

"There's somewhere else I want to go first. I'll be right back." Devon stepped away to go to Small World Books, a place she liked to visit whenever she was at the beach. It was a tradition her mother had started. First they would buy a few books, then they would hit the sand. This was her beach. Nowhere did she feel safer. She trudged across the sand to the colorful strip of shops and apartment buildings lining the boardwalk. She wanted to have a place of her own here someday. It would be like living in a pastel painting.

The calm space of the bookstore was a relief, a break from the sun. She pretended to care about the covers of the serious books staring at her but wound up surrounded by graphic novels, as usual. Devon had spent most of her money on lunch and didn't have enough left over for a book. Maybe her mom would buy her a copy of *Anya's Ghost* someday. A tabby cat with white paws started rubbing against her ankle but something scared it away, and Devon took this as her cue to leave. She wanted to get back to her friends.

"I've been dreaming about you," the woman said as Devon walked outside into the blinding sunlight.

"Oh, it's you." Devon tried to sound casual though her whole body grew tense.

"Your hair." No compliment, no criticism. Devon put her fingers to her scalp and knew the bleach had been a mistake. It was such a bad dye job. She felt foolish and adolescent. The woman started laughing. "Don't worry," she said, pointing to her own black locks. "I dyed mine too, recently. That's something we have in common. Everybody wants to hide their roots. Only your true friends know who you really are."

"What color is your real hair?" Devon asked. Her mouth had gone dry. She couldn't help staring at the woman, who was wearing a sheer white cover up dotted with little black beads. She was tiny, without an ounce of fat, but she had curves in the right places. When she smiled, her face didn't break out in wrinkles. Was she just another committed Westside woman who refused to age? What was her story? Devon wished the twins could see her talking to this woman. Or Reina. She should have dragged Reina to the bookstore with her. If her friends could see her, they could help her decide if the woman was interesting or dangerous.

"Are you down here all by yourself?"

"No. I need to get back actually. All my friends are here." It sounded like she was bragging about a big group, but they were down to four. Madison had abandoned them for a group of theater kids.

"That's unfortunate. I would love to sit with you. Treat you to a cool drink."

Why not? It wasn't bad to have a drink with someone, was it? "Okay. I have a few minutes." She texted Reina. She hoped everyone would pack up and come looking for her, but texts didn't always go through at the beach.

They sat down at the café right next to the bookstore. Devon was hungry but she didn't want to make this stranger spend too much money on her. They both ordered lemonade. The woman picked up Devon's glass and held it for her.

"What are you doing?"

"Drink. Take a sip. One little sip."

Devon leaned forward and took a sip from the straw and then instantly regretted it. This was creepy. She felt manipulated. "I don't even know your name," she said, to break through the awkwardness.

"You have to guess it."

"Like in that fairy tale where she has to guess his name? Who's that little man? Rumpelstiltskin?"

"Something like that."

"You're serious? Okay. What do I get if I guess your name?"

"You will become your true self."

The hairs stood up on Devon's scalp. "But this is my true self," she said. Was she lying? She didn't know what was true, but she had to assert herself.

"No. This isn't you. I know you, Devon, and I can make you a queen."

"What are you talking about? How do you even know my name?" I need to get away from here, Devon thought. I shouldn't have done this. They had never introduced themselves, she was sure of it.

"You needn't be afraid. I know you."

"How?"

"We met once before. When you were little. You don't remember."

"I don't think so. You're not one of my mom's friends. I don't know you."

"I know you. I know everything."

Devon stood up, splashing the lemonade all over the table. She was afraid to speak but tried her best to make eye contact, to pretend fearlessness at least.

"We've met many times. I am always the same, even when you don't see me. Our next rendezvous will be crucial. You must choose wisely. The survival of your family depends upon it." Then she rose and kissed Devon's lips. She tasted like woodsmoke.

"You're insane."

"No. I am your only truth."

"Stop it. I'm going."

"I know what you want. What you need. We can get around that mother of yours. You will leave your family behind, safe and sound. I will not harm them. You will be free. You will transform, finally and forever. Don't be a coward. Come with me."

Devon rushed out of the café and bumped into a group of girls standing in line for henna tattoos. She could not stop shaking, not even when she crossed the sand to find her friends again. Thank God the twins hadn't witnessed her humiliation. That woman kissing her on the mouth.

"Dude, what happened to you?" This was from Samantha.

"I ran into someone."

The twins were suspicious. Reina sat next to her and stroked her arm. It was getting late now, and they had to figure out how to get themselves home. Melissa was willing to pick them up, but they would have to wait a while. Devon considered texting her mom even though she hated it when anyone got sand in the car.

"What happened?" Reina asked her in a whisper.

"Nothing. I mean, I can't talk about this." It was too hard to explain. How could she describe what the woman had done to her, what she had said? It was a threat, but it was also a promise, and the promise scared her more. The woman's talk of transformation had struck a chord. What did it mean? She hadn't considered that her whole family might be in danger, and now she was under pressure. She had to be smart.

Should she talk to the police? And say what? The woman had not hurt her. There was no direct threat of violence. It was all so skillful and subtle. Devon was too embarrassed, of course, to mention the kiss. For a second she thought of transcribing what she remembered of the conversation on her phone, but her hands were still shaking.

Had they really met before? Devon tried to remember. What about the woman in the park that night? Were they connected? But her mom had seen a homeless woman with white hair, not a sleek young brunette. In any case, Devon felt sick all over. She had no one to confide in. She couldn't tell her mom about the lemonade incident, for fear she would take away Halloween.

Everything depended on Halloween night.

She had to stay one step ahead of evil. She had to get back to childhood, to her younger self, to that self the woman said she knew. *We met once before. When you were little.*

There was only one way out of this. The answers were in the past, in that summer at the chalet.

Devon made a plan and committed to it.

She wiped her lips again but could not erase the woman's kiss. Her mouth tasted like a campfire.

* * *

Counting down the days of Halloween week was hard, a long slow march to Thursday night. Devon spent too much of her life waiting for time to pass. She was always trying to get to the end, spurred by her terrible anxiety.

In English she got back the first draft of her Transformative Event essay. She had tried to write about the fire, which was a real challenge because she could not remember much. They were supposed to write about an event that had changed them, and most of her classmates were focusing on disappointments, accidents, and trauma. Divorce. Cross-country moves. For a full week she had stared at a blank page, her first real experience with writer's block. She had even considered interviewing her parents, and maybe her grandparents, but that was like cheating.

Besides, she could not rely on them to give her the real story.

I see myself as a little girl in a white nightgown. In one arm I'm holding my bear while the building in front of me is consumed by flames. My parents are trying to comfort me. My mother, in her pajamas, clutches her computer. My father is holding his briefcase but wearing only his jockey shorts.

All lies. Certainly, she was holding a stuffed animal. The one thing she could remember was the sensation of hanging onto something soft. Was it her bear or Henry? Weren't most of her toys lost in the fire? There was a picture, though, of her having a tea party with Bear and Henry in the back yard of the chalet. She hadn't seen that photo in years, but she could swear to its existence. Yes. She had brought it to school once when she was still in lower elementary. Did she lose it? The image of her parents on the night of the fire was completely fabricated, but it still felt truthful. They would have been wearing whatever they had slept in. They escaped the fire with their computers and phones. That was a fact she had heard repeated many times. Was her mother actually holding a laptop, or was it simply impossible to picture her away from her computer? She had been sitting and working at her computer all these years since Devon was born.

She wanted to write about the most important thing the fire gave her: a sense of urgency, as if something very important could happen at any minute. "That's your anxiety talking," one therapist told her. "Also, you shouldn't believe everything your mind tells you."

Then what should she believe?

In any event, there were so many details she had to make up. She could still hear the neighbors' cat screaming in his carrier because that was the official story. Every living thing in the building had made it out in time. Was it really a black cat? Did it matter? *Excellent description*, her teacher had written, *but you don't actually address how the event changed you.*

How could she address something that was still happening to her every day? How could she write about these things her own parents preferred to forget? She hadn't even told her mother about the essay. That would never work.

Everything changed after meeting the woman in Venice. Devon made her decision and stopped being afraid. She wasn't going to let the mystery woman scare her. She refused to run away and hide. She became powerful. It was like magic. Game on. She went to school each morning feeling calm and in control. She was going to make something happen without any outside help. It was her idea; she was in charge. It was not simply anxiety, as the doctors would claim, this terrible thing that sometimes forced her to make extreme, inflexible decisions. Now she was ready.

She stepped onto campus like a secret queen, like Carrie from the movie, but this time Carrie was in the know and the mean girls had become loyal helpers. Even the twins, feared by so many, were on her side. They waved her over to them as soon as they saw her so they could go vape before class. Devon was pretty sure Sierra was more addict than rebel. Sierra already knew how to drink, savoring those few inches of brown liquid in a crystal tumbler like a divorcée in an old movie. She could swallow it without wincing. Sam, on the other hand, hated alcohol. It was funny how different the twins were.

Madison was gone, which was kind of sad, but it left her alone with Reina, the friend she would keep for life. Reina understood everything. Reina saw Devon for who she really was. When she'd first heard about Devon's Halloween costume, she had said, "Of course you have to have real feathers! How else will you be able to fly?"

Angels were meant to fly, obviously. The girls laughed until they cried. They were lying on the fuzzy rug in Reina's room while Astro circled them. Reina touched Devon's hair and asked her if she was sure.

"Sure about the bleach?"

"No. Sure about the transformation. Because there's no going back. Once you become an angel, you leave the devil girls forever."

Devon laughed. "I'm ready."

"Why is it so important to you?"

"I need to be seen. It's kind of like a performance."

"For your mom? You shouldn't ruin your hair for your mom. You shouldn't ruin anything for your mom."

"I promise you I'm not going to ruin anything."

Reina had stood by her on that first white-haired morning back at school when everyone else stared and wondered why Devon would do something so drastic. The twins were surprised. Madison looked away. The boys told her both that she used to be hot (before the bleach) or that she was now suddenly hot (after the bleach). Teachers raised their eyebrows. Reina took responsibility. Yes, she had helped Devon bleach her hair, and yes, it was beautiful.

It was no big deal. It was hair. Dead cells. Why so much drama? Halloween was supposed to be fun and this was their last year of middle school. They could do whatever they wanted.

This was the story Devon let herself believe.

* * *

The blood was disappointing. There wasn't very much, to tell the truth, and if it hadn't been for the awful cramps, Devon would have felt like she was exaggerating once again, or even lying about her period. She was the last of all her friends to get it. She really wanted to have her period on Halloween and now she feared the timing was off. She was so new to this she couldn't even guess how many days her cycle was. She didn't want to resort to an app. In this one instance she wanted to be like her mom, who always claimed she could tell where her body was in its cycle, right down to ovulation.

Nothing, not even the blood, could interfere with her plan.

She stopped taking the sleeping pills and instead stored them in a little velvet bag in her underwear drawer. It had to look like she was taking them in case her mom checked. Now that she had her plan, she was more hopeful about her future. Ideally she wanted to get back to the trance at the twins' house, or to the night under the skylight, or to her dark walk in the park. She was trying to recapture all those precious moments of lost time. If she closed her eyes, she could sometimes get to a place so quiet and menacing that she scared herself.

She tried one afternoon before her mom came home, while she was still alone in the house. Where did she go? To the woods, as usual. Obviously. Everything started in the woods, all the great stories. There were no woods where they lived though. It was urban and dry and kind of dirty. A nice enough street, but it was only a short walking distance from a big road. She should ask her mom to take her into the Santa Monica Mountains. She should ask someone to hypnotize her.

It was no use. She opened her eyes wide and then closed them again. It didn't work. There had to be a way to empty her mind and make it free of thought. Quiet. Peaceful. She wanted to travel or be visited. Why couldn't she have a vision? Didn't people study this? Not in yoga studios in Los Angeles, but in India or someplace real.

She tried deep breathing. She could get to a certain point of drifting, but then something always yanked her back to full consciousness. Again, she closed her eyes and pictured a forest. Massive trees. A walk uphill. She felt so small. She had a terrible thought: What if she, Devon, never came back?

What if someone hostile appeared to her?

Devon opened her eyes. Her mom was standing in her bedroom.

"What's going on, Dev?"

"Nothing. I didn't know you were home. I was meditating."

"Good. How have you been feeling?"

"Mom, stop asking me that. It's so condescending. What about you, how have you been feeling?"

"Me? I'm fine. Don't worry about me."

"Mom, I have a question. Who were our neighbors when we lived in the chalet?"

"What made you think of the chalet? We didn't really know our neighbors. The houses were far apart, at least back then. The nearest neighbors were only there on the weekends or something. There was a little store, but we weren't there long enough to become part of the community."

This sounded like a rehearsed speech, which meant her mom didn't want to talk. It was intimidating. Devon pushed herself to ask, "Was there someone who lived nearby? A lady?"

Even saying the word—*lady*—was dangerous. A betrayal. Devon knew this. Her whole body grew hot.

"Devon, is something wrong?"

"Mom, what happened when we were living out there? You have to tell me."

"What do you mean?"

"Didn't something happen to you? Something medical?"

Her mother avoided Devon's eyes and instead looked at that mysterious empty space to the left. "I had a miscarriage."

"You did?"

"I've told you this before."

"No! You haven't. I would have remembered."

"I could swear I told you. Anyway, I was more worried about you, Devon. You kept disappearing at night. Sleepwalking. I know I've told you that."

"Mom, the miscarriage. You never told me."

Her mother gave her a warning glare. "Look. Please don't make a big deal out of this. It happens all the time. It's nature's way of taking care of things. Don't look at me like that, Devon. It's very common in the first trimester."

"What do you mean about nature's way?"

"Maybe there was something wrong with the fetus, or maybe it wasn't meant to be."

"So that was why you went to the hospital?"

"Yes, I suppose so."

"And me? You can tell me the truth now. I'm almost in high school."

Her mother sighed. "Hang on. It's hard to remember. You were lost."

"Lost?"

"On the hill behind the chalet. I had to go looking for you."

"Was it dark? Was I sleepwalking?"

"Well, it got dark eventually. It must have been the end of the day. Your dad wasn't home yet."

Devon stared into her mother's eyes and wondered how much she was holding back. "So you found me?"

"Actually, no. I was bleeding too much. Your dad found you."

"And what was wrong with me?"

"Nothing."

"Mom, come on!"

"Nothing, I swear. They put you on an IV. I'm sure you were lost and scared. I would never let anything happen to you—I would die first. How are the pills working out, by the way? It seems like you're sleeping normally. There aren't any side effects, are there?"

"I'm fine, Mom. So, when we lived at the chalet, there weren't any neighbors. Did I have any friends?"

"You were really little. That's why I was trying so hard to get you into preschool."

"What did I do all day?"

"You played outside with Henry."

"How did Henry get that scar on his stomach?"

"What scar?"

"There's a place where you stitched him up. I can tell."

"Devon, I don't know. It's hard for me to keep track of your toys. That's supposed to be your job. My memory is blurry, honestly, around the fire, and the miscarriage didn't help things. And then the divorce."

"What happened to my bear?"

"Oh, Devon, I don't know. He disappeared. Things get lost. You should ask your grandmother when she gets here. She gave it to your dad.

Anyway, a new bear should be arriving soon, and if you don't want it, you can save it for your own child. If you ever want to have a child, that is."

Her mom left to change out of her work clothes, but Devon knew it was because she didn't want to talk anymore. Something had ruined the progress she was making there in her bedroom. She had been drawing closer to someplace important, maybe even magical, and then her mother appeared and erased it. Her mom always put up a wall when they talked about the chalet. It never failed. Devon got scared off and gave up too easily. This time, though, she had learned new information: her mom was pregnant when they were living at the chalet. Still, there was something more her mother wouldn't tell her, something that scared the both of them.

She couldn't push things away like her parents did. It was because of all this secrecy that she was in this terrible, dangerous position.

Maybe her grandmother would have some answers. She certainly liked to talk.

* * *

Reina put one hand over her solar plexus. "Go like this whenever you encounter a toxic person," she told Devon. "See? It blocks the bad energy."

Devon raised her hand to cover the anxiety spot in her stomach. "Like this?"

"Hold it there when you have to deal with someone who gives off bad vibes. You know what I mean."

"Shouldn't we be walking around school like this all the time?"

"Come on, it's not that bad. If you're putting out negativity, only negativity will come back to you. You get back what you put out."

"Seriously? You think I put out negative vibes?"

"I think you're really worried about something. I've never seen you so stressed out. You need to cheer up. Halloween is tomorrow. Hey, are you wearing your costume to school?"

"No. I need to wait until sundown."

The girls were supposed to be studying but they hadn't even bothered to take out their books. They were on their phones, trying to find inspiration for Reina's costume. She had decided to go as a devil, in contrast to Devon's angel, but she didn't want to look ridiculous. So far she had pointy horns, a tail, and a cape, all in red. She had made a black pitchfork in her art class. "Who even knows what the devil looks like?" Reina said. "I've never really thought about it before."

"At least you won't have your cleavage hanging out."

"Never. I'm going to wear a long black dress and boots."

"Then you're all set. It's close enough. I'd better go home."

It was already getting dark when she left Reina's apartment. Devon loved walking at dusk in October. Too much of her life was spent in cars, and she didn't really feel close to the city unless she was on foot. When Devon got home, her mom was already there, scrubbing and vacuuming for Grandma Elaine. She was too busy to grill Devon about coming home so late.

"I can clean the bathroom, Mom."

"Thanks, but that's where I started. I'm more interested in you getting your homework done and going to bed at a reasonable hour."

"When is Grandma Elaine supposed to be here?"

"Around three tomorrow."

"Are you going to pick her up?"

"She told me not to bother but I want us both at home to greet her."

"Mom, that's not possible."

Devon knew a fight was coming on. She went ahead and put her hand over her solar plexus, but then her mom told her to invite her friends over.

"That would never work, Mom. The twins are having a big party at their place. Our house isn't big enough. Don't be sad. I promise I'll be home early."

"Do not walk home alone. Call me or make Melissa drive you. Devon, listen, Halloween night is special."

"I know all this."

"Do you? What would Grandma Elaine say?"

Devon recited dutifully, "It's when the veil between our world and the other side is at its thinnest." Her grandmother had taught her this when she was little, so that she would understand where all the important rituals came from.

"I don't want you going near the park."

"Which park?"

"Carlson. By the twins' house."

A cloud passed over the conversation. "Mom, what? We're trick-or-treating, or at least walking around. Probably for the last time."

Her mother left the room and came back with a necklace and earrings. "Smoky quartz. Will you wear these?" she asked. "I mean all the time. Don't take yours off and I won't take mine off either."

"Did you get a set for Grandma Elaine?"

"No. I'm sorry. I didn't know she was coming when I ordered them. I'm sure she won't mind."

"It would be better if Grandma had one too."

"I didn't intentionally exclude her, Dev. If you'd like, I'll order her a set tonight. Look, I've been so busy trying to get this place clean. Dinner is almost ready."

Devon put the jewelry on and went to her room. There was a rumor about an algebra quiz ready to pop out and ruin Halloween, and she still had to read that story about the man who outwitted the devil. It was impossible to concentrate, but if she didn't finish her homework, she would never be able to go to sleep. Wasn't she still a student, after all? She planned on graduating, which meant she planned on surviving Halloween.

Surviving. She grabbed Henry and stroked his fur.

Then she put her head down for one second. Just one second.

She was walking up a hill in the woods again and her body felt very small. She could smell the trees all around her, a familiar smell from early childhood that brought tears to her eyes. The sky was a deep, dark blue. Her bear was leading the way and he was even smaller than she was. They were on a mission, looking for someone. She was not afraid. She knew she was home.

A voice whispered in her ear. *Not much longer now, my love.*

And then a hand on her shoulder. She sat up and it took a second for her to remember where she was. Henry was in her lap.

"It's time for dinner, Devon. You need to come to the table before it gets cold."

"Wait. Did you say something?"

"I've been calling you. Didn't you hear me?"

"Sorry. I was dreaming."

"That means you're sleep deprived. If you start dreaming as soon as you close your eyes, it's a sign you haven't been sleeping enough."

"Mom, I have so much homework."

"Come and eat. It will make you feel better."

The dinner was pleasant enough. Her mom was oblivious to everything, as usual, but Devon knew the truth. She was in one world while her mom was in another. She would never be little again. Dinner would never make her feel better again. The battle had already started between her and the dark force that was after her family.

* * *

"It's been so long since I was at your house," Reina said.

The place was spotless. There was even a fresh bouquet of white anemones on the kitchen table. Devon led Reina to her room. "You have to help me with the wings. I can't do it by myself."

Devon brushed her hair and put on some powder and pink lipstick. Then she slipped on the nightgown.

"That's it?" Reina asked. "You're ready?"

"All I need is my wings."

Devon shivered as the wings settled across her shoulder blades. She turned before the mirror, checking the angle. Reina was already taking pictures.

"Don't post anything! Not yet."

"All right, all right." Reina adjusted her devil horns and put on more red lipstick. "What about shoes?"

"I was planning on pink ballet flats but we're going to walk so much. I kind of want to wear my Doc Martens. Unless you think they would kill the look?"

"No! That's totally metal. The black ones with the red roses. Hey, can I leave my backpack here?"

"Sure. I'm only taking my keys and my phone."

Reina flew down the hallway to the front door. It was a long walk to the twins' house. She turned around and asked, "Wait. Are we really trick-or-treating? Do we need bags?"

"I don't know. Are we still little kids?" Devon locked the door behind her and stepped outside with her devil-girl best friend. If only they could be little kids playing. If only she didn't have to leave behind her entire childhood tonight.

Where should she do it? She still hadn't decided. It wasn't dark yet and she needed darkness. She couldn't risk involving Reina. She had to be alone. This is really happening, Devon reminded herself. I will remember everything. I will get back to my childhood. This is real. Now. Tonight is real.

She was going to the Other Side.

The solution had come to her, slowly but surely, creeping up from her unconscious, so obvious as to be laughable. The sleeping pills. One day she transferred her stash of pills to a tiny plastic baggie, which she then hid in her backpack. On the morning of Halloween, she tucked it into her bra. The pills could take her where she needed to go. And fast.

"Dude, you are so quiet."

Reina was frustrated with her. Devon was afraid of losing Reina like she had lost Madison, and all because of these secrets she had to keep. She tried to swing an arm across Reina's shoulders, but it was too complicated with her wings. They linked arms at the elbow instead, and soon cars were honking at the angel-girl devil-girl duo. Devon's heart was light and happy for a few minutes. If only she could be free like this always.

Halloween. Her last year of middle school. The twins' house was decorated like a theme park. Melissa had gone all out, as usual, and this time the display made Devon tear up. She had to get control over her emotions before the sun went down. Life-size *Addams Family* figures dominated the front lawn, where tree branches dripped with cobwebs. A row of fuzzy bats dangled from the eaves of the house, and a laughing grim reaper met her at the front door. Next to him was a witch stirring a cauldron filled with dry ice. Inside, skulls of all sizes were spread across the tables and countertops. An elaborate miniature Scaresville, with a haunted house and its own museum, covered the dining room table. Devon turned away from the others and pretended to study the details of Scaresville while she dabbed at her tears.

"You should see what we did with your table, Devon."

"My table?"

Sierra and Samantha each grabbed one of Devon's hands and dragged her upstairs to the coffee table the girls had raised together. It was covered with a red velvet cloth on top of which sat a crystal ball.

Devon blushed. "I hope your mom didn't spend a lot of money on this. I'm not really a psychic. I can't tell fortunes or anything."

Nobody was listening to her. Everyone was running around and getting into their costumes while eating too much sugar. Melissa kept urging the kids to eat the pumpkin soup and potato pancakes she had made. Other moms arrived to help Melissa, whose house served as the headquarters for the neighborhood festivities.

Devon wondered what it would be like to have Melissa for a mom; Melissa, who lived to entertain her kids. She wondered what kind of mom *she* would be, or if she would be one at all. If she would survive.

"Everybody! It's time to take the picture." Melissa made all the kids stand together for the yearly photo. Sundown was less than an hour away and yet true night felt like a distant world. Devon checked her phone to find that her grandmother's plane had been delayed. She wouldn't be in LA until late.

Devon was overcome by sadness. She wanted, needed, Grandma Elaine to be somewhere nearby.

"K. talk later," she texted her mom. Then she turned her phone off.

Let's get this over with, she thought, looking around at everyone, the adults and the children. Which group did she belong to? Neither. There was nobody here who understood her.

* * *

"Hey, angel baby!"

"There's my devil girl!"

Everybody wanted them. Devon and Reina walked by themselves through the twins' neighborhood. They had lost the others at the park, which didn't matter because they all agreed to meet up later at the twins' house. That was the plan.

"You're so sad tonight. Sad again."

"No. Just because I'm not smiling doesn't mean I'm sad."

"You know what I'm saying, Devon. You're not all there."

"Hot! Hot! Hot!" called a man from a car.

"What a fucking creep," Reina spat. "Isn't this supposed to be a family neighborhood?"

They kept walking, side by side, white against red-and-black, good alongside evil.

"We're two archetypes," Devon said.

"Stereotypes, maybe? Anyway, we're not that creep's type. We're not anybody's angel. And we're for sure not anybody's devil."

Devon laughed and the two girls joined hands.

Reina sighed. "This is such a cute street. Do you ever think about where you want to live?"

"Not really. I mostly worry about staying alive."

"Oh, Devon. Sometimes you scare me."

"Don't be scared. And don't be sad. You know what? I really need to go home."

"Now? Are you serious?"

"My grandmother is waiting for me. She's visiting us. I have to talk to her, but I'll come back later. I'll see you at Sam and Sierra's."

"You shouldn't walk home by yourself," Reina said. "Not tonight."

"It's not far. I'll bring you your backpack tomorrow—if I don't see you, I mean."

"I don't think I'm even going to school tomorrow. I always miss the day after Halloween. It's a tradition."

"Okay then. I'll see you later."

"Devon?"

"What?"

"Be careful, girl."

Now she was on her own. There was still time to back out of her plan. She could go home and see her mom and grandmother. She could finish the reading for tomorrow. Or she could find a place, take the pills, and see if they plunged her into a deep sleep.

She headed home, crossing Overland. There was no other way. Instead of turning on her street, she kept walking, past her neighborhood and across the bridge that went over a little trickle of the LA River. She felt like she was doing something wrong, walking alone at night in her angel costume. She had blisters by the time she reached Lindberg Park. Not very private, but it would have to do. Her mother would never think of looking for her here. They had stopped coming to this park when she was still little. She walked over to the picnic tables and sat down facing away from the street. A few other people were wandering around. Maybe they were trying to have fun on Halloween night. Maybe they were looking for drugs or a place to sleep. Devon didn't care; this was her turf, or close enough. She hoped nobody would bother her, but she knew her white wings were like a neon sign in the night. She was an angel. She buried her head in her arms.

This would never work. She couldn't fall asleep in public, and she could never swallow pills without water. She needed to get away from other people. She hated living right in the middle of a giant metropolis. She needed to be surrounded by trees, walking up the hill from her dreams. Where was that hill? How could she get back there? It was up to her now. Nobody else in her family had made the journey.

They were all cowards. She could not let them stop her.

Devon got up and went over to a tree.

This would have to be good enough. She would not take off her wings, that much was certain. She closed her mouth and let the saliva build. Then she took the baggie out of her bra and opened it with shaking fingers. Three. That would do the trick, right? She wasn't trying to overdose, but she couldn't have anyone interfering with her plans. Maybe five? Six would definitely be too many. No. Three it was. She lay down on her side with her wings behind her. If only she could have found someplace more hidden. This was creepy. She felt too exposed.

The pills stuck in her throat.

She closed her eyes, but she had never been more awake. She was so alert, so lucid. How unfair this was. All day long at school she could barely stay awake and now this. It wasn't even dark in the park, not with the illumination from the streetlights.

Did she ever fall asleep? No. It wasn't sleep. She crossed over, instantly gliding into another consciousness. She was back on the hill, walking, but this time her bear was nowhere to be found and she was no longer little. She was her true, present-day self, wearing her wings and nightgown and Doc Martens. Up and up and up. She was panting. And then she found the place she didn't know she was looking for, a hut in the woods, as familiar as her mother's face.

The hut was glowing. Someone was cooking over a fire inside. Devon heard a low growl from a large beast, but she could not see anything. There were no animals around her, no insects buzzing.

"Bear?" she called.

No answer.

She knew she had to go inside the hut. Her whole life had been a journey to this moment. She was beyond fear.

She approached the hut from the left and went around the back to a black metal door decorated with roses like the ones on her boots. She grabbed the knocker and her fingers sizzled with a familiar pain. When she dropped the knocker, the door opened, and she saw a cauldron over a fire pit. There was a little round table covered with a white cloth. There were two little chairs. A teapot with a blue flower pattern sat on the cloth. There were two teacups. She had been to this party once before, but she hadn't been able to stay. Now she was here to finish something.

All at once she felt blood running between her legs. She was having her period, here, in earnest. It would get all over her nightgown. Her burned fingertips stopped throbbing and went numb.

The Lady stepped out of the shadows. She had long hair, parted down the middle in a straight line. One half was snow white and the other half was ink black. Her nightgown matched Devon's perfectly, and she was wearing an elaborate headdress like a bride from Eastern Europe.

"I am Verushka. And you, Devon, are here! Look how lovely you are. I am so glad I waited. So glad you remembered. I knew you would come back. I knew you were the one."

"I'm not staying."

Verushka smiled. "You certainly look as though you are. I do love your hair, and those wings are precious. You must sit and have tea with me. You know all this."

"I won't eat or drink anything while I'm here."

"It would be very rude of you not to join me. That is not how it is done. Don't you remember?"

"Not everything, but it's coming back to me. Especially the fact that you cheat."

Verushka smiled even wider. "No. I always play fair. Your family, however, is full of sore losers. You're not going to be like all your relatives, are you, Miss Woodward? Sit and rest. At least for a minute. You must be so weary after your thirteen years of journeying."

"I am." Devon found herself sitting at the little table, where she shut her mouth so tightly her back molars clicked together. She watched Verushka take the teapot and pour what looked like black tea into the two cups.

"Now, do you remember what comes next? We each drink, but you don't want it to be tea. Happy girls find blood in their mouths. That makes you the winner. Last time you lost Bear, your valiant protector. Maybe this time your luck will change."

"And what, exactly, do I win?"

"You get to live forever. Like me. You will become me."

"And if I should lose?"

"You will die instantly. It's only fair. Last time I let you get away."

"It sounds like I lose either way."

"Not at all. You should be honored to be my successor. It's a great blessing to be able to pay off an old family debt."

"But you always, always cheat."

"Let me make it easier." Verushka took a teacup in each hand and switched them. Then she did it again. And again. She did it until the cups hovered in the air, spinning in a circle. The table began to spin next, followed by the hut. Devon closed her eyes and grabbed her head with her hands. Verushka commanded, "Open your eyes and choose."

Devon tried to rise from the chair but couldn't. The blood gushed from between her legs. Her wings weighed a ton.

"You came to me, Devon. You always come to me. Now drink."

"I did not choose this."

"None of us choose our family. Blood is never a choice. You must understand. Blood is running down your legs right now, the same blood that can make you a mother. I know you. I have always known you. You are Elaine's granddaughter. The only granddaughter in your family. I have been waiting for you for such a long time."

Devon put her hand in front of her solar plexus as Reina had shown her and said, "I am not yours! I can't be yours."

"You were mine the minute you were born. Now drink."

"So that you can kill me?"

"It is not death but the beginning of a life that will last forever. You will forget all about your past, your world. You can have a different kind of child if you become like me. A special child. Don't you want to live forever?"

"No. I want to go home."

"You can't leave here without drinking."

The wings became light again. Devon grabbed a teacup in each hand. She held them up in front of her. "There is no difference, is there?" she asked. "Either way my life is over."

"Taste and see."

Devon downed each cup without pausing, without thinking.

A bear roared somewhere. Devon's Bear.

Verushka smiled with all her teeth, a true predator. She was suddenly covered in bites and scratches, like someone who had been mauled by a wild animal. Devon remembered this happening before. In her mind she saw a bear, her Bear, but he was enormous. He was protecting her. Where was he now? What had become of him?

Was nobody going to help her?

It wouldn't be enough to escape. Or to sacrifice herself. She had to undo the curse. She had to save her whole family, even the ones yet to be born. But how could she do this by herself? How could she kill this woman who was not a woman?

She had to believe that Bear would not abandon her, wherever he was. She could channel his strength. He was a powerful ancestor. He was family. He had always known what she was up against.

Her stomach gurgled. Whatever she had ingested was snaking its way deep into her body, her insides, making sure she never came back, never regained consciousness. Never returned to where she belonged. It's now or never, she told herself. I have to expel this.

At first she couldn't step forward, as if her boots were glued to the ground, so she wrenched her feet free of them. She took Verushka's ice-cold face in her hands and kissed her full on the mouth, tongue to deathly tongue. And then she regurgitated the contents of the two cups of tea down Verushka's throat.

The fluid burned her on the way out. Her throat and lips would be blistered, she was sure of it. Verushka struggled, thrashing her head back and forth and emitting a deep, guttural groan. They fell to the ground together, where they rolled, upsetting the table and chairs as the tea set shattered around them. The fire was dying but Devon could see Verushka dissolving and shrinking before her. The groaning stopped and was replaced by the sounds an infant would make, and for a second Devon felt remorse. She was afraid. She had never killed anyone or anything before. She could not imagine killing a child.

Verushka was the size of a toddler now. In a tiny voice she said, "You can still save me and redeem yourself. I will forgive you for what you did. I will forgive your family members. I will reward you. You will be a queen. The Queen of the Forest."

Devon shook her head. Her throat was sore and she didn't know if she could speak.

"You are the one I have been waiting for. You and only you. You must save me."Verushka spoke in the voice of a little girl, and Devon recognized it. It was her own voice from childhood. She remembered it. It was definitely her voice. "Save me," Verushka chanted as her face melted. Her body curled up at both ends. One strand of white hair remained, and Devon grabbed it and tossed the remains into the fire below the cauldron.

On the other side of the world, Davor smelled smoke and felt his mother die. He went blank for a moment, like a field covered in snow, and then he went off in search of a baby to feed to the river.

The walls of the hut fell over. Devon's wings flew off her back and disappeared into the night sky. She stood in the darkness in her stained white nightgown. Where was she? How would she get home? She knew the old place they called the chalet was nowhere near here. This was a different kind of forest. She was in a world she could escape only by waking.

But what if she couldn't wake up? She raised her face to the sky and saw the stars.

* * *

When Devon came to in the hospital, she could not immediately recall Halloween night. Her memories stopped and started in random fragments. She remembered staring at the little creatures of Scaresville on Melissa's dining room table. She remembered walking with Reina. She saw herself at Lindberg Park. She knew something had happened, she sensed she had done significant things, but there was a blank spot in the space where her most important memories belonged. Like a sleepwalker, she had lost some time.

Panic and shame fell over her. What had she done? And why were her mother and grandmother so happy and grateful? Why was her father flying in from New York? She had done nothing to earn this. In fact, she was sure she had done something wrong. Something terrible.

Tiny blisters covered her lips. It hurt to swallow.

They talked to her about her blood oxygen level and heart rate and how lucky she had been. They talked to her about drugs. The remaining sleeping pills, in the little baggie, were still tucked inside her bra when they found her. A social worker came to talk to her, which was incredibly embarrassing and awkward. They told her she would have to see a therapist every week. Devon said very little because she knew they would never believe her.

Her mother said she was sorry but that someone had stolen her wings and her shoes. She promised to replace everything.

Devon wanted to talk to Grandma Elaine alone, so she asked her mom to get her a bag of Doritos. After Caroline left the room, Devon said, "I'm trying really hard to remember what happened to me, but it keeps slipping away. I know you know something. You're the missing puzzle piece in my life. If you tell me your story, I think I'll remember where I went and what I did."

"You really don't remember anything? It sounds like a lot has been going on since the school year started. Your mother told me everything she knows."

"It's so close but I can't grasp it. Each time I start to remember, it slips away from me. I know there's a woman."

"With hair like yours." Grandma Elaine touched Devon's hair.

Devon waited. "You have white hair too now. Yours is natural, but it still matches hers. What does it mean? Who was she?"

"I haven't thought of her in years. Not since your father was a boy, and even then I was able to chase the idea out of my mind."

"What idea?"

"That someone from your past could come back to haunt you and your loved ones. That someone could curse you and it would stick."

"What was her name?"

"I haven't said it out loud since I was a teenager. I don't even like to say it in my mind."

"Please tell me, Grandma. You have to. What was her name? I have to hear you say it. Then I'll know it's true."

"Verushka."

Devon was unable to breathe for a second, like she was underwater, and then she opened her mouth and gasped. She remembered strange words being forced through her lips at the twins' sleepover; she saw the white-haired woman beckoning to her from the skylight in the kitchen; she heard the same woman in the park telling her to come away with her now, while they were all alone. She remembered buying the cookie at the Mini Mart, and the fateful sip of lemonade in Venice. She remembered both dark tea parties, the one from when she was little and the one on Halloween night. She saw what happened to Bear, how he went from toy to mighty beast, from beloved friend to fierce protector.

She saw Verushka young and beautiful back in San Francisco when her grandmother was a teenager, and she saw her ancient and scarred. She saw her decimated.

"I killed her," Devon said. "You won't believe where I've been or what I've done. You'll think it was all a dream."

"I do believe you, Devon."

"You do?"

"I thought you looked exactly like her when I first walked in the room. The white hair. She tried to get to your father too, when he was a boy."

"So Dad knows about her?"

"Not everything. Not exactly."

"Why did she want to hurt us so badly? What did we do?"

"We didn't do anything. Some people are parasites. Vampires. They live off others. Don't waste your energy trying to figure them out. Don't blame yourself."

"You're sure it's not because I did something wrong? Like, maybe a long time ago, when I was little?"

"Devon, please, this is not your fault," Grandma Elaine said. "You didn't do anything. I didn't do anything. We got unlucky, that's all."

"Was she human?"

"I'm not sure what to call her. I don't know where she got her terrible power."

Her mom came back in the room, followed by the nurse, who checked Devon's vital signs while a heavy family silence hung in the air. When the nurse left, Devon said, "I'm sorry I ruined Halloween."

"It doesn't sound like you ruined it, Devon," Grandma Elaine said. "Quite the opposite."

Caroline took Henry out of her bag. "Here. I brought your rabbit. He's your oldest toy."

"Henry," Devon said. "Look at you."

"And you know what? That Steiff bear arrived but it smells like smoke. I'm going to get a refund."

"Mom, don't! I want him."

"Oh, Devon, you do not. He smells like someone dragged him through a campfire."

"Mom, please. Let me keep him and I won't ask for anything else ever again."

Her mother and grandmother laughed at her.

"I'm serious. Don't get rid of that bear. And what happened to my necklace?"

"They probably cut it off you in the ER, but don't worry. I can get you another chain," Caroline said. "We've been wearing smoky quartz to get us through this, Elaine."

"Smoky quartz! Don't tell Jack or he'll blame me when he gets here."

"When will Dad be here? And why is he coming at all? I'm fine. He always shows up when it's too late. Always."

* * *

Back in her bedroom, Devon pressed her nose into the fur of the Steiff teddy bear. It looked like Bear, but she knew it wasn't him. Bear had moved on to the Other Side forever, leaving behind the smell of smoke as a kind of message. A nod to her, a blessing. The face of the new bear wasn't quite right. Every teddy bear in the world has its own face, even if it is a mass-produced toy, and every child with a bear knows this. They could find each other in a crowd.

The other face Devon would know anywhere was Caroline's, of course, a face she had turned away from for weeks. It wasn't all her fault. Her mother had been avoiding her as well. Verushka had come between them. Fear had pushed them apart instead of uniting them.

Devon still had some questions. She went into Caroline's bedroom and closed the door. Grandma Elaine was napping on the couch.

"Devon? You should be lying down."

"I'm fine. I want to talk about what happened."

"Why don't you let yourself rest? We can talk about this later."

"I just want to know one thing. Do you want to be my mom?"

Caroline turned white, and Devon instantly regretted the question.

"What are you talking about, Dev?"

"I've been worried you would leave ever since we lived at the chalet. I could feel you pulling away."

"That's because I was trapped. You might understand when you're older. I was trapped and I had to rearrange my life to make it work again. Devon, look, I'm sorry. I'm sorry about the things that happened when you were little. And I'm so grateful you're all right. I hope you don't ever hurt yourself again."

"Mom, I wasn't trying to kill myself. I don't care what the doctors think. Ask Grandma Elaine."

"I know what you were trying to do."

"You do?"

Caroline held her daughter's gaze. "I know who you were trying to find. I saw her once, in the past. It was when we were living at the chalet."

"I killed her, Mom. I don't think she's coming back."

"I hope you're right," Caroline said, wrapping her arms around her daughter. "I need you to know that I always, always wanted to be your mother. And I always will, but I won't lie. I was relieved when I miscarried. It was more than I could handle. I don't regret the divorce even though I know it hasn't been easy for you. What I regret is how ugly things got before we separated. I didn't want you to have to see that."

"And now Dad's back. Everyone's in LA all of a sudden and it isn't even a holiday."

"It could be an early Thanksgiving," Caroline said.

"They don't call it that anymore, Mom."

"Well, we can have our own celebration."

* * *

Devon had to go back to her old life. Homework. Clubs. Volunteering. Reina. The twins. Art class. Next year she would be in high school. As usual, nobody would know what she had been through. As usual, she was alone. She couldn't tell Reina all the details of Halloween night. Something held her back. She trusted her best friend, but she knew her story, her family history, wasn't for everyone.

She wondered if there was someone out there for her, someone she could share the story of Verushka with. Who would ever believe her? She had never seen a psychic before that Amber woman. She read her horoscope every Sunday, but she usually forgot it right away. Mercury in retrograde, always a big topic in So Cal, meant nothing to her. Was this the way Christians felt, isolated from non-believers? The difference was, those people usually couldn't stop talking about their faith, whereas Devon wanted to keep her recent experiences as quiet as possible.

The lady with long hair, white or black, was gone, but Devon was still afraid to say her name out loud. What would life be like now that she knew scary stories were true? They were true and they were also survivable. She had survived. What was more, she had saved the ones she loved.

"Devon, your dad's here!" her mom called from the living room.

She squeezed the new Steiff one last time before running to the front door and handing him to her dad. It wasn't the same bear but it would do. She could tell from her father's face that he had no idea what she had been through. It didn't matter. She knew what was important.

She was a hero.

Acknowledgments

A novel is always a leap of faith, and I could not have written this one without the support of the following people: Scarlett R. Algee of JournalStone for giving this book a chance; Sean Leonard for the attentive edits; my dedicated critique group, Fish Tank 2.0 (I know you did not sign on to read entire novels, but here we are): Mary Crawford, Josh Jones Lofflin, Lori Sambol Brody, and Ruth LeFaive; my dear friends: Betsy, Diane, Jonna, and Valérie; my courageous and indulgent family: Kurt, Marco, and Sabrina Miller.

About the Author

Jan Stinchcomb is the author of *The Kelping* (Unnerving), *The Blood Trail* (Red Bird Chapbooks) and *Find the Girl* (Main Street Rag). Her stories have appeared in *Bourbon Penn*, *The Horror Is Us* (Mason Jar Press) and *Gamut*, among other places. A Pushcart nominee, she is featured in *Best Microfiction 2020* and *The Best Small Fictions 2018 & 2021*. She lives in Southern California with her family and is an associate fiction editor for *Atticus Review*.